BUMPY LANDINGS

In his debut novel, Donald J. Carey has crafted a gripping and warm coming-of-age story. With a deft hand, Carey elevates the ordinary ups-and-downs of life into a richly textured, surprisingly suspenseful, deeply touching novel. I was drawn in from the beginning and quickly found myself caring about the characters.

—Braden Bell,
author of *The Road Show*

There is nothing rough about *Bumpy Landings*—it's a fresh story in a fresh setting with a fresh voice and a fresh perspective. Carey does a great job bringing this story to life!

—Josi Kilpack,
author of the Culinary Mystery series

Bumpy Landings is a delightful tale of a young returned missionary trying to find himself, and finding love in the process. Adorable story, fun characters, and all set against the backdrop of the incredibly romantic Hawaiian Islands. You're sure to enjoy this tale!

—Julie Wright,
author of *Eyes Like Mine*

In his debut novel, *Bumpy Landings*, author Donald J. Carey brings us into a different world and shows us romance with a tropical flavor. I greatly enjoyed this book and recommend it to any reader who's looking for a story they haven't already read a million times.

—Tristi Pinkston,
author of *Agent in Old Lace* and *Secret Sisters*

Bumpy Landings is a dual love story, fusing a young man's determined passion to become a pilot and his longing for the heart and love of a beautiful woman. Donald Carey's compelling narrative drives the reader in rapid-fire and seesaw fashion, yet always with the opportunity to get acquainted with the flawed, fun, and faithful young characters along the way.

—Jim Weaver
Executive Director Emeritus, Angel Flight West

BUMPY LANDINGS

donald j carey

Bonneville Books
Springville, Utah

To my girls:
Kara, Anna, and Alyssa

© 2010 Donald J. Carey

ISBN 13:978-1-59955-413-6

Published by Bonneville Books, an imprint of Cedar Fort, Inc., 2373 W. 700 S., Springville, UT 84663
Distributed by Cedar Fort, Inc., www.cedarfort.com

LIBRARY OF CONGRESS CATALOGING-IN-PUBLICATION DATA

Carey, Don, 1968-
  Bumpy landings / Don Carey.
      p. cm.
  Summary: Against his mother's wishes, a young Mormon in La'ie, Hawaii, earns his pilot's license in order to impress his girlfriend.
  ISBN 978-1-59955-413-6
  1. Mormons--Fiction. 2. Laie (Hawaii)--Fiction. I. Title.

PS3603.A738F58 2010
813'.6--dc22

            2010019531

Cover design by Danie Romrell
Cover design © 2010 by Lyle Mortimer
Edited and typeset by Heidi Doxey

Printed in the United States of America

10 9 8 7 6 5 4 3 2 1

Printed on acid-free paper

one

Jordan MacDonald eased the rusty old van into a too-small parking space and quickly killed the engine. He glanced at his watch and groaned—the perfect chance to make a good impression, and he was late.

Squeezing himself out of the van, he inched past the faded flowers painted on its side and began running through the parking garage. As he reached the road in front of Honolulu International Airport, he heard a small plane fly overhead. Instinctively he glanced up but found his view of the sky blocked by the interisland terminal building. Shaking his head, Jordan darted across the road and through the doors.

The baggage claim area bustled with people greeting one another and hurrying toward the exit, most of them locals with dark skin and hair. During the two years he'd spent in Oregon, Jordan had forgotten what it was like to be in the minority. Now that he was home, however, his fair skin and light blonde hair set him apart from many of the people around him.

Pulling a scrap of paper from his pocket, Jordan set off to find his passenger. Normally his trip to the airport as the driver for Pua's Tuberose flower shop would only involve picking up boxes of roses and strange alien-looking protea shipped in from Maui. But today he was doing a favor for his Hawaiian coworker, Malia, by picking up her Auntie Kehau.

Jordan had known Malia before his mission, although at the time she had been just one of his sister's stupid little friends. She had grown up nicely in the two years he'd been gone, though, and Jordan practically tripped over himself offering to help her out. But now he was late and in danger of messing up the whole excursion.

Taking his paper to one of the arrival monitors, Jordan scanned the list, looking for Hawaiian Air flight 181 from Hilo, so he could see which baggage carousel they had used. He hoped Auntie Kehau would still be there waiting.

When he found the flight information, Jordan learned the plane had left nearly half an hour late, which meant it wouldn't arrive for another ten minutes. He exhaled, letting his shoulders relax. This errand for Malia needed to go well. Jordan had developed a bit of a crush on her, even though she told everyone who would listen that she was waiting for Robert Tu'aia and planned to marry him when his mission ended the next year.

It was probably Malia's devotion to her missionary that gave Jordan the nerve to talk to her at all. He'd always been quite shy around girls, especially if he had any romantic interest for them. Jordan had been particularly concerned when his mom got him a job in a flower shop with three attractive coworkers, afraid he'd spend every day as a red-faced, babbling idiot.

But Malia was waiting for Robert. Amber, the tall blonde volleyball star, already had a large male following, and Jordan didn't even consider her a prospect. And his boss, Lani, was cute—with her short dark hair and thick New Zealand accent—but she had to be pushing forty. So, without any romantic pressure, he found himself able to function quite well and actually enjoyed the job.

After making his way to baggage claim C on the far end of the terminal, Jordan stopped and sat down to wait. The luggage from several other interisland flights crowded the carousel, and dozens of travelers met their loved ones, many receiving flower leis and the traditional kiss on the cheek. Jordan looked at the lei Malia had sent with him for Auntie Kehau. It was a double strand tuberose lei—the namesake of Pua's Tuberose flower shop. The long, creamy, trumpet-shaped blooms were known more for their scent than their appearance, and Jordan couldn't help but open the bag to sneak a whiff of their rich, spicy aroma.

The smell brought back a flood of memories: greetings, partings, special events, and a particularly disastrous prom night. *That was a long time ago*, thought Jordan. *You're a different man now.* Although just how different still remained to be seen.

Jordan checked his watch and realized the people from flight 181 would be arriving at any moment. He stood and began looking for his passenger. He didn't have much to go on—just a name, a flight number, and a vague description: "She's about my height with shoulder-length black hair," Malia had told him before he left. It didn't take long for Jordan to spot a woman matching this description. In fact, he quickly saw several dozen women about Malia's height with shoulder-length black hair.

This was not going to be as easy as he first thought. He looked at the paper and read through the scant information again, hoping to find something that might help his search, but he had nothing. He reached for his cell phone to call Malia but found it missing from his pocket. With a twinge of panic, he realized he'd probably left it plugged in at home, and with no way to call Malia, he'd have to find Auntie Kehau on his own.

Nearby, a group of kids in purple T-shirts clustered around a big man holding a sign that read Pearl City Elementary, and Jordan had a flash of inspiration. Hurrying to a rental car counter, he asked the man behind the desk, "Do you have a piece of paper and a marker I could use?" The man pulled a nearly blank sheet from a stack near his printer and then rummaged around in his desk before handing Jordan a large, red Sharpie.

Jordan thanked the man and then copied the name from Malia's little scrap, starting out neatly but cramming the last half of "Pulakaumaka" against the right side of the page. He returned the pen and made his way to baggage carousel C, where he stood with his makeshift sign, smiling at every middle-aged, dark-haired woman who passed. He got a lot of smiles in return, but nobody stopped.

As he looked over the crowd, he noticed a girl across the baggage claim eyeing him. She was a local girl about his age and quite attractive. He smiled at her nervously, and she smiled back, filling Jordan with a mixture of excitement and panic.

The girl turned her attention to her backpack, from which she produced a cell phone. As Jordan continued his search for Auntie Kehau, he kept stealing glances back at this girl. After a few minutes, she put her phone away and wheeled her suitcase toward him. His heart pounded in his chest as she approached, and he thought to himself, *You're a different man, now. You can do this!* Gathering all of his courage, Jordan managed a smile and said, "Hi."

"Hi, Jordan," she replied.

Jordan drew in a quick breath. How did she know his name? He searched his memory frantically but couldn't remember ever meeting this girl before. He looked at her luggage for a clue but without success. Finally he had to admit defeat. "Um, I'm sorry," he stammered. "What was your name again?"

The girl raised her eyebrows and then smiled. She took the sign from his hand and held it under her chin so that the top of the paper brushed her black, shoulder length hair.

Jordan had found Auntie Kehau.

Once the initial surprise wore off, Jordan remembered the lei he held in his hand. He pulled the fragrant strand of creamy white flowers from the bag and said, "This is from Malia." He slipped the lei over her head and paused. Tradition dictated a kiss on the cheek, but Jordan froze, the pounding in his chest making him dizzy. *If she were some old woman, you wouldn't hesitate*, he thought. But several moments passed in awkward silence with Jordan unable to move.

Kehau knit her brow. "Are you okay?"

"Yeah, I'm fine. Why?"

"Well," she said, "your ears are so red . . ."

At the mention of his red ears, Jordan's entire face flushed bright crimson, and Kehau stifled a giggle. Jordan recovered by smiling at his own embarrassment, giving Kehau permission to laugh.

Jordan was sure he had never heard a more beautiful laugh in his life.

He grabbed her luggage and quickly led her out of the terminal building to the parking garage. "Thanks for coming to get me," she said as he opened the van's passenger door.

Jordan's heart pounded in his chest. "No problem."

Kehau moved toward the open door but hesitated. Jordan followed her gaze to the white pastry box sitting on the seat.

"Oh, sorry," he said, grabbing the box. "*Malasadas.*"

"Oh, I love *malasadas*," Kehau said as she climbed into the van.

Jordan hesitated before offering her the box of fried pastries. "Here, have some."

"Thank you." The smile she gave him more than made up for the trouble he'd be in when he got home.

As they drove out onto the highway, Jordan fidgeted with the gearshift, building up the nerve to try his hand at small talk. "You can have the rest," he said, indicating the two remaining pastries.

"Really? Thanks. Do you want one?" she asked, offering the box to Jordan.

"No, I already had three," he answered.

Kehau ate the *malasadas* as they drove through lush mountain valleys on the H-3 freeway, but when she had finished, their conversation didn't resume the way Jordan had hoped. He couldn't bear the thought of driving the hour to La'ie in silence. *C'mon!* he thought, *You can do this! After two years on a mission, talking to a girl should be no problem at all.*

Taking a deep breath and gathering all of his courage, he asked the first question that came to mind. "So, um, how is it that you're Malia's auntie?"

"Well, I'm the youngest of eleven kids, and Malia's mom is my oldest sister, Lanea." Kehau paused, her mouth curling into a grin. "I was born halfway through her wedding reception."

Jordan smiled. "Nice. Let me guess: Malia was born a year later, right?"

"Ten months. We were like sisters until her family moved to La'ie. We're still like sisters, really."

Jordan congratulated himself on breaking the ice and said a silent prayer he could keep the conversation going. "So, you're a student at BYU—Hawaii?"

"Yes. And you?"

"Yeah," he said. "I just got back from my mission in Portland." They passed through a long tunnel to the other side of the mountains, and the view of the windward coast opened up in front of them. Jordan quickly thought of another question. "What's your major?"

"Secondary education, with a minor in Hawaiian studies. What about you?"

"Computer science. No minor—not yet, anyway." Relieved that

the conversation was coming together, Jordan continued. "Okay, let's see. Do you work?"

Kehau nodded. "PCC luau and night show." Jordan half expected this, knowing many of the students at BYU—Hawaii paid tuition by working at the Polynesian Cultural Center, which sat just to the east of the school.

"Live in the dorms, or off campus?"

"Dorms, Hale 5," Kehau replied. *Hale* was the Hawaiian word for house.

"Have a boyfriend?"

Silence followed, and Jordan felt his ears go red, unable to believe he'd actually asked the question. He'd meant for this to be light-hearted small talk, and instead he was turning it into an interrogation.

But after a few seconds, Kehau just smiled coyly and said, "Not at the moment."

As they continued chatting, the conversation came more easily, and they drove slowly but steadily with the heavy H-3 traffic. As they approached Kaneohe, Jordan took the opportunity to brag a little.

"You see that condo over there? The one with the blue around the top?"

"Yeah?"

"I helped build that."

"Really?"

"Yup, I worked with 'Ano Maika'i Builders my sophomore and junior years in high school—during the summer. My sophomore year we built that condo, and my junior year we went to Kauai and worked on the Hale Pakela subdivision."

"Oh, cool," she said. "I know a guy who worked on the Hale Pakela. He just started dancing in the night show at the beginning of summer. Do you know Scott Sauaga?"

Jordan caught a hint of admiration in her voice that made his throat tighten. This was certainly not a turn he wanted their conversation to take. "Oh, yeah," he said, trying not to sound too resentful. "I know Scott." Jordan wasn't really in the mood to discuss him, though—especially not how Scott's idea of a good time usually involved discomfort and embarrassment on Jordan's part.

They drove on in silence for a few miles, the interstate giving way to a narrow, two-lane highway before Kehau asked, "So, what about you? Where are you from?"

"Me? I'm from La'ie. We moved here from Colorado when I was eight, after my parents divorced. My mom teaches business."

"Wait—is your mother Beth MacDonald?" Kehau asked.

"Yeah, that's her," Jordan said.

"I had her for my economics class. She was a good teacher." Kehau smiled at him. "She told a lot of stories about her son on a mission."

"Oh, great." Jordan blushed again.

He managed to keep the rest of the drive filled with light-hearted small talk and Kehau's intoxicating laughter, which he found he could trigger quite easily. All was going well until they neared La'ie, where a loud mechanical scream caused him to jump. Looking into his side mirror, Jordan saw something shooting toward him. An electric-blue motorcycle flew past his window and cut into his lane just inches ahead of him, barely avoiding a tour bus coming the other way.

The bus driver let loose a blast from his horn, and Jordan hit the brakes hard, locking up the tires and skidding halfway off the road. The large white flower boxes crashed forward, and the van bucked violently before shuddering to a halt. Tires screeched behind them, and Jordan braced for an impact that fortunately never came. The rider with the blue bike and matching helmet sped away, oblivious to the near pile-up he'd caused and was now leaving behind.

"You idiot," Jordan muttered as the bike disappeared around a curve in the road. Noticing the line of cars stacking up behind him, he quickly restarted the van. Spraying gravel as he pulled back onto the highway, Jordan fumed silently for the last few minutes of the drive.

When they entered the parking lot near the girls' dorms, his head still buzzed with adrenaline. This gave him the extra dose of courage he needed to act on a thought that had been forming for the last half hour. Quickly, before he could stop himself, he said, "*Peanut Gallery* is the campus movie this week. Have you seen it?" The words came tumbling out quickly, as though they were spoken by a stranger instead of himself.

"No," she said. "Is it good?"

"I don't know, but I'm willing to chance it if you are." Jordan's heartbeat pounded in his ears, but he managed to stick with the commitment pattern he'd learned as a missionary. "So should I pick you up at, say, nine-twenty?"

Kehau's smile broadened. "I think I'd like that."

Jordan grinned widely as he drove back to Pua's Tuberose, feeling quite pleased with himself. He'd asked a girl out on a date, and she'd accepted. He really had changed.

The heady aroma of a thousand flowers greeted him as he walked into the shop. Malia was on her phone, and she giggled when she saw him. After he had brought in all of the flower boxes and began unloading them in the back, she moved close to him and, with mock indignation, said, "Hey, lover boy. When I asked you to 'pick up' my auntie, that's not what I meant."

two

Jordan quickly finished his work at Pua's and hurried home. A sweet aroma permeated the air along his short walk from the shopping center to Iosepa Street. The scent of countless flowers filling yards and lining streets was a sensation Jordan had taken for granted before his mission, but now he relished it as the smell of home. He stopped in his front yard and held a small cluster of white and yellow plumeria to his nose before continuing into the house.

"It's about time," Julie said as Jordan opened the screen. She sat in the easy chair that faced the door, wearing her swimsuit and a green and yellow flower-print *lava-lava* wrapped around her waist. Her long, sandy blonde hair was twisted into a loose bun. "Hurry up and change."

Jordan stopped and looked at his sister. "Change? What for?"

"Hello—we're going to the beach, remember?" Julie leaned forward in the chair. "You were supposed to be home, like, two hours ago. And it'd be nice if you kept your phone with you once in a while." She flung it at him, and he barely got his hands up in time to catch it.

"Oh, man, I forgot. I'll be right back."

He turned to leave the living room when Julie said, "And where are the *malasadas* you promised me?"

Without turning to look at his sister, Jordan said, "Um, I forgot those too."

Once Jordan had changed into his swimsuit, he returned to the living room. "You know, you're lucky I waited for you," Julie said. "If Mom had given me the keys, I'd have been long gone." Julie was a couple of years younger than Jordan but often treated him as if she were the older sibling.

"I said I was sorry."

Jordan and Julie climbed into the family's little white Honda. "So, where to?"

"Well, I really wanted to go to Waimea, but it's so late. By the time we get there we'll just have to come right back home. It's my last day here, and all I wanted to do was go to the beach." Julie folded her arms and pouted.

Jordan looked at her and frowned. "So, the question is still the same. Where to?"

"I don't know. Temple Beach, I guess." She turned her head and looked out the side window.

Jordan scowled. "You could have walked to Temple."

"Okay, fine," she said, turning back to face him. "We'll go to Hukilau then. Just go already."

It only took a few minutes for them to arrive at Hukilau Beach on the north side of town, site of the fishing party made famous in the classic song. Julie walked along the sand, looking not at the waves, but the houses that sat with their backs to the ocean. She came to one with a collection of bicycles, surfboards, and fishing spears on the patio and announced, "This looks good."

"Who lives here?" Jordan asked.

"What? I don't know," Julie answered, though Jordan didn't believe her.

Several dozen people were spread across the seashore, enjoying a near-perfect afternoon. It was just warm enough with the sun hanging in the western sky and trade winds supplying a gentle breeze. Compared to Sunset or Waikiki, the beach was nearly deserted, but this was actually a pretty good crowd for a Friday afternoon in La'ie.

Julie, well tanned after a summer of sunbathing, applied some lotion to her arms. The smell of the sunscreen and the ocean hit Jordan and brought back memories of fun in the sun—and sunburns long past.

"Julie, can you do my back?" he asked as he took off his shirt.

"Ow! The glare!" she teased. "I need darker glasses."

"Yeah, so funny," said Jordan. "Let's see how tan you look after a brutal Chicago winter."

"Not a problem," Julie said. "There's at least sixteen tanning salons within three miles of campus."

Jordan considered sharing his favorite tanning-booth horror story but decided to let it slide. Instead he said, "Okay, let me ask you something. Why Chicago State? I mean, as much as you hate the cold, I would have expected you to pick someplace warmer."

Julie shrugged her shoulders. "I had three criteria," she said. "Number one: It had to be on the mainland. There's not enough room on this rock for both Mom and me. I seriously need to get away on my own."

Jordan nodded.

"Number two: Not BYU. Not Provo, not Idaho, and certainly not here. If I was using Mom's faculty brat discount, I know she'd find some way to hold that over my head. I've got to make a clean break.

"Three: A reasonably decent marketing program. That narrowed it down to, like, two hundred schools. So I started filling out financial aid forms until I thought I'd puke. Chicago State gave me the most money, so here I go."

"Oh, so that's it," Jordan said. "Sold to the highest bidder." He meant it as a joke, but Julie apparently didn't see it that way.

"Oh, look who's talking," she shot back, "Mr. Cop-out himself. You know, with grades like yours, you could have gotten into just about any program at any school you wanted. But, no. You're going to stay here and be Mommy's Little Helper."

"Hey—I promised Dad I'd take care of Mom, and that's what I plan to do."

"Suit yourself, but she did just fine without you for two years. The real reason she wants you around is so she can run your life exactly the way she thinks it should be run."

Jordan was about to object, but before he could say anything, Julie suddenly grabbed his arm and let out a frantic, "Oh my heck!" She ducked her head behind Jordan, but it was too late.

"Hey, Julie!" a male voice called out. Jordan looked up to see a tan, athletic guy with a surfboard several yards down the beach, walking toward them.

"Hi, Todd," Julie called, adding under her breath, "Don't come over here, you big jerk."

Todd had dark hair and a handsome, square-jawed face—just the kind of guy Julie was always chasing after. Or, as seemed to be the case here, running away from.

"Julie, hey! Where were you this morning," Todd said as he reached them. "I stopped by to pick you up, but nobody was there."

"Oh, was that this morning? I must have totally forgotten."

The brush-off was blatant, but Todd seemed undeterred. He turned to Jordan and shook his hand with the vigor of a town council candidate. "Hi. You must be Julie's brother. I'm Todd Jameson."

"Yeah, hi—I'm Jordan."

"Good to meet you, Jordan." Todd turned back to Julie and said, "You really missed out. It was a perfect day for flying."

Jordan felt a jolt of excitement. "You're a pilot?"

Todd looked the part. "Yes, sir. You ever been for a ride in a small plane?"

Before he could stop himself, Jordan said, "Oh yeah. I have thirty-one hours in my log book."

Todd nodded approvingly, but Julie's jaw dropped. "Oh really? When did this happen?"

Jordan's face flushed red, but he couldn't think of any way to unsay what he'd just said. "The summer before my mission, when I was . . ." Jordan paused for a moment, a wave of sadness washing over him. "When I was in Texas, working with Dad."

"Oh, Mom's gonna love this."

"Mom doesn't need to know, does she?" Jordan replied quietly.

"Hey, that's cool, man. You need to hurry and finish up your ticket. Roach, the guy where I rent, he's probably the most affordable on the island. You should really think about it," Todd said. " 'Cause you know, chicks dig a pilot."

Julie rolled her eyes as Todd winked at her. "Maybe next time, Julie. Good to meet you, Jordan."

As Todd walked away, Jordan turned to Julie. "Not a word about this to Mom."

Julie smiled at him coyly. "Who, me?"

"Listen," Jordan said, a sense of foreboding twisting his gut. "I've kept I don't know how many of your secrets. I'm begging you—"

"Oh, all right. Your secret's safe with me." Julie lay back down on her bamboo beach mat and covered her eyes with the end of her towel. "Probably."

That evening, Jordan sat down for dinner across from his mother, Beth. She was a tall woman, just shorter than Jordan's six-foot height, with short silver hair that had once been long and blonde like his sisters'. "So, Jordan, what are your plans for tonight?" she asked after the dinner prayer.

"I thought I'd go to the movie up on campus."

"Romeo here has a date," Julie said.

That got Beth's full attention. "Really? With who? Where's she from?"

Jordan shrugged his shoulders. "It's nothing, Mom. I met this girl today, and I asked her out. That's it."

"Ooh, sounds serious," said his youngest sister, Rebecca.

"Jordan is a real lady's man now." Julie said as she got up from the table. "'Chicks dig a pilot.'"

Jordan felt a surge of rage mixed with cold panic. He'd expected Julie to get back at him for the whole *malasada* thing, but this was brutal, even for her.

Beth's eyes flashed as she watched Julie walk from the room. "Wait, what do you mean by that?" But Julie was gone. Beth knit her eyebrows. "Jordan, what did she mean by that?"

"Oh, it's nothing." Jordan tried to look at his mother but couldn't meet her eyes. "It's . . . well, we met a friend of hers while we were at the beach, and he's a pilot, and, um, I think she has a crush on him."

"She was talking about you."

He could feel the weight of his mother's gaze. "Oh, well that's probably, um . . . we talked about flying, and I mentioned that I thought it might be kinda fun to be a pilot, you know, and—"

"No," she said shaking her head. "No way. Don't you even think about it, young man. You can just forget it—right now."

"Yeah, Mom, I know," Jordan said in a futile attempt to stop her lecture.

"This is all your father's fault. The nerve of that man. Flying off in that little death trap with wings, knowing full well how I felt. He did it just to get to me, you know. And I have no doubt he would have crashed and killed himself if he hadn't had that heart attack first—"

"It was only talk, Mom," Jordan said, desperate to end the conversation. "Look, I gotta go."

Jordan walked from his house in the center of town to BYU—Hawaii, which sat barely a mile to the south. A gentle breeze blew through the warm evening air, and Jordan grew more and more anxious as he walked past the large empty fields at the school's entrance. He'd avoided giving his mother any information about Kehau, but nothing in La'ie stayed a secret for long.

So what if she doesn't approve, Jordan thought. *This is your life, not hers.* Yet having his mother's approval meant a lot to him, and he hated keeping things from her.

Jordan checked his watch and saw that it was just after eight. With over an hour to kill, he wandered around the campus, giving himself a much-needed pep talk.

What was he so afraid of? Jordan knew his mother was concerned about her children dating anyone who wasn't *haole*—white like them—but she probably wouldn't pitch a fit unless it looked like things were getting serious.

Would things get serious between him and Kehau? As he thought about it, Jordan certainly hoped so. There'd been an obvious chemistry between them on the ride back from the airport. Now it was just up to him to keep that momentum going.

By the time he arrived at the collection of two-story dorms near the back of campus, he'd decided this was a relationship he wanted to pursue. Still a few minutes early, he watched several couples playing tennis on the courts separating the boys' and girls' dorms and took deep, cleansing breaths to try to calm his nerves. He kept stealing glances at the entrance to Kehau's *hale*, and when she finally arrived, Jordan was unable to hold back a smile. She wore a loose green shirt with light-weight white pants. The lei Jordan had given her at the airport hung around her neck.

"Wow, you look great," Jordan said.

"Thanks."

Walking the short distance to the McKay Auditorium at the center of campus, Jordan smiled in relief as their light-hearted small talk picked up right where it had left off earlier in the day. Kehau's laughter came easily, and Jordan was intoxicated by her smile and the smooth, rich sound of her voice.

He picked out some seats just as the lights dimmed, and, acting before he could lose his nerve, Jordan took Kehau's hand in his. She tensed slightly at his touch, and he feared he might have overstepped his bounds. She didn't pull her hand away, though, and soon he felt her relax.

Throughout the movie, Jordan found his attention wandering to the girl at his side. She was pretty—quite pretty. Not drop-dead, supermodel gorgeous, but he couldn't keep his eyes off her round, warm face and smooth black hair. What was more important, though, she seemed to genuinely like him.

About halfway through the show, Kehau's head began to nod, and soon he suspected she was asleep. Deciding to try his luck once more, he reached up and gently eased her head onto his shoulder. He noticed a hint of guava as he breathed in the scent of her hair, and Jordan smiled at the feeling of her head resting against him. By the time the movie finished, Jordan's arm had gone numb, but he let her sleep all the way through the end credits.

Kehau finally stirred when the house lights came up. "Why didn't you wake me?"

"Because it was kinda nice sitting here with your head on my shoulder." He squeezed her hand and gave her a smile. "But now I'd better get you home before you turn into a pumpkin."

They walked in silence, arriving at her dorm all too soon. Jordan said, "Thanks for coming with me. I had a good time."

"Yeah, me too." Kehau smiled. "I can't believe I fell asleep. You make a good pillow, though." They laughed and then stood silently in the cool night air. Jordan tried to decide if he should kiss her. After all, she'd let him hold her hand. But a kiss? *Just do it, you idiot*, he thought.

He leaned in toward her but stopped himself. Somehow it just didn't feel right to try to take a kiss on their first date, so he settled for giving her a hug instead. "Good night. And thanks again."

"Good night." The heady aroma of tuberose lingered in the air as Jordan watched Kehau disappear through the doorway and around the corner. He turned and walked home slowly, trying to keep the magic of the night alive as long as possible.

three

Malia accosted Jordan as soon as he entered the shop. "So, how'd it go last night?"

Jordan shrugged, trying to appear indifferent. "Good," he said. "But I'm sure Kehau already told you all about it."

"Yes, she did." Malia punched him hard in the shoulder. "So, what? You gonna send her some flowers now, right?"

"Of course," he said quickly, trying to hide the fact that the thought of sending flowers hadn't occurred to him, even though he'd been working in a flower shop for several weeks.

"What are you going to send?" asked Amber.

"I don't know—what do you think?" Jordan said, turning to his boss.

"That depends," said Lani. "How much do you like this girl?"

"Um . . ." Jordan wasn't quite ready to define his feelings for a girl he had met only the day before, especially not publicly—and with Malia present. His ears burned, and he silently wished a customer would come through the door and take the attention off of him.

Amber stifled a giggle, and Lani said, "That much, huh? Well, you can hardly go wrong with roses. A half dozen, maybe?"

The thought of giving Kehau one of Lani's six-rose bouquets seemed a little much. "How 'bout just a single," he said.

"Chicken," said Malia. "I'm sure she'll like it, though," she added quickly.

Lani wrapped a single red long-stemmed rose in heavy cellophane with a spray of baby's breath and then handed it to him. But Malia immediately snatched the flower from his hand. "Girls' dorm—my delivery."

"Hey!" Jordan looked at Lani for help.

"Sorry—she's right. You know that if flowers are going to the ladies' dorms, one of the girls makes the delivery."

"Besides," added Amber with a smile, "wouldn't delivering your own flowers be some kind of conflict of interest?"

Lani opened the lock box and took out the keys to the van. "Malia, why don't you go ahead and take care of all the deliveries. Jordan can stay here and finish your leis."

Jordan helped Malia load up the day's flowers before he took her place at the workbench in the back of the shop. Up until that point, Jordan had only made a few single tuberose leis, where the flowers were simply strung end-to-end in a thin, sweet-smelling strand. But Malia had been working on a double tuberose lei, with the flowers assembled sideways to create a two-inch-thick rope of fragrant, creamy whiteness, accented every six inches with bright red rosebuds. Jordan hesitated for a moment, and then started in. Taking a trumpet-shaped bloom from a bag on the table, he peeled away a couple of outside petals that were turning brown and slowly pushed the needle through the side of the flower.

"Yeah, just like that," said Amber. Jordan smiled, feeling strangely comforted by her simple words of encouragement.

For over an hour, Jordan strung flowers, moving on to red and white carnations once his tuberose leis were finished. He grew more and more anxious for Malia's return, excited to get her report on Kehau's rose delivery.

His cell phone rang, and he fumbled as he took it out, thinking perhaps it might be Kehau. But it was his mother.

"I've decided the whole family is going to take Julie to the airport. We need to leave in fifteen minutes."

Jordan looked at the pile of flowers in front of him, and then out the store window at the van's empty parking space. "Mom, I'm working. I can't just drop everything and go." As soon as he said the words, though, a wave of guilt rose up inside him. This was family—*ohana*—and nothing was supposed to be more important than that.

With a heavy sigh he said, "I'll see what I can do."

"Thank you. We're down to fourteen minutes now," she said. The end-of-call tone beeped in his ear.

Jordan took a deep breath. "Um, Lani?"

"Don't worry about it, love," Lani said, barely looking up from her arrangement. "Malia will be back soon. Go ahead. We'll be fine."

"Thanks, Lani."

■ ⬛ ⬛

The next day, after Jordan's church meetings ended, he found himself walking through campus, looking for Kehau around every corner. Once, as he walked along the covered walkways that opened out onto a large courtyard, he thought he saw her on the sidewalk that ran perpendicular to his. But as he looked over his shoulder, trying to make sure, he collided with a large metal support pole, sending his scriptures flying.

The sound of laughter from behind him made Jordan's face burn, but he refused to look. He gathered his books, but as he stood up, the laughing voice called, "Hey, *Pono!*" A knot formed in the pit of his stomach. Only Scott Sauaga called him "*Pono*," and Jordan was in no mood for Scott.

The muscular Polynesian passed Jordan, his arm around a girl with a pretty face and long brown hair. As soon as Jordan looked up, Scott grabbed the girl, leaned her back, and gave her an overly dramatic kiss. The girl giggled and slapped Scott on the shoulder. Jordan frowned and shook his head. *Why is he still doing that?*

Jordan's face still burned as he walked past the cafeteria entrance, where he saw a girl in a red dress looking at the notices on the three-sided bulletin board. From the back, it looked like it might be Kehau, and his heart sped up. On closer inspection, his suspicions were confirmed.

"So, see anything good?" he asked.

Startled, Kehau jumped.

"Sorry," he apologized.

"Oh. Hi, Jordan," she said, smiling. "No, it's okay. And thanks for the rose. That was so sweet."

"No problem," said Jordan. "So, what are you reading that's so interesting?"

"Just this," she said, motioning to a page in front of her. It was an announcement for the school's "Welcome Back" dance, and Jordan noticed that her smile grew when she looked at the sign.

"That's this Friday," said Jordan. "Are you going to go?"

Kehau looked at Jordan, eyebrows raised. "Of course. Aren't you?"

"Oh, yeah. Absolutely," he said. *I am now, anyway.*

"Good. Well, maybe I'll see you there."

"Maybe," said Jordan, though he planned to make certain she did.

Before Jordan could start a new line of conversation, a group of girls emerged from the cafeteria, and one of them called to Kehau.

"I've gotta go," she said. "But I'll see you Friday."

"Friday—if not sooner." He watched her walk with her friends and breathed deeply, a warm feeling running through his body.

Jordan's moment of happiness was interrupted when he felt a hand on his shoulder. A deep voice behind him said, "You know you're not supposed to talk to the girls, Elder!"

Jordan turned and recognized his former mission companion Brandon Mendes. "Mendes? What are you doing here?"

Brandon was tall, a bit on the large side, and thinning black hair covered his head. "I transferred from Provo this semester. I heard you talk about BYU—Hawaii so much, I thought I'd come check it out. Now all I have to do is get you to set me up with a pretty Hawaiian girl like that. Is she an old friend of yours?"

Jordan shook his head. "Nah, I just met her yesterday on my airport run for the flower shop."

"Flower shop?" Brandon hit him playfully on the shoulder. "Dang—why couldn't I get a cool job like that? I'm stuck in the computer lab showing people how to plug in their thumb drives and helping them 'find a Google.' You wouldn't believe some of the questions I get."

Jordan laughed. "Yeah, I can imagine. That's what I really wanted to do, though—computer lab assistant."

"Well, why aren't you doing it, then?"

"I can't—I haven't had CS 350 yet."

Brandon shrugged. "I haven't had 350, either."

Jordan's smile dimmed. "Really?" He'd told his mother he wanted to work in the lab, but she'd insisted the advanced programming class was a requirement for the position. So instead, she'd gotten him the job at Pua's.

"Aw, c'mon," said Brandon. "The lab's not nearly as cool as a flower shop. But if you want, I'll let you know if any spots open up."

"Thanks, Brandon. I'd appreciate it."

Later that night, Jordan walked from his home to an off-campus student house. He carried two pans of *pani popo*—sweet rolls baked in coconut milk—which he had volunteered to make as part of the refreshments for his family home evening group.

He rang the bell and, following custom, removed his slippers— what the mainland kids would call "flip-flops"—adding them to a pile growing on the small porch. The door was answered by Solomi, a Samoan girl who had been one of his home teachees before his mission.

"Hi, Jordan! Come in. Come in," she said, taking the pans from him. "Oh, your *pani popo* looks delicious. Is this my recipe?"

"Just like you taught me," Jordan said, following her into the warm house. The air smelled of curry and rice, and Jordan found his way over to a petite girl with extra fair skin and unruly blonde hair. "Hey, Stacie."

Stacie turned and gave Jordan a hug. "Welcome back, Jordan. How was your mission?"

Before Jordan could answer, Solomi's voice carried from across the room. "Stacie—can you help me for a minute?" Stacie left with a promise to return, and Jordan took the chance to look around the room. The group was rather diverse: half from various Polynesian islands, a handful of Asian kids, Mdeleshi from Zimbabwe, and the rest were *haoles* like Jordan.

One of the *haole* guys stood next to him, fiddling with his blonde hair, the sides combed together so it stuck up in the middle in a faux-hawk. Jordan introduced himself, and the guy shook Jordan's hand. "Spencer Hoven," he said. Spencer leaned in and whispered, "Check out this freak show, man. I've never seen a bigger group of weirdos in my life." Jordan looked around at the diverse group and thought they looked perfectly normal. He assumed that by "weirdos" Spencer meant "people who don't look like me."

four

Anticipation built up in Jordan as he walked from his house to the dance on campus. Although Jordan went to church dances during his youth, they had done more to feed his insecurities than anything else. The dances his freshman year at BYU—Hawaii had been little better, and Jordan tended to avoid them altogether. As he approached the Aloha Center student building, a wave of anxiety swept over him. He took a deep breath, reminding himself how much had changed since his awkward youth, and bravely entered.

Jordan walked the length of the Aloha Center, looking for a friendly, familiar face—someone to help bolster his confidence—but all he saw were strangers. When he reached the back of the building, he took one more steeling breath and then walked out.

The school's ballroom occupied its own building, connected to the rear of the Aloha Center by a small, partially covered courtyard. A cluster of students loitered off to the side, and loud, throbbing music filled the warm night air. Jordan showed his student ID to the girl at the door and walked in.

A handful of colored lights shone on the small group jamming to music Jordan didn't recognize, while a slightly larger crowd milled around the perimeter of the ballroom. Jordan joined the non-dancers and watched the action out on the floor, trying to build up his nerve while waiting for a slightly larger group to hide in. As he scanned the crowd, looking for Kehau, it occurred to him that she wouldn't be there until the PCC night show let out, so maybe he should find someone to dance with in the meantime.

The crowd grew steadily, and after four songs the number of people on the floor had tripled. Jordan was still hanging with the wallflowers when he heard someone say "Hey, are you gonna dance or what?"

He looked over to find Stacie, the girl from his family home evening group, grooving next to him in a style that could only be described as unique. "C'mon, Jordan. Show me your stuff."

"Hey, Stacie," he said, smiling. As near as he could tell, Stacie was by herself, so he joined her. They danced for a couple of songs, and then he thanked her and Stacie danced away. He noticed Amber standing not far from him and decided maybe he'd dance with her too. Jordan danced with several other girls after Amber and found by just getting out and interacting, he actually enjoyed himself for a change.

The mass of students out on the floor now spread nearly to the wallflowers, which made it difficult to move through the crowd. The air hung thick and heavy, the air conditioners on the roof struggling to keep up with the overheated throng. Jordan noticed there were significantly more Polynesians on the floor and figured the PCC night show must be out.

With that realization, he resumed his search for Kehau and finally located her on the opposite side of the ballroom. He worked his way around through the crowd, but by the time he'd traversed the floor, she was nowhere to be seen.

After completing another fruitless circuit of the dance floor, Jordan slipped out into the cool night air, where a steady breeze felt like heaven. He walked around the outside of the ballroom and then through the halls of the Aloha Center. Every place he looked was the same: no Kehau.

While in the Aloha Center, he ran into Brandon, hot and sweaty and standing at a drinking fountain. "Hey, bud. What are you doing in here—the dance is over there."

"I'm looking for someone," Jordan replied. "What are you doing here?"

"Oh, man. I needed a drink." Brandon wiped his lips on his arm and asked, "So who are you looking for? That girl you I saw you with Sunday?"

Jordan smiled. "Yeah."

Brandon raised his eyebrows and smirked. "I'd be looking for her too."

Together they worked their way back inside the ballroom. "Hey," Brandon said. "Who's that guy dancing with your girl?"

Jordan followed Brandon's gaze, and he quickly drew a breath. Kehau was smiling intently, dancing with her arms around Scott Sauaga. Jordan felt as though he'd been punched, and the room spun as he watched them. "That's not good." He walked outside and began circling the ballroom with Brandon following close behind.

"What? Do you know him?" Brandon asked.

"Yeah. His name's Scott, and he has a habit of ruining my life." Jordan remembered the admiration in Kehau's voice when she asked about Scott on their drive back from the airport. "Did you see the way she was looking at him?"

"I, uh . . ." Brandon stammered. Then he stopped, put his hand on Jordan's shoulder, and said, "You know what, dude, it was only a dance. The way she looked at you was way more than that, you know? Now go in there and get your girl back."

Brandon clapped him on the shoulder, and Jordan smiled. "You're right. Thanks."

"Now if you'll excuse me, there are a couple of cuties over there I need to introduce myself to."

Jordan walked back into the ballroom and, to his relief, saw that Kehau and Scott were dancing with other people now. Jordan stood near Kehau, and once the song finished he moved quickly to intercept her before anyone else could get in the way.

"Kehau," he called, trying to make himself heard above the noise without sounding as desperate as he felt.

She turned and smiled when she saw him. "Hi, Jordan."

Seeing her smile sent a thrill up his spine. With mock formality he asked, "May I have this dance?"

"Why, certainly."

Kehau was a good dancer—really good—and next to her, Jordan felt more awkward than ever. Yet Kehau smiled broadly, clearly enjoying herself, and if she even noticed Jordan's inept moves, she failed to show it.

The next song began with a slow, soft drum beat, and Jordan said, "Um, would you mind two in a row?"

"Sure" she said. Kehau took the elastic from her ponytail and slipped it on her wrist, letting her hair fall down over her shoulders. Jordan put his right hand on her back and took her hand in his left. The tingle he'd felt earlier was now ten times as strong and shot all through his body. His heart pounded as he looked down into her deep brown eyes. He leaned close to her, smelled the guava in her hair, and enjoyed the warmth of her body close to his. Jordan felt light-headed as they moved together to the music.

Dancing with his arms around Kehau in the middle of a crowded floor, he felt a sense of triumph. The last two years had changed him; he was a new man. And the new man had found his woman.

Jordan walked Kehau home after the dance. He wanted to hold her hand and kiss her at the door, but something held him back. After all, it was just a dance and not a real date or anything.

So as they stood at the door of Hale 5, Jordan decided a real date was just what he needed. "What are you doing tomorrow night?"

"Work," she said. A cool breeze blew a strand of hair across her face, and Kehau reached up to pull it behind her ear.

"Just work?" Jordan asked. "What about after?"

"Homework. Why?" she asked, the corners of her mouth turning up into a slight smile.

"My friend Brandon and I are going to catch a late showing of a movie down in Kaneohe, and I thought you might like to come."

"A late show? I don't know—I might fall asleep again."

Jordan smiled. "I'm counting on it." Kehau's face flushed as she laughed. "I'll meet you here at nine thirty?"

Kehau bit her bottom lip for a moment, and Jordan could tell she was thinking hard. His insides twisted, and he feared she might turn him down. But then she smiled and said, "Okay, nine thirty."

"Great," said Jordan.

As he walked home, Jordan called Brandon to let him know their trip to the movies had just become a double date.

"Gee thanks, MacDonald. 'Hurry up and find a date for tomorrow night—no pressure.'"

Jordan smiled as he walked down the long, straight sidewalk flanking the main campus drive. "Oh, c'mon. You were a dancing fool tonight. Don't tell me none of the girls you danced with would be willing to go see a movie with you."

"I can think of one or two," Brandon said. "Let me see what I can come up with."

■ ■ ■

What Brandon came up with was Crystal, a talkative girl of average height, with a round face and mousy hair that hung limply from her head as though she hadn't quite figured out how to manage it in the humid tropical air.

Brandon, who'd just gotten a new camera, insisted on taking pictures of everyone before they left. From what Jordan could see in the camera's little display, the picture of him with Kehau was a real keeper.

Jordan had borrowed his mother's car for the evening, and the forty-minute drive to the theaters at Windward Mall seemed to drag on forever, with Crystal sharing her opinion on everything from the quality of the cafeteria food to the diminutive size of her dorm room to the cockroach she caught eating food from between the bristles of her roommate's toothbrush. "I probably should have told her, but I was kind of mad at her that night."

Jordan tried steering the conversation to include Kehau, but she seemed distant and distracted. When they sat down in the theater, he took her hand and asked, "Hey, are you okay?"

"Yeah, I'm fine. Just tired." Still, she managed to stay awake through the movie, although she fell asleep on the way home along with Brandon and Crystal.

Jordan parked by the dorms, and Brandon escorted Crystal to Hale 3, while Jordan walked Kehau to Hale 5. She still seemed distracted, and Jordan again asked her if everything was all right.

"It's just that . . ." she began, pausing for several seconds before saying, "I'm really tired."

"Okay," said Jordan. He had set up this date hoping to finally get a kiss, but when he turned his face toward Kehau, she looked down, and Jordan had to settle again with giving her a hug. *Next time*, he thought.

"I'd better go now," Kehau said

"Yeah," said Jordan. "You get some sleep."

Kehau smiled weakly at him. "I will. Thanks."

Jordan watched her walk through the doors, disappointed the night hadn't turned out better. *Next time*, he thought again.

five

"**W**ho's Kehau?"

Jordan froze mid-bite and turned to look at his mother. She sat at the end of the table, leafing through a magazine, an air of practiced indifference about her. When he didn't answer right away, she looked up at him and cocked her head.

"Just a girl," Jordan said, returning to his breakfast and trying to match his mother's casual demeanor despite the icy feeling that spread through his chest.

"And were you with this girl last night?"

Jordan felt his ears flush and knew there was no point trying to keep the truth from her.

"Yeah, at the last minute Brandon and I decided to take some dates to the movie. But she's just a friend, Mom."

"Just a friend, huh? Are you sure? It didn't look that way to me." The icy feeling in Jordan's chest wrapped tightly around his heart, and he looked up in alarm. His mind raced as he watched her casually turn the pages of her magazine. Had she followed them onto campus? No—the family only had one car, and she refused to walk around town after dark.

Then Jordan had a thought. "Can you excuse me for a second?" Pushing himself away from the table, he hurried to his room. Just as he feared, he had forgotten to lock his computer screen. At the top of his email list was a message from Brandon—a message he

26

had never seen, but which showed as having been read.

With his heart pounding in his ears, Jordan brought up the message. There on the screen was the picture Brandon had taken of him and Kehau, and the way Jordan held her, it was clear he thought of her as more than a friend.

Jordan covered his face with his hands and let out a low groan. How could he have been so careless as to leave his computer unlocked? Struggling to keep his irritation in check, he sat back down at the table. "Mom, please don't read my email."

His mom looked up from her magazine, her casual air replaced with one of mild disappointment. "I don't like you keeping secrets from me, Jordan. And I can't believe you lied to me about why you wanted the car last night."

"I didn't lie to you, Mom. We just decided at the last minute to take dates to the movies." Jordan fidgeted with the cereal in his bowl, suddenly lacking in appetite.

"And yet you never said anything about going out with your girlfriend. Jordan, that's a lie of omission, and I expect better from you." The look on her face was more hurt than angry. "I don't know who this girl is, I don't know anything about her, and I don't like that you're sneaking around with her and lying to me about it."

Jordan sighed and sat back into his chair. "Fine. I'm sorry. It won't happen again."

"I'm sure it won't," she said. "But still, given the circumstances, I think it might be best if you not use the car this week."

Jordan looked up in surprise. "What? You're grounding me from the car?"

His mom raised her eyebrows. "Considering the way you've been behaving, I think it's a fitting punishment. Don't you?"

"No. Why are you doing this to me? I'm not a little kid anymore, Mom. I'm twenty-one."

"Then I suggest you start acting like it."

Jordan sighed. For the first time since he'd returned from his mission, he thought living at home might possibly be a mistake. But since he didn't have any plans that required a car, he decided it would be best to just let the subject drop. Shrugging his shoulders, he looked down and said, "Okay."

Closing his bedroom door, Jordan began changing for church.

The picture on his computer screen caught his eye, and he sat down at the desk. A warm feeling rose up inside him as he looked at the photo, pushing aside the disappointment he felt at his mother's reaction. Turning on his little inkjet printer, he printed the image while he finished dressing.

Once his tie was cinched up around his neck, he took the paper and looked at it. Then he grabbed a tack from his bulletin board and pinned the picture over his desk.

The next day Jordan walked quickly from his computer class to the small courtyard between the little Natural History Museum and the school's security offices. As he approached, he could see Kehau up ahead. A small flock of butterflies danced in his stomach, and he couldn't help smiling.

After a quick greeting, Kehau said, "Um, Jordan? Can I ask you a favor?"

"Yeah, sure—anything."

Kehau's smile broadened. "Okay. Tomorrow is my roommate's birthday, and Malia was going to take me to the mall to get her this book she really wants, since they don't have it in the bookstore here. But her brother was working on their car, and now it won't start or something. I'd take the bus, but there's no way I could get back in time for work. Do you think you could take me?"

The butterflies in Jordan's stomach all turned to rocks. "I'd love to, but, um, my mom said I can't use the car for a while." Embarrassment rose up inside him at the lameness of his situation. "You know, Lani might let me take the van—I can ask her at work."

Kehau's smile didn't dim, but her shoulders fell just a little. "No, don't worry about it," she said. "There's other people I can ask. Thanks." She put her hand on his arm and said, "I should probably get to class."

As she turned to go, Jordan said, "Oh, wait. Let's do something this weekend."

"Okay, um—let me see what my schedule is, and I'll let you know."

As Jordan walked away, he began to simmer at the thought of his mom treating him like a child and taking away the car. What he needed were some wheels of his own—today, if possible.

Jordan stopped at the bulletin board outside the cafeteria as soon as his class was done and looked at the cars listed for sale. Taking a chance that it truly was easier to ask forgiveness than permission, he wrote down the information for several and realized that three of the cars had the same contact number. So he called it.

"Hello! This is Chad; how can I help you?" Chad's voice definitely had a used car salesman quality about it.

"Hi, yeah, um, I'm looking for a car, and I saw you had a few posted."

"Yes, I do, as a matter of fact. What are you looking for?"

"I was hoping you had something less than four hundred." Although Jordan's dad had left him some money when he died, Jordan felt sure the less he spent, the easier his mother's forgiveness would come.

"Ooh, I'm running a bit low on the economy models. Um . . ." There was a pause on the other end. "Tell you what. I do have one car—a little Toyota hatchback. It's a bit rough, but it gets really good mileage. There's a guy who said he'd give me five-fifty for it, but he hasn't come back with the money. It's been several days . . ." Chad paused again, and said, "If you can match his price, I'll let you have it. I'll just tell this other guy he took too long. Why don't you come by and take a look?"

Jordan started to protest. He really didn't want to spend more than four hundred, but he also really needed the car, and he didn't have much time to look around. Suddenly, he had an idea. "I can be there in half an hour."

■ ■ ■

Jordan approached the house carrying a box and saw quite a few cars parked in the street and the driveway. He found the little blue Tercel and had to agree it was indeed fairly rough, with ripped seats and nearly as much rust as paint. But it was cheap.

He set the large box down on the porch and knocked. The door was answered by a tall, slender guy with curly red hair and a pointed chin that angled off to the right. Jordan recognized him as one of the regular customers of the flower shop.

"Hi, you must be Jordan. I'm Chad," he said with a large smile that revealed a slight underbite. "This is it right here. Like I said, it's a bit rough, but in your price range that's about all I have. If you can come up with a grand, I've got this nice Maxima," Chad motioned to a black car, "or there's a blue 626 around here somewhere . . ."

"Where did you get all these cars?" Jordan asked.

Chad gave Jordan a proud, toothy grin. "I buy them up the end of the semester, when everyone's getting ready to leave, and then sell them again when the new semester starts." He rubbed his hand along the roof of the Maxima. "It's a good little side business. I pretty much make fifty percent profit every time."

"Wow," said Jordan. "That's a great idea. I wish I'd thought of something like that."

"Yeah, it works. So, are you sure I can't sell you this beauty?" Chad said, indicating the Maxima.

"No, I think the Tercel will work. But, um, before we do anything else, I was wondering if . . ." Jordan trailed off, and he could feel his face flush red. So much for expert negotiating skills. "It sounds like the five-fifty price is pretty firm?"

"Yeah," said Chad.

"Well," Jordan bent down and opened the box. "I wondered if you might consider this." He reached in and pulled out his old computer. He'd bought his fancy new laptop when he first got home, and he hadn't even turned this old one on in over a month. "It's an iMac. I did a check on eBay, and you could easily sell it for five-fifty. I'd do it myself, but I really need the car today." Jordan cringed at how desperate he must sound. "So, anyway, I was wondering if you'd be willing to make a trade."

Chad stood with his arms folded, lips pursed, and his finger tapping his chin. After what seemed like an eternity, he said, "For two hundred and the computer, I think we have a deal."

As soon as the paperwork was complete, Chad gave him the keys, and Jordan drove straight to work. Although he was late, he sat in his car for a minute so he could call Kehau. "Hey, it looks like I'll be able to take you to the mall after all. What time do you need to leave?"

There was a brief pause on the line. "Oh, um, actually I already have a ride. But thanks for letting me know."

"Yeah, no problem." For the second time that day, Jordan's excitement turned to disappointment. "Hey, look—I'd probably better get to work. Have fun shopping."

"I will," said Kehau. "Thanks."

Jordan brought his fist down on the dash as soon as the call ended. He didn't hit it hard, yet the cheap, sun-bleached surface cracked into a spider web of broken plastic. Jordan leaned back against the head rest, closed his eyes, and let out a long breath before hauling himself out of the car and slamming the door shut.

As soon as his shift at Pua's ended, Jordan got into his car, turned left on Kamehameha Highway, and started driving. To his relief, the ugly little car ran pretty well, and soon his forward motion acted like a relief valve, allowing his anger and frustration to slowly bleed away.

By the time he reached the small surf town of Haleiwa, his emotions had diminished to a dull ache and were nearly overpowered by the growling in his stomach. Jordan checked his watch and realized that his little excursion was going to make him late for dinner. He turned into a small shopping center and found a parking spot in front of the grocery store.

As he walked in to pick up a snack, he called home. "Hi, Mom. I'm going to be a little late for dinner. No, I'm okay. I just . . . I'll be back in about an hour." Jordan picked up a package of dried cuttlefish and walked to the checkout. "I've got something I need to talk to you about when I get home."

He paid for his snack. Then as he was walking toward the exit, he spied a pamphlet advertising glider rides at the nearby Dillingham Airfield. A grin stole across his face as he took the flier from the rack and headed for his car. Although he had no interest in gliders, he always enjoyed a trip to a little airport.

Fifteen minutes later, Jordan parked outside the tiny airstrip and walked to the fence. On the other side, several gliders were lined up near the runway, each tilted so the end of one wing touched the ground. Across the field, a couple of small planes cast long shadows as the sun inched its way toward the western horizon.

Then Jordan heard the sound he was hoping for. He looked out into the sky above the ocean where a small white plane with a red tail buzzed over the waves, flying parallel to the runway. As the plane flew past, Jordan imagined he was the one at the controls, with one eye on the airport and the other on the altimeter, waiting for just the right moment to turn into the base leg of the landing pattern.

Jordan watched as the plane banked to the left and then turned to line up with the landing strip. The engine sounded like it was barely running as the pilot gently touched the gear to the runway, and Jordan remembered the mixture of relief and sadness that came with the end of every flight.

The plane taxied to a tie down on the opposite end of the field, and

Jordan roused himself to begin the trip home. As he drove, his mind jumped back and forth between memories of flying and thoughts of Kehau, but before those thoughts could fully form, his mother's voice popped into his head and chased them out. "I expect better from you."

Jordan chafed at the memory. Why was his mom still treating him like a child? He was old enough to make up his own mind and live his own life. And he wanted that life to include airplanes. By the time he reached La'ie, Jordan had talked himself into asking his mom about flying lessons. It was what he really wanted, after all, and he needed to stand up for himself.

He parked the little blue car on the street in front of the house. His mom stood in the driveway, talking to their neighbor, Sister Talaki. It was too dark to make out his mom's face at first, but as he approached, he could see her eyebrows were raised.

"Is this what you wanted to talk to me about?" she asked, indicating his car.

"Yeah. That, and . . ." Jordan tried to form the words to bring up flying lessons, but they caught in his throat.

"And what?" Her eyes kept glancing past him to the car parked in front of her house.

Jordan hesitated, and Sister Talaki said, "Listen, Beth—I'll catch up with you tomorrow." She turned and walked toward her house.

"Okay, Mom. Promise me you won't get angry."

"I'm already angry, Jordan." Beth's voice was soft but edged with irritation.

Jordan drew a deep breath, and let it out slowly. "Well, tonight after work, I took a little drive, just to see how my new car runs—and it runs very well." Jordan shifted his weight from one foot to the other, and made a futile effort to look his mom in the eye. "Anyway, I ended up past Haleiwa, over at the Dillingham Airfield."

"Stop," said his mom. "I know where this is going, and the answer is no." She cocked her head, and her brow furrowed. "I can't believe you'd even ask that. You know how I feel. I mean, what has gotten into you? Running around behind my back, lying to me, and now this," she said, gesturing at the car again. "I thought you'd come back off your mission a better person, but instead you're turning into your sister."

Fighting disappointment, Jordan walked into the house and muttered, "Well maybe Julie had it right."

six

The next week, Jordan lingered at the bulletin board outside the cafeteria where he had seen Kehau the Sunday after their first date. He stared unseeing at the flyers and announcements, his mind instead focused on his sudden change in fortune. When he called Kehau to firm up their plans for the previous weekend, she told him something had come up. He'd called her again earlier in the week, but she claimed to be busy with school and work and unable to make time for a date. The thing that had Jordan feeling more than a little bit paranoid was that he no longer saw her between classes. His vast experience with unrequited love told him he was getting the brush-off, yet he just couldn't bring himself to give up hope.

Jordan moved around to the other side of the kiosk, and his eye caught a poster for New Student Day at the Polynesian Cultural Center. *This'll be great*, he thought. He could go and see Kehau at work.

Jordan looked at the poster for a date and was greatly disappointed to find the event had already passed. Still, the thought had been planted in his mind, and Jordan decided to go to the night show that very evening.

As soon as he finished his last flower delivery, he raced home for a quick early dinner of frozen burritos, and then drove to the PCC. Jordan found a spot in the north end of the massive parking lot, which was nearly a third the size of the park itself.

The PCC's main entrance occupied a long, narrow building with a steep thatched roof that curved inward to a high point. Inside, the ceiling sloped up, mirroring the roof outside. Set into the walls were deep glass cases with models of Polynesian voyaging canoes, carvings, weapons, and other artifacts. Jordan bought a ticket from a girl he vaguely recognized from school and began wandering through the grounds.

He had come to the PCC with his family when they first arrived in La'ie and again when his grandparents came for a visit. But that had been at least a half-dozen years earlier, and Jordan saw everything as if for the first time. Immediately inside the entrance was the Gateway Restaurant, where, up until just a few weeks ago, his sister Julie had worked, feeding the teeming hordes of park visitors who opted not to attend the more expensive Ali'i Luau.

Jordan circled around behind the restaurant near the gift shop, where, as a child on their first visit, he had been fascinated by the little carved tikis offered for sale. He walked past the full-sized carvings of the ancient Hawaiian gods outside and then moved along further into the Center. With over an hour before the night show began, Jordan followed the path toward the right, which led past the Hale Aloha Theater, site of the Ali'i Luau dinner show.

As he walked over a bridge that crossed the Center's lagoon, a group of tourists in a double-hulled canoe passed on his left, pushed along by a muscular, pole-wielding Polynesian. To his right, Jordan could hear the music and drums from the Luau entertainment, and the realization that Kehau was probably dancing there made him smile.

Standing on the bridge, listening to the show inside, Jordan suddenly felt a strong arm around his shoulders. He looked up and found himself face to face with Scott.

"'Sup, *Pono*?" Scott asked, with a mischievous smile.

"Hey, Scott," said Jordan, stiffening.

"So, what? You here all by yourself? Still all alone?"

"No, as a matter of fact, I'm here to watch my girlfriend dance in the night show." Jordan knew referring to Kehau as his girlfriend was a bit of a stretch, but Scott didn't need to know that.

"Girlfriend, huh?" said Scott, slapping Jordan on the back. "I guess maybe there are still miracles today." Scott punched Jordan in the arm, just a little too hard to be considered playful. "Hey, do yourself a favor: Keep her away from Rich Mekila." With that, Scott howled with laughter and walked away.

Jordan's face burned red. Somehow Scott managed to reference that terrible night nearly every time they met.

He walked slowly along the pathway, past the Samoan village, but he was no longer enjoying himself. He turned around and made his way to the other side of the park, to the Pacific Theater where the night show was held. Jordan walked up one of the long, sloping cement ramps that led into the theater and gave his ticket to a small Asian girl with short hair and an impish smile. Then he continued on into the seating area.

Jordan looked around, a flood of memories returning to him. Although he had only been to the PCC night show twice before, he had been in the theater several times for regional church meetings and community activities. The stage floor was a large, circular area covered in green artificial turf and backed by a high wall of simulated lava. The seats rose in a semi-circle from the stage, and the whole affair was covered by a large, open roof that extended from the back of the auditorium to just above the stone backdrop, effectively shielding the theater from all but the most torrential rains while giving the audience a view of the sky beyond the back stage wall.

Jordan found his seat, which was on the top level and closer to the right side than the middle. But for a discount ticket, he decided he really shouldn't have expected much else. At least he was on the front row of his section, so he wouldn't have to worry about someone with big hair sitting in front of him.

As the crowd filed in, eventually filling most of the theater, Jordan awaited the show with anticipation. An older couple sat on his left, and there was no one to his right. Soon the lights dimmed and the stage filled with performers, some dancing, others carrying torches. In the flickering light of the fire they held in their hands, Jordan searched in vain for Kehau's face.

A large, white banner fell from the ceiling, and onto it was projected a stylized animation, depicting the desperate escape of a young couple from deadly volcanic fire, followed by the birth of their son, Mana. The story then showed this family as they journeyed through the different Polynesian islands and Mana grew into a young man.

Jordan intently watched the performers, constantly looking for Kehau, but after the introduction and Tongan section, he still hadn't seen her.

As the Tongan performers left the stage and a traditional Hawaiian chant announced the next section, Jordan sat forward in his seat. He knew Kehau danced in the Hawaiian part of the show, and he watched intently as the performers made their way onto the stage. An uneasy feeling grew within him as he examined the face of each dancer, yet failed to find Kehau. Had he accidentally picked her night off to come to the show?

As the Maoris from New Zealand took the stage, Jordan's heart fell. Kehau wasn't there. He had a clear view of every performer, and none of them even resembled her. Jordan sat back in his seat with a groan. He fidgeted as the Maoris taught Mana the skills of a warrior, and when intermission came, Jordan decided to go home.

As the house lights came up, and he stood to leave, the show's announcer drew his attention to workers in the aisles selling Pineapple Delights—guava sherbet in a half-pineapple shell. Jordan had wanted one of these treats desperately when his family came to the show years before, but his mother had absolutely refused. "You kids will be up half the night if you eat all that ice cream." But now at the show as an adult, and with Mother nowhere around, Jordan decided to indulge himself.

With a mouth full of ice cream, Jordan's frustration ebbed, and he decided to stay and watch the rest of the performance. As the house lights went down and the next section began, a girl wearing a white dress wandered onto the stage while others in the background did a traditional Samoan seated dance. Jordan scanned the dancer's faces, but didn't find the one he was looking for. Then the girl in white made her way to his side of the stage, and Jordan's heart leapt in his chest.

Kehau.

Jordan hadn't realized she had a starring role in the show, yet there she was, front, center, and in the spotlight. She was playing the main love interest to the young man in the story, and Jordan couldn't take his eyes off of her the rest of the evening.

Kehau danced with Mana twice during the Tahitian section, the second time as part of a wedding scene. After the wedding, Kehau and her partner presented themselves to the audience as a newly married couple. Jordan reminded himself it was all part of the show, but he still found himself fighting off a touch of jealousy.

Once Kehau and the other performers took their final bow, the stage lights went down and the house lights came up. Jordan tried to hurry through the bustling masses, wanting to catch Kehau as she left the Center. He knew the employee exit was on the back side of the PCC, leading straight onto campus, and he toyed with the idea of trying to get there from the inside but figured it would probably be blocked off from the rest of the park.

Instead, Jordan made his way to the visitor's exit and started walking toward his car. Already, the line of vehicles trying to leave had ground to a halt, and Jordan realized the only way he could make it would be to walk. He hurried down the park's long east side, across the end, and back up the road between the college and the Center, toward the employee gate at the back.

Moving south along the road, he saw a few people walking west from the Center to the campus dorms. He was about thirty feet from the stream of people when he heard a familiar laugh and saw Kehau in a small group walking beneath a street lamp. He knew he could catch her if he ran, but then he decided calling out would appear less desperate.

"Kehau!" She turned, and he waved at her. The group stopped, looked his direction, and Kehau waved back. "Hi, Jordan," she said. It was too dark to see her face, but Jordan imagined her smiling at him, and he smiled back. His smile soon left, however, as Kehau and her friends turned and continued walking. Jordan stopped, confused and hurt, and he watched until she and her friends were out of sight.

This was not good.

The next night, Jordan wore a path in the grass as he paced nervously, waiting for the night show to end. He always preferred to try to make his meetings with Kehau appear spontaneous and accidental, but he'd decided to abandon that strategy. He had little reason to be standing in the field behind the Cannon Activities Center other than to try to catch her on her way home from work. The thought of being so forward made his stomach hurt, but his need for information was strong enough to require the direct approach.

Jordan rehearsed in his mind what he would say, trying to

anticipate every avenue the conversation might take, and applying the "resolving concerns" skills he learned as a missionary to make sure he could get the time and answers he needed. He planned to ask Kehau out and not leave until they had set a date.

When at last he heard the musical finale and the applause of the audience, Jordan took up his position where the sidewalk leading from the PCC employee exit to campus passed the racquetball courts. It was the only structure near the sidewalk, and Jordan somehow felt comforted having it at his back.

Students alone or in small groups had been leaving the PCC sporadically ever since Jordan arrived, turning into a steady stream about fifteen minutes after the night show ended. He braced himself, and it didn't take long for Kehau to appear.

Jordan was disappointed but not surprised to see her with her usual group of friends. Her laughter drifted on the cool night breeze in painful contrast to the dread growing inside him. With as much courage as he could muster, Jordan walked toward her.

"Hi, Jordan," she said as he approached. He tried to read her expression but couldn't.

Jordan went numb. His brain and his body disconnected, and he seemed to be moving and speaking by remote control. "Kehau. Hey, could I talk to you for a minute?"

The group stopped, and Kehau said, "Yeah, sure." Her friends shot each other glances and little smiles, but to Jordan's horror they made no move to leave. An uncomfortable moment passed before Kehau turned to her friends and said, "You go on ahead. I'll catch up."

Thank you, thought Jordan as her friends smirked their good-byes and slowly walked off. They burst into a fit of giggles when they were several yards down the sidewalk, and Jordan's confidence eroded even further.

A look of concern now replaced Kehau's usual smile. Groups of PCC night show workers continued to stream toward them, and while Jordan didn't quite know what he wanted to say, he was sure he wanted to say it in private. "Can we walk this way?" he asked, indicating the open field between the old gym and the Cannon Center.

"Sure," she said, and they moved off together in an uneasy silence.

The field was not large, maybe an acre, and Jordan's thoughts were still a jumble of fear and pain when they reached the middle.

Despite not knowing what to say, Jordan stopped anyway so as to avoid the crowds in the parking lot behind the Cannon Center.

"Kehau, I, um . . ." Jordan's mind was a mess of thoughts and questions, yet his mouth refused to use the words his brain gave it: I really care about you. Why are you avoiding me?

He made himself look at Kehau, to search her eyes for some sign of hope. But in the harsh, dim light he saw only pity. Jordan felt a sudden urge to disappear from the face of the earth. *Just get it over with, you idiot.*

Finally forcing his mouth to work, he managed to say, "Um, I know you're busy and everything, but there has to be some time that we can go out. It doesn't have to be anything fancy—just a movie or whatever. But I want to set something up—tonight—before you go back to your room." There! He'd done it. He'd told Kehau what he wanted, and he wasn't taking no for an answer.

But Kehau just looked down at her hands. "I like you, Jordan. Really, I do. It's just . . ." She paused, and the knot in Jordan's stomach tightened. "Jordan, I'm seeing someone else right now. I'm sorry."

The knot in Jordan's stomach leapt up and became a lump in his throat. "Oh," he said, trying to hide the hurt in his voice. His head spun, and his eyes begin to water. He wanted desperately to leave before tears could come and embarrass him further. "Okay, well, um—I guess I'd better go then."

He turned and began walking quickly away. "I really am sorry," he heard her say, but all he could think about was finding some solitude so his heart could break properly.

seven

Jordan drove the Flowermobile to an off-campus student house on Moana Street and parked in the shade of a large breadfruit tree. He had hoped working would take his mind off the heavy, dull ache in his chest, but delivering flowers only served to deepen the hurt.

Reaching around behind his seat, past the little tropical bouquets and single-wrapped flowers, he grabbed a dozen long-stemmed red roses arranged in a large white vase. Chad's little used car business must be doing pretty well if he could spend that kind of money on flowers for his girlfriend. Lifting the arrangement gently out of a bucket, he shook his head at all of the deliveries still left to make. "Student Romance Season—four weeks after the start of every semester," Lani had said as she prepared the day's orders.

Jordan double checked the card and forced a smile as he knocked on the door. "Hi. I have a delivery for Heather Martin."

When Heather came to the door, Jordan recognized her as a girl from his biology class. She was a cute, petite girl, and Jordan enjoyed seeing her smile, even though he knew it was for the roses and not for him. "Hey, Erin," she called out. "Come take my picture with the flower guy."

The girl who had answered the door approached with a little silver camera, and Heather put her arm around Jordan's waist. Her unexpected touch caught him off guard, but Jordan liked it. Feeling her close to him, he realized if he wanted to get over Kehau, he needed to find someone to take her place. There had to be a girl out there for him—he just needed to keep looking.

"Hey, flower guy." Erin's husky voice brought him back to the present. "How about a smile?"

As Jordan finished his delivery rounds, he thought about the girls he knew and might be interested in asking out. He decided to start with Angie, a Filipina girl who sat near him in his computer class. She was taller than most Filipinas he knew, with short black hair and piercing brown eyes, and Jordan had enjoyed talking with her after class a couple of times. The fact that his mother probably wouldn't like her any better than Kehau made her just that much more alluring, so the next day he went to the computer lab in the library where Angie worked as a lab assistant.

Angie was talking with Brandon when Jordan arrived. They soon finished talking, and Brandon came over to see him.

"Hey, bud. How are you doing?"

"Doing good," Jordan said. "How 'bout you?"

"Not too bad." A little smile crept up on his face, and he lowered his voice. "You know Angie, right?"

Jordan nodded.

"I just got a date with her for Friday." Brandon raised his eyebrows and the little smile grew huge.

Jordan did his best not to show his disappointment. "Cool."

"Yeah. Hey, so what about you and Kehau? How's that going?"

Jordan winced but quickly tried to shrug off his discomfort. "It didn't work out."

Brandon scowled, bringing his wolf-man eyebrows almost to his nose. "Ah, man. Sorry to hear that, bud."

After a brief, awkward silence, Brandon said, "Hey, do you still want to be a lab assistant? One of our guys was let go, and we're real short right now."

Jordan's eyes opened wide. "Yeah. I would." Maybe this trip to the lab wouldn't be such a downer after all.

"Really? Cool. You'll be great at this. I'll have the lab supervisor give you a call. I know he really wants to fill this spot before the term paper rush hits."

"That sounds great, Brandon. Thanks."

The next day Lani asked Jordan to take Amber to the floral supply warehouse on his way to the airport. Jordan hadn't spent much time one-on-one with Amber, but on the drive he found her to be friendly, funny, and quite nice to look at. Although her extroverted personality was a little intimidating, she was very easy to talk to, and Jordan opened up to her as they drove. Soon he had told her the whole Kehau saga.

"It's just frustrating. I thought things were going along so well, but then it just fell apart. And it didn't help that my mom was getting all freaked out about me dating a local girl." Jordan shook his head. "I should have done like my sister and gone to a school far away."

Amber smiled at him. "Just hang in there. Things will work out. And the sooner you get out there and start dating again, the sooner you'll get over her."

Jordan knew this; it was what he had been telling himself all week. Yet his false start with Angie had killed his momentum. The thought of putting himself actively in the dating world sent his heart racing. Jordan took a moment to gather his courage. Then he turned to Amber and said, "You know what? You're right." Before he could stop himself, he added, "What are you doing tomorrow night?"

■ ■ ■

Jordan took her to the movie on campus, and it felt good to be out with someone as fun as Amber. "You know what?" he said as he stood with her on the porch of her off-campus house. "I think my mom would be okay with you as my girlfriend. What do you say?"

Though he'd said it half as a joke, the thought of being Amber's boyfriend held a certain appeal, and he was disappointed when she simply smiled and ruffled his hair. "Thanks for a fun night. I'll see you at work on Monday."

Although Jordan's date with Amber helped ease his pain, the effect only lasted for the next twelve hours until he saw Kehau with her roommate, Zoe, walking home from church the next day. Kehau wore the same red dress he'd seen her in after their first date. But Jordan stayed back, not wanting to open himself up for any more heartache, and simply watched from afar. Kehau laughed her clear, beautiful laugh, and Jordan's heart turned to lead.

His sour disposition the past few days had not gone unnoticed by his mother, and when he returned home with a long face that afternoon, she was waiting for him.

"I know there's something bothering you, Jordan. Do you want to talk about it?"

"No, I'm fine." Jordan felt embarrassed at being so upset over losing a girl who was never really his in the first place and certainly didn't expect any sympathy from his mother.

"All right; well, I think I might have an idea what's going on, and if you want to talk about it, I'm here, okay?"

Jordan looked at her and forced a smile. "Thanks, Mom."

"Now," she said, her voice changing from soothing to enthused, "what I think you need is a hobby—something to keep you busy and help get your mind off your troubles." His mom picked up a small box from the floor next to her and set it on the table. "When your father left, I looked a lot like you do now. And your Uncle Charles gave me this to help me out." She opened the box and pulled out a worn leather case.

"Your camera?"

"Mm-hmm. He gave me one of his old ones and some books on photography." She took it from its case and handed it to Jordan. He reached to take the outdated silver camera. "I put it away for several months, not really appreciating what I'd been given. Then one day I was feeling particularly down and I came across the camera in the closet. I took it out and started looking through this book, and seeing the pictures I realized that there was beauty all around me, and I felt a sudden, strong desire to find it and capture it and make it a part of me."

Jordan looked around the room at some of the pictures his mom had taken. He always thought her photos were good enough to sell. She gave a few away as gifts, but for the most part she used them to decorate the house, enlarging her favorites and hanging them on the wall.

"I haven't used this camera for quite a while. I could never go back to film now that I have digital, but I learned things with this old girl that made me a much better photographer. I like the auto focus and all of the other fancy features on my digital when I'm taking quick shots, but for the pictures that really matter, I turn off the automatic stuff and do all the settings myself, just like I did with this one."

Jordan looked at the camera in his hands. A touch of excitement tried to break through the gloom he was feeling, but it wasn't getting very far.

"The best part about learning to take pictures, though," she said, the softness returning to her voice, "was that it gave me something to think about besides myself and all of my problems." Beth took the camera from Jordan and looked at it as if it were an old friend. "This little gal got me through a really, really tough time." She stared at it for a second more and then quickly handed it back to Jordan. "I thought it might help you too."

She pushed the box at him and said, "Now, look. It's a gorgeous day outside. Go out and take some beautiful pictures."

She stood and patted Jordan's back. He smiled in spite of himself and said, "Thanks, Mom."

Slipping the camera and a couple of books into an old backpack, Jordan decided to make the most of the beautiful afternoon and ride his bike to the temple. The La'ie Temple sat high on a hill on the western side of town, looking down across eleven acres of beautifully landscaped grounds that teemed with poinsettias, bougainvilleas, royal palms, and dozens of other flowers and trees. In addition to the flora, there were fountains, sculptures, and the building itself. Modeled after Solomon's temple from the Old Testament, the La'ie Temple was one of the few Mormon temples built without spires. Like nearly every other temple, however, it faced east, down across the lush grounds, along Hale La'a Boulevard, and right on to Temple Beach and the ocean.

Armed with two rolls of film, Jordan set up the camera and started shooting. He took close-up pictures of flowers, pictures of the fountain with various shutter speeds, and wide angle shots of the temple itself. The more pictures he took, the more excited he became, and he quickly burned through both rolls of film. With just a few exposures left, he set a course for a large banyan tree that grew behind the building.

Jordan walked through the gate that led to the small garden at the back of the grounds. A sidewalk curved to the right, connecting the gate with a back door Jordan had used dozens of times as a youth doing proxy baptisms in the temple. To the left, a giant banyan tree dominated one corner of the garden and towered over a small, round sitting area. The wooden bench was a favorite photo site because the dark, twisting mass of the banyan made an excellent backdrop from which the subjects stood out clearly. Jordan quickly realized, however, that the tree itself was too large to fit in a photo, and while the trunk made for an interesting backdrop, it wasn't a very good subject itself.

Jordan tried framing some of the nearby flowers against the tree, but he just didn't like what he saw. He sighed. Looking around to see what else he might be able to shoot, his eyes were drawn to the top of the temple. The building was designed in the form of a Greek cross, and at the top of each of the four sides were intricate frieze murals depicting people and events of scriptural importance. Most photos of the temple Jordan had seen were straight on from the front, but as he studied the back of the building, he was struck by the interesting pattern the walls made when viewed from the corner.

He worked his way around the banyan tree to get a good angle for a shot. As he maneuvered himself behind the tree, trying to frame the temple between some of the vines hanging from the branches, he heard the gate open and close. At first he hoped whoever came in wouldn't block his shot, but it soon became clear he wasn't going to find a good angle anyway.

Moving from behind the tree to look for a picture worthy of the end of his roll, he suddenly froze. Kehau sat on the bench beneath the banyan tree, and a man stood in front of her, his back to Jordan. She looked up at this guy, holding both of his hands and smiling in a way that made a knot in Jordan's chest. Up until now, the photography ruse had worked to take his mind off of his heartache. But seeing her with this dark-haired stranger shattered everything.

Grateful Kehau hadn't seen him, Jordan slowly moved back behind the tree where he would be out of sight. Through a gap in the trunk, Jordan could still see Kehau, and he watched as the guy sat down next to her, put his hand under her chin, and kissed her.

Jordan's stomach did a back flip, and the knot in his chest jumped to his throat. Fortunately, the kiss was short, and Jordan felt a touch of relief as Kehau stood to go. His relief was short-lived, however, as her new man turned to follow.

Kehau had just been kissed by Scott Sauaga.

eight

Jordan waited until Kehau and Scott were well out of sight before making his way from the temple grounds over to his bike. Anger, pain, and frustration coursed through his body and fueled his legs as he quickly pedaled the short distance home. Once in his room, he dropped the camera into the old box and unceremoniously shoved the whole mess under his bed. He flopped onto his back, breathing heavily.

After just a few short seconds, though, his aggravation forced him back up. Jordan looked aimlessly around the room, and soon his eyes came to rest on the picture Brandon had taken during his date with Kehau. He walked across the room and ripped it off his bulletin board, sending the pushpin flying. Studying Kehau's face, he remembered the way he'd felt when he thought things might actually work out between them.

He crumpled the picture into a ball and threw it in the trash. But then, with a sigh, he fished the picture out and straightened it as best he could. Looking at it one more time, he took a long, cleansing breath and slipped the photo into his desk. He slammed the drawer closed and stood staring at the empty spot on his wall where the picture had been. Then something he had glimpsed in the drawer registered in his brain, and he opened it again. From beneath the picture, he pulled out his pilot's logbook.

Jordan looked at the book, and the words of Julie's friend Todd hit home: "Chicks dig a pilot."

Maybe that's what his dad had been thinking when he'd pushed Jordan to start flying lessons. "If nothing else, it will help you build confidence," his father had told him before he started. "I just want you to get your license—that's it. What you do with it after that is up to you, but please, as a favor to me, see this through to the end."

Jordan had intended to finish his lessons, but his father's heart attack cut that short. As he looked at the entries made by his instructor in Texas, he remembered each of the flights, and the desire to return to the sky overwhelmed him. Not only because his father had wanted him to, but because he thought that doing so just might help him get over Kehau.

Maybe his mom was right. Maybe he did need a new hobby—flying. With the money his dad left him, he was sure he could afford it. He barked out a short laugh as he imagined asking his mom for access to his money. But the more he thought about flying, the more he knew he needed to find a way.

Maybe he could withdraw a little at a time without attracting her attention, and combine it with his computer lab pay. After talking to Brandon, he knew that the lab paid significantly more than the flower shop, so it just might be enough. He could even set up his own private bank account.

A sense of reckless rebellion flooded through him. Quickly, so he wouldn't have the chance to lose his nerve, Jordan carefully returned his log book to the drawer and hurried outside where he climbed into his car and sped away.

Jordan knew that Todd Jameson, being from a family of relative privilege, lived in one of the higher-rent houses nestled between the highway and the beach. Jordan peered down each driveway until he spied the little black Mazda he'd seen Todd driving around campus. Nervously he approached the door, trying to hurry before the frustration and angst that propelled him forward were replaced by good sense. Jordan could hear laughter inside and hesitated, nearly turning away. He knew this was crazy, but remembering Scott and Kehau at the temple pushed rationality aside, and he quickly knocked.

An overly tan blonde answered the door. "Hello, may I help you?" she asked in a phony British accent, eliciting giggles from somewhere within the house.

"Um, I'm looking for Todd Jameson." said Jordan.

The girl turned her head and yelled, "Todd! It's for you."

"Hey, Brother MacDonald. C'mon in." Todd opened the door, and Jordan entered the living room. "It's Jordan, right?" Jordan nodded. "What can I do for you?"

"I was wondering about where you rent your plane."

"Oh, yeah," Todd said. "I rent from La'aloa Aviation, down at Honolulu International. Why, you thinking about starting lessons again?"

Jordan almost said yes, but then he realized that if he were to keep his lessons secret from his mom, he'd have to keep them secret from everyone. "No, I, uh, I was just curious. Do you know if there's anything at Dillingham?" Jordan had figured he'd be flying out of the small airfield on the west coast of O'ahu and not all the way in Honolulu. But Todd shook his head.

"There might be a guy with a plane and instructor's license over there, but I'm telling you, you won't find a better value than La'aloa. I'll be flying the day after tomorrow. You want to come?"

Jordan took in a quick breath. "Yeah, that'd be great."

"Excellent!" said Todd, slapping Jordan on the shoulder. "We'll leave here Tuesday morning at five thirty. That'll give us a jump on traffic, and we'll be back on the ground before the air gets too rough. Want me to pick you up?"

"No," Jordan said quickly. "I'll meet you here." Driving home, he began making up his excuse for leaving the house before dawn.

Jordan had an interview for the lab assistant job the next day. Although still a student himself, Hisaishi, the beefy computer lab supervisor, looked to be in his mid thirties. "Nice to meet you, Jordan. Sit down, please." Jordan took a seat across from Hisaishi. "I'll get right to the point," he said with a heavy Japanese accent. "I'm very busy right now. We have one student who missed too many days work, and we had to let him go. He was married student, so he was working thirty hours in the labs. I have already one new lab assistant—single student who can work twenty hours, and I still need student to work other ten hours."

Hisaishi handed the job description to Jordan, but as he read it, his heart sank. Even though the hourly rate was significantly more than at the flower shop, working only ten hours in the lab would mean an overall cut in pay.

"I need someone very dependable, someone I can count on to be at work on time, every time. I already talked to Dr. Maran, and he agree you would be a good lab assistant. But one thing, I need someone who can start right away. Can you do it?"

Jordan's mind raced. If he took this job, he could never afford to fly. *Unless I stay at Pua's too.* With this sudden realization, Jordan quickly made his decision. Barely giving a thought to the burden two jobs would be, Jordan smiled and said, "I can do it."

"Great," said Hisaishi. "You come start Friday night, six to nine shift. Same on Saturday. I'll have next week's schedule up Saturday morning, and we give you your full ten hours starting next week."

Jordan felt a bit let down that suddenly his whole weekend, or at least the evenings, would be taken up by work. But his disappointment came with a sense of relief—he hadn't put much effort into finding a date for the weekend, and with his new work schedule, he didn't need to bother.

Jordan walked out of the main computer lab, past the library, and toward the Little Circle—the small road that ran in front of the central buildings on campus. At the middle of the circle lay a round grassy field surrounded by flags from dozens of countries represented by the student body. A strong breeze from the ocean lifted the banners, and Jordan heard the familiar chiming chorus as the flags' hardware clanged against the poles.

As he cut across the road, another sound filled the air—the mechanical whine of a motorcycle. Jordan jumped as a blue bike sped past him—the same bike that had run him off the road on his way back from the airport. But this time the rider wasn't wearing a helmet, and Jordan recognized the spiked fauxhawk of Spencer Hoven, the guy from his family home evening group.

"He's going to kill himself one of these days," Jordan muttered to himself. "Idiot."

■ ■ ■

The following morning, Jordan slipped quietly from the house, making a clean get-away before anyone else was up. As he rode with Todd, his excitement at going flying again after all this time was tempered by concern that his mom wouldn't accept the cover story he'd come up with in his note to her—that he was going to

La'ie Point to watch the sunrise.

Jordan had never been to the general aviation section of the Honolulu airport before. It sat to the south, across the runways from the main terminal. They drove past a number of flight schools and aircraft businesses and parked in a little area at the end of the road.

"Here we go. This is gonna be great." Todd led Jordan toward La'aloa Aviation, which consisted of little more than a small office built into the corner of an aircraft hangar and a metal desk set near the back. The hangar door was up, and as they approached, Jordan saw a girl with short, honey-colored hair sitting at the desk with her back to them.

"Roach has someone working the desk today. That either means he's out or hung over. He's too cheap to hire someone full time."

As they entered, Jordan saw that the hangar continued off to the side, where a couple of partially assembled airplanes sat. Todd stopped short and pointed at a faded blue Cessna with no engine. "That's not good." Before he could elaborate, his phone began playing the theme song from Top Gun. Todd looked at the name of the caller, smiled, and shook his head. "Hello."

"Hello, Mr. Jameson? This is Tonya at La'aloa Aviation." It took Jordan a second to realize the voice he heard came, not from Todd's phone, but from the light-haired girl sitting at the desk.

"Hello, Tonya at La'aloa Aviation. What can I do for you?" Todd walked toward her.

Tonya still sat with her back to the door and didn't see them approach. "Well, the plane you were supposed to rent this morning is not available."

Todd stood directly behind her and said, "I see."

Tonya jumped and spun around, her hand to her chest.

"That would have been nice to know before we drove all the way to the airport."

"I'm sorry," Tonya said, her lip quivering. "I'm just filling in for today, and Mr. Roach gave me this list of people to call, and—"

"Hey, don't worry about it," Todd said, quickly changing his tone. "It's not your fault." Todd flashed the girl his winning smile, and she smiled back weakly. "I'd better let you get back to your list before anybody else shows up." He winked, and Tonya's smile grew. As she turned back to the desk, Todd asked, "So, is Roach in today?"

Tonya faced them and bit her lip. "Yes, but I don't think he's in a very good mood this morning."

"So what else is new?" Todd said. "Thanks."

Jordan followed Todd as he walked toward the office. "Well, sorry about that. But while we're here, you should at least find out about signing up for lessons."

Jordan looked back at the old planes sitting in pieces across the hangar. "So, um, are those the only planes here?"

"Huh? Yeah," said Todd. "There's the gold Bonanza, and the Cessna's called The Blue Bomb." Todd must have noticed the concern on Jordan's face, because he quickly added, "They don't look like much, but Roach is a top mechanic. He keeps 'em in great shape."

They reached the office door, which stood slightly ajar. Todd knocked, and a deep voice called out, "Come in."

A large black man paced behind the desk with a cell phone to his ear. As they approached, he began speaking loudly. "Listen, you tell that—" He paused at the sight of Todd and Jordan, and then continued with words that were likely not his first choice, "—boss of yours that I will be in his office in thirty minutes, and we will get this worked out once and for all. I need my planes in the air by Friday."

Roach ended the call, looking first at Todd and then at Jordan. "Sorry about that—my friends, the parts guys. They've been jerking me around for weeks now. You must be Jameson's friend."

"Yes, sir. Jordan MacDonald. I, um, I'd like to find out about finishing up my ticket." Jordan's head buzzed as he made this announcement, not quite believing what he was saying. Somewhere in the back of his mind, Adventure cheered while Reason sounded alarm bells. Jordan ignored them both.

"Hmm. Do you have your log with you?"

Jordan nodded and handed it to Roach.

Roach looked through Jordan's log book and tapped away at his computer. Jordan looked around the office to keep himself occupied. On the wall, several bits of roughly cut fabric dangled above the door, while a poster with the words *Angel Flight* hung next to the light switch. On one corner of the desk was a model airplane. It was different than any Jordan had ever seen—a twin-engine prop plane with a big canopy and a high twin tail. On the wall, Jordan saw a photo of two men standing in front of a plane that looked like the model.

Roach spoke, pulling Jordan back to the present. "Well, I think we can probably get you your ticket with another thirty hours of flight time, plus maybe ten of instruction." Roach looked at Jordan over the top of his glasses. "I don't know if Jameson told you or not, but my main business is the shop. I like to keep a few students, just to stay current. It's really only worth my while if you're serious about finishing, and I've found that getting payment up front goes a long way toward that." Roach turned, catching a couple of sheets of paper as they fed out of the printer. "The total for you, because of the hours you already have, is going to be around four thousand."

Jordan's shoulders slumped. He could easily cover that amount with his savings, but his mom would certainly notice if he spent that much all at once. It would take forever to pull enough out a little at a time, even if added to his wages. "Um," Jordan began, but Roach continued.

"We can set you up with a student loan if we need to. The guys I use are pretty quick, and they're a little more liberal than most lenders. Plus, they actually still have money to lend, which isn't too common these days. All I need you to do is sign here and here and initial here, and we'll get you set up with a training schedule."

Jordan didn't quite know what to say. "Can I take these home and look over them?"

"Yeah, sure," Roach said. "Now, if you'll excuse me, I better go find out what's happening with my parts."

On the way home, an overwhelming sense of doubt hit Jordan. What was he doing? Todd didn't seem to notice. "You've just gotta do this. You won't regret it, not one bit."

But Jordan felt quite certain he would be full of regret, no matter which decision he made.

nine

"Jordan, what's this I hear about you dropping your programming class?"

Jordan poked at a pile of mashed potatoes and avoided his mother's gaze. He'd expected the BYU—Hawaii grapevine to deliver news of his adjusted schedule but not that same day.

"I needed to free up some time now that I'll be working at the computer lab." He felt bad lying to his mother, but he couldn't let her know his real reason—to create a block of time in the morning for flying lessons.

"I don't understand why you need that job. Aren't you still working for Lani?"

"Yeah, I am. But I figured working in the lab would be good experience. I mean, I am getting a degree in computer science, you know."

"Which is why I don't understand your decision. Dropping your computer class so you can work in the computer lab? If you needed to drop a class, why not bowling or something?" Jordan just shrugged. This was not an argument he could win, so he just let her vent. And being reminded of how fast news traveled through the small community further convinced him to keep his flying ambitions secret from everyone so word would not get back to his mother.

With his computer class dropped and biology shifted to the afternoon section, Jordan had time to meet with Roach that Friday

53

during his next airport run for Pua's. The payments on the four thousand dollar loan Jordan took out represented a large chunk of his monthly earnings.

The following Monday, Jordan got a call from a girl named Brooke at La'aloa, letting him know that The Bomb had been fixed and that he could have his first lesson Wednesday morning at seven. She asked if that would work.

"Of course!" he said.

The alarm on Jordan's phone rang promptly at five thirty that Wednesday. He quickly turned it off, dressed as silently as he could, and crept out into the hall. Easing the door closed, he turned to find himself face-to-face with his mother.

"You're up awfully early again this morning," she said.

Jordan's heart leapt into his throat. "I, uh . . ." Jordan's mind raced. What excuse could he possibly make about being up before the sun? "I just thought I'd get up and watch the sunrise."

"Mm-hmm." Beth nodded her head but did not look convinced. "Just like you did last Tuesday?"

"Uh, yeah. It was so beautiful, I thought I'd watch it again, you know, and, um, take some pictures this time. You know. Up at the Point. I love watching the sunrise at La'ie Point."

"Really?" Her eyes narrowed. "And wouldn't you need a camera for taking pictures?"

Jordan's mind raced. He could pretend he'd forgotten it in his room, but she was probably expecting that. "Oh, yeah. It's actually out in my car already. I was just coming back to, um, get my jacket. It's a little cooler out there than I expected."

Beth stared at him, but Jordan just smiled back. His story was solid, and after a moment she smiled and said, "Have fun on your shoot. I expect to see some amazing pictures later."

"Amazing pictures. You got it." Jordan quickly slipped past her and practically ran to his car.

His stomach was a tangle of excitement and nerves as he drove toward the airport for his seven o'clock lesson. The guilt he felt for sneaking around tempered the thrill of his impending flight, but those emotions were both overshadowed by his concerns about Roach, who had been sullen and distant their first two meetings. The thought of trying to fly with the man intimidated Jordan.

When he arrived at the hangar, Jordan approached the blue Cessna cautiously. "Mr. Roach?"

Roach poked his head out from behind the plane and smiled. "Hey, MacDonald. Glad you could make it." The man's deep, resonant voice rang through the hangar and surprised Jordan with its friendliness. Roach wiped his hands on a rag before shaking Jordan's. "Meet The Blue Bomb. We'll be using her for your lessons."

The hesitation Jordan initially felt at the thought of flying in a plane with a foreboding nickname quickly tripled as he looked closely at the ancient Cessna. Covered in heavily oxidized powder-blue paint and filled with an equally worn interior, the plane did not inspire confidence. However, Jordan's faith in the machine improved a bit as he examined the crucial parts during the preflight inspection and saw that they all looked sound.

"Okay," Roach said. "You run through the startup checklist. I'll get us out to the training area, and then we'll see what you've got."

Jordan followed the checklist carefully while Roach watched. As soon as he brought the engine to life, Jordan felt the familiar rush of excitement that always came with a flight. The sun beat in through the windshield, but as they taxied toward the runway, a cool morning breeze slipped in through the cockpit vents.

As the ground fell away from the plane, Jordan realized that, despite the ancient plane and controls, the thrill of flight was still the same—the feeling of floating above the ground; the view of the world from the sky; the nagging, low-grade nausea that always dogged him in the air.

They flew up to the practice area, and Roach asked Jordan to do some maneuvers: turns, stalls, and straight and level flight. It seemed to Jordan that he was getting a review instead of a lesson, but he decided that was probably just as well. He must have done okay, though, as Roach directed Jordan to fly back to the airport instead of taking the plane himself. "You fly it in. I'll talk to the boys and girls upstairs," he said.

Jordan tried to maneuver for the landing but soon ran into trouble. He didn't line up very well on the downwind and turned too late on the base leg, so he had to add power to get closer to the runway when he turned into his final approach. The turn from base came early, so he had to fly more to the right and try to keep the airspeed up. Jordan expected Roach to take over at any minute, but he didn't. He didn't offer any suggestions, either. He just let Jordan fly.

Jordan overcompensated for being low by adding too much power, and he flew way past the '4R' runway marker. He floated down the runway, struggling to get the plane to settle down while keeping the speed above stall. The stall horn sounded when they were still too high above the ground, and Jordan pushed in on the yoke to lower the nose. He finally got the plane down, bounced several times, and then stopped near the far end of the runway.

"Good thing we had a full nine thousand feet to work with," said Roach drily. "Next time you should probably try to set her down in the first mile of the runway."

"Sorry." Jordan followed the directions from ground control off of the runway and back to the hangar. Roach remained silent until Jordan brought the plane to a stop and cut the engine.

"Not bad on the flying, MacDonald, but we're going to need to work on the landing. However, here's the first lesson for today: don't apologize for the landing or anything else. If you make a mistake, just fix it. Okay?"

Jordan nodded, wondering how doing something that made him feel so inadequate was supposed to build his confidence.

ten

Fierce wind whipped his hair as Jordan leaned on a railing at the top of Pali Lookout. Looking down at the tangle of brush beneath the thousand-foot cliff, he remembered a painting he had seen of King Kamehameha driving the army of Kalanikupule over the edge during his conquest of O'ahu. *I guess things could be worse*, he thought.

Raising the camera to his eye, he snapped several photos of the panoramic view of Kaneohe. As long as he kept showing his mom pictures, she pretty much let him go where and when he wanted. As far as he could tell, his efforts to keep his flying lessons secret were a complete success.

At least these photos would actually be his. He'd taken a lot of pictures on these little excursions with Brandon, Angie, and a few others from the lab. For the mornings of his flight lessons, however, he'd been using other people's vacation photos, finding them online and having them made into prints at Foodland.

Glancing at his watch, Jordan decided to round up the gang. "Hey, Jordan," Brandon called as he approached. "What do you think about Maui?"

"I think it's a very lovely place," Jordan said.

"No, I mean what do you think about going over Thanksgiving?"

"Yeah, that'd be fun." Jordan tried to sound interested, but lately he'd been too tired to get excited about anything. "Hey, listen—are we about ready to go? I'm ignoring a ton of homework right now, and I really need to get it done."

As he checked his email later that evening, Jordan noticed a message from his bank—the one where he kept his secret personal account. As he opened the electronic statement and looked at the balance, a knot formed in his gut. Even working two jobs and transferring small amounts from his main savings, his balance had been dropping precariously. Certain there must be a mistake, he scanned the transactions. But after a quick review, he had to admit the amount was correct, and the only mistake had been the way he was spending his money.

If he was going to make his next loan payment, he would need to cut back on his spending, and that meant no trip to Maui or any other extra activities.

■ ■ ■

During the month of October, about the only thing Jordan did outside of work, school, and flying was go with his sister to the Kahuku High homecoming football game.

Rain fell on and off during the evening, as it had for most of the previous week, and the field was a sloppy, muddy mess. Jordan enjoyed watching Kahuku easily handle rival Waianae, and by the time the game ended, he was glad he had come.

While Jordan waited after the game for Rebecca to congratulate her boyfriend—the team's star running back—he visited with Dana and Leiana, a couple of surfer girls from the Sunset Beach area he'd known during high school. Jordan was just getting caught up with his former classmates when he heard, "Hey, *Pono!*" Instinctively he turned, just in time to see Scott lean Kehau back and give her a kiss. To Jordan's relief Kehau didn't giggle or really even smile afterward, but that didn't help the giant knot that twisted his insides.

"Who's *Pono?*" Dana asked, running a hand through her short, sun-bleached hair.

"Scott likes to call me that," Jordan said. "It's a long story,"

"He did that to me our senior year. Do you remember?" Leiana asked.

"I remember," said Jordan, giving her a weak smile.

Leiana flipped her long brown hair back over her shoulder. "Is that because of what happened with Tiffany Camillo at the prom?"

Jordan felt his ears burn. "I don't know. Maybe," he said, although he knew full well it was.

"Wait—what happened to Tiffany at the prom?" asked Dana.

"You didn't hear this? Oh, Jordan, you've got to tell Dana the story."

Jordan sighed. Telling this story to Dana was the last thing he wanted to do, but he knew if he didn't, Leiana would, and she'd probably get all of the details mixed up. Jordan's entire face flushed as he began. "What happened was, I had this tremendous crush on Tiffany. And somehow, I got up enough nerve to ask her out to the prom. She agreed, but she didn't seem all that excited about it, and I didn't know what to do—I'd never even been on a date before."

Jordan looked around, afraid that the entire crowd was suddenly listening to his tale. "So anyway, she wanted to double with Scott and Olivia, which was a big mistake, but I agreed. And then, about halfway through the dance, Tiffany disappears. I mean, I could tell she wasn't enjoying herself." Jordan paused, the embarrassment of the memory flooding back to him.

"Anyway, I looked all over for her, and when I finally found her, she was . . ." Jordan paused. "She was off in the corner, making out with Rich Mekila."

"No way! Jordan, that's terrible," Dana said. "What did you do?"

"What else could I do? I left. I called my mom and had her come get me. Then the next Monday, when I see Scott, he gives Olivia this great big kiss and starts laughing like it's the funniest thing in the world."

"That girl he kissed tonight didn't think it was very funny. She kinda looked mad—did you see that?" Dana said.

"The blonde hanging all over him at the Jack Johnson concert last week would have liked it, I bet," Leiana added.

Jordan stared at Leiana. "Scott was with another girl last week?"

"Oh, Jordan, he's with a different girl every time I see him. And I see him a lot."

The next night as Jordan walked toward the library for work, the trade winds blew strongly from the ocean, carrying music from the PCC night show across campus. Jordan remembered the night he had gone to see Kehau dance. He remembered what Leiana had told him about Scott and wondered if he should tell Kehau. Was it his place to say anything? Maybe Kehau already knew and didn't care. Girls complained and moaned about jerks like Scott all the time, and yet they just kept going back to those same guys.

Jordan walked into the library and worked his way to the lab, where he found Brandon slouched in a chair, his face drawn down into a frown.

"Hey, Brandon. You don't look so good—what's up?"

"Oh, nothing. It's just, well, me and Angie kinda broke up today."

"Whoa," Jordan said. "Is she seeing someone else?"

Brandon shrugged. "Nah, it's nothing like that. It's just, I don't know. Things didn't work out. I mean, at least it happened now, so I was able to cancel my stuff for the Maui trip." Brandon fidgeted a bit, clearly trying to keep his emotions in check. "Hey, so, what are you doing over Thanksgiving break?"

Jordan shrugged. "I'll probably work at Pua's part of the time, but I'll mostly just hang out at home. A regular old boring Thanksgiving."

"Oh." Brandon sounded like he'd hoped for something more.

"Hey, why don't you come over to our house Thanksgiving Day?"

Brandon's eyes lit up, but then he shook his head. "Nah, man. I wouldn't want to intrude on your family time."

"No, really. It's not a problem. My mom always invites a bunch of people, and then after dinner everybody plays games and stuff. I mean, about the only thing that might be an issue is she doesn't let anyone watch football, but other than that . . ."

Brandon's eyes opened wide, and he looked truly shocked that anyone could even suggest such a thing as Thanksgiving without football.

Jordan smiled. "Nah, I'm just kidding ya."

"Well, okay. Yeah. I'd like that. Thanks, Jordan. Thanks a lot."

"No problem."

A couple of weeks into November, Jordan got up early to prepare for his trip to the airport. The weather had been cooperating, and he'd made great progress with his lessons.

Later that morning, after two touch-and-go landings at Kalae-loa airport, the training field west of Honolulu International, Roach said, "Make this one a full stop." Jordan's heart jumped—a full stop meant Roach was getting out.

Jordan taxied to the general aviation terminal area, and Roach exited. "Just go around the pattern a few times. Make sure you come back for me before you go home." Roach patted the side of the plane, and Jordan smiled. When Roach closed the door, Jordan looked over at the empty seat and said a quick prayer. This was it. His first solo flight. A huge grin stole across his face as he pushed in the throttle.

Flying alone was neither as eerie nor exhilarating as Jordan had expected, though he was surprised at just how quickly the little plane leapt into the sky without the weight of his instructor. He wasn't really alone, as he still had to talk to the controllers in the tower, and it was as if he could feel Roach in the seat next to him. His first landing was pretty good, but he bounced the second, and the third was even worse. Roach called to him with his portable radio. "Hey. Don't make me regret turning you loose up there. Do you think you can bring it down smooth one more time before you come and get me?"

"Yeah, I'll try."

"Just relax, MacDonald. You bounce when you're tense."

Jordan's fourth landing wasn't as good as the first, but better than the other two, and he wore a giant grin on his face as he stopped to let Roach in the plane.

When Jordan and Roach got back to La'aloa, several of Roach's buddies were there.

"Man, you wore the wrong shirt today." Jordan looked down at his shirt. It was a nice one Julie had picked out for him shortly after he got home from his mission.

"Why's that?" Jordan asked.

"Because," said Roach, approaching with a pair of scissors, "tradition dictates we cut your shirt tail after you solo." Jordan couldn't believe Roach was serious, but with a quick snip of the scissors and hearty laughs all around, the bottom third of his shirt was hanging above the door with the shirt tails of Roach's other students.

eleven

Thanksgiving Day arrived sunny and warm at the MacDonald's home. A large box fan sat in front of the louvered windows, trying to coax some air through the house, which was filled with the heat and aroma of cooking turkey. Jordan used a large spoon to scrape at a bucket of frozen mango puree, scooping the shavings into a glass, which Brandon filled with Sprite and set on the table. The guests had nearly all arrived, bringing a variety of ethnic side dishes from Asia and the South Pacific. Viti, one of Beth's students, brought a large pan of baked sweet potato and pineapple.

"It's traditional in Fiji for festivals," he said.

The digital thermometer monitoring the turkey began to beep, and as Beth had Viti help her lift the heavy bird from the oven, she called out, "Rebecca, can you let everyone know it's almost time for dinner, please?"

When there was no reply, Beth called for her again. "Rebecca? Jordan, have you seen your sister?"

Jordan stopped his scraping and looked around the room. "Now that you mention it, no. She borrowed my car this morning, but that was hours ago."

"Well, call her and see where she is. We're almost ready to eat."

Jordan reached for his phone, but before he could begin dialing, he heard the front door open and someone shouted, "Happy Thanksgiving, everyone." The voice sounded almost like Rebecca, but not quite.

"Julie?" he asked, just as both of his sisters walked into the dining room.

"Hey, bro," she said, walking over to hug him. "Happy Thanksgiving."

"Oh, my goodness—Julie!" Beth said. "What are you doing here?"

"Mom!" Julie said, giving Beth a hug.

Beth looked at Julie and then at Rebecca, who wore a huge grin. "Well, Rebecca, see if you can fit another place at the table." She looked back at Julie and furrowed her brow. "I thought I bought your ticket for Christmas."

"You did," Julie said. "But I found a Thanksgiving Day deal, and I thought it would be fun to surprise everyone?"

"A deal? How much?" Beth asked.

Julie smiled and changed the subject. "Hey, so are we ready to eat, or what?"

Beth looked like she wanted to press the issue of Julie's "deal," but after glancing around at the room full of guests, she just shrugged her shoulders and motioned everyone to the table. "Let's eat."

Once the guests were seated, Beth said, "Jordan, you're the man of the house. Will you do the honors?"

Jordan stood and said, "Hi. I'd like to welcome everyone here today. It takes a certain kind of person to eat MacDonald's food on Thanksgiving." Jordan paused for a moment, and the guests laughed politely once the joke set in. "In many homes, it's a tradition to go around the table at Thanksgiving and have everyone tell something they're thankful for." The room instantly fell silent, and as Jordan looked around, seeing concern and even panic, he fought to keep a straight face. "And I am thankful that we don't have that tradition here." Visible relief flooded over the table, and Viti even clapped. "So I'll just bless this food, and then we can eat."

After dinner, Brandon helped Jordan and his sisters do the dishes. Then as a group they made their way to the family room where they played Wii games until Rebecca's boyfriend called, and she excused herself to go to his house. Jordan sat on the couch, and Julie rested her head on his shoulder while Brandon took up residence in the easy chair. Long fingers of orange light streamed through the west windows, and Jordan said, "Wow, it's late already. There might still be a game going if you want to check."

Brandon shook his head. "Nah, I watched a couple of games early this morning. I'm still getting used to being six hours behind the east coast. Football before breakfast is cool but kind of weird." He paused for a moment and then said, "So, Julie, when do you go back?"

"Saturday night. Why?"

Brandon shrugged his shoulders and looked at his hands. Jordan noticed a crimson flush creeping up his cheeks. "I just wondered if you'd like to go out to a movie with me tomorrow."

Jordan felt Julie tense and caught his breath. He couldn't think of a more mismatched pair, but to his relief Julie said, "Um, yeah, we could do that." She spoke in a halting, sing-song voice. "And, um, maybe Jordan could find a date and we could all go together. Right, Jordan?" Julie poked him hard in the ribs, her head cocked and eyes pleading.

"Oh, yeah. Yeah, that sounds great. I could ask . . ." Jordan thought about Angie first, but that would be wrong in so many ways, and he was glad she was gone for the weekend. "I don't know. I'll think of someone. This will be fun."

Jordan first asked Amber out for his double date with Brandon and Julie, but she already had plans for a day at the beach with her friends. So he decided to take Stacie, his friend from his family home evening group because despite any lack of romantic spark, he always enjoyed her company.

"Where are we headed?" Jordan turned around to face Brandon, who sat next to Julie in the back seat of the MacDonald family sedan.

"It's a place called Sam Choy's, down in Chinatown," Brandon said. "Here—hand me the GPS and I'll program it in." Jordan unclipped the little moving map and handed it back to Brandon.

Sam Choy's restaurant sported a large white and yellow fishing boat in the middle of the dining room, with tables set up inside. Jordan and his little crew sat around a small square table near the bow. Since Brandon and Julie had used up much of the available small talk during the hour drive to town, it was up to Jordan and Stacie to keep the conversation going.

About the time the entrees arrived, the subject had turned to books. Stacie was an ardent Harry Potter fan and could quote just about anything from the stories. "In high school some girls thought I looked like Luna Lovegood, so they started calling me Looney, which I guess is better than 'Spacey Stacie,' but not much."

Julie apparently had never heard this nickname before, and Jordan saw her stifle a laugh that made her choke. But Brandon didn't seem to notice. "Luna was always my favorite character in the series, he said.

"Really?" Stacie asked. "Did you like her better in the books or the movies?"

This launched Brandon and Stacie into a discussion of young adult fantasy that soon left Jordan and Julie far behind. Brandon and Stacie continued their conversation through the rest of dinner and dessert and were still going strong as the group walked through the parking lot. As they approached the car, Jordan asked Julie, "Are you thinking what I'm thinking?"

"Oh, yeah," she replied.

Jordan stopped at the car and said, "Hey, um, Stacie? Why don't you go ahead and ride in the back with Brandon."

Brandon looked at Jordan with a furrowed brow before his eyes widened with understanding. Flustered, he said, "Oh, wait. No—dude, I'm sorry! I didn't mean to—"

Jordan held up his hand. "Brandon. Brandon, my good man." Jordan smiled at him. "It's okay."

Brandon glanced quickly between Jordan and Julie, who pursed her lips in a smile and nodded. His face turned so red, Jordan thought he would explode, but then Brandon looked at Stacie, smiled, and said, "Okay. Thanks."

Later that night, after they dropped Brandon and Stacie at her off-campus house, Jordan and Julie sat down in their living room, and Julie said, "That was interesting."

Jordan smirked, Julie smiled, and soon the two of them were fighting back the giggles. Rebecca came into the room, looked at her siblings, and asked, "What's so funny?"

Jordan and Julie both broke into hysterical laughter, causing Rebecca to shake her head and walk back out.

twelve

A light rain fell on Jordan as he walked from the van to Pua's, carry-ing several boxes full of pikake, ilima, and ginger leis, the making of which was a little more specialized than what Lani wanted to tackle in-house. The scattered showers had lasted through most of December, bringing Jordan's flight training to a halt.

As he stepped onto the covered sidewalk in front of the shop, a familiar voice said, "Hi, Jordan."

He looked around his stack of boxes to find Angie. "Hey, what's up?" he said. Jordan had been so busy with school and work that he hadn't seen her since before she and her friends had gone to Maui. "So, how was your Thanksgiving trip?"

"Great. We had a lot of fun," Angie replied. "Except for nearly getting blown off our feet at the Iao Needle. I hear you had quite an interesting weekend with Brandon."

Jordan shook his head. "Yeah, that was different. But it turned out okay. Brandon's planning to fly to Canada to meet Stacie's family at Christmas."

"Wow, already?" she asked. "That sounds serious." She ran a hand through her short black hair, and Jordan remembered why she'd caught his attention earlier in the year. "Good for them," she said. "Brandon's a nice guy. I'm glad he found someone. Hey, I should let you get back to work. It's good to see you, Jordan."

"Yeah, you too. Take care."

Jordan entered the shop, where the smell of tuberose hung heavy in the air as Amber and Malia both strung lei after lei in anticipation of the upcoming winter semester graduation. Without a word, Jordan took the leis he was carrying and unpacked them in the cooler, his mind drifting from work to the exams he had to study for and homework he needed to finish.

As he came out of the large walk-in fridge, he noticed Malia helping Chad place his regular order of roses for his girlfriend, Heather. Then he overheard them talking about a Teleflora order for someone on the mainland. While Malia ran his credit card, Chad poked his head into the back and said, "Hey, Jordan. I'm thinking about bringing on some partners in my car business. Stop by later if you're interested."

Jordan felt a surge of excitement. "Yeah, okay. That sounds great." He would soon be getting his scholarship money for the next semester, and the prospect of additional income from a used car business brought a smile to his face. He could put the extra money into his secret account, which had been hovering just above zero.

When Chad left, Malia returned to the bench, and all three girls worked stringing leis. Jordan wanted to help, but there wasn't really room for him, so he busied himself sweeping up and making sure everyone had enough flowers to keep working. After a while, Amber said, "Dang. My neck is so sore." She leaned her head forward and rubbed the base of her skull with her hand.

Jordan hesitated and then asked, "Do you want me to rub your neck?"

"Oh, please! Be my guest," Amber replied.

"Come do mine next, Jordan," said Lani.

"Hey! What about me?" Malia chimed in.

Jordan spent the rest of his shift kneading shoulders and working knots out of muscles. He left Pua's that afternoon with sore, achy hands, the likes of which he hadn't felt since his days working construction. As he walked, the thought of Chad's "investment opportunity" intrigued him, and Jordan decided to visit him later that evening.

When Jordan arrived, Chad was sitting at a table covered with dozens of flyers advertising cars around campus. "Are you planning to buy all of these cars?" Jordan asked.

"Not all. Just the ones I think will turn a tidy profit." Chad smiled and put his hand on Jordan's shoulder. "But I've got a little problem this semester. You see this? There's kind of a bumper crop of good cars for sale right now, and I can't afford to get all the ones I want. So I'm looking for investors to help me pick them up. What do you think? Are you interested?"

Jordan thought about this. His gut wasn't sure, but his mind was already figuring that if he could put up two thousand dollars, that would become three thousand by January. "Yeah, I think I'd like to. Let me just talk to my . . ." Jordan stopped himself from finishing the sentence. It wasn't his mom's money; it was his. "I've got a couple thousand I can invest."

"Excellent! You won't be disappointed."

Jordan went back later that night to give Chad the money. For the next few days, he closely watched his primary account online, and as soon as the check showed up on his statement, he told his mom what he'd done. Jordan had prepared himself for a tirade and he wasn't disappointed.

"I can't believe you would go behind my back and spend that kind of money before clearing it with me first." Beth stormed into the living room and pulled her laptop from its bag.

"But it's my money, Mom."

" 'It's my money, Mom,' " Beth repeated in a mocking voice. "Not if you keep pulling stunts like this, it's not." She set the laptop on the table, whipped open the lid, and pressed the power button. "There's a reason this money is in a joint account, and that's so I can keep you from doing anything stupid with it—like this."

Jordan worked to channel his frustration, presenting his argument just as he had rehearsed. "This isn't something stupid, Mom. It's an investment—you know, like you teach about in your business classes."

"An investment? Really?"

"Yes. C'mon, Mom. I'm not a little kid anymore. I do know a few things. Why can't you just trust me once in a while?"

His mother glared at him, but Jordan held her gaze, unwilling to back down. Finally her pursed lips relaxed into a frown. "Fine," she said. "You want trust? Here's your chance to earn it."

thirteen

Julie MacDonald stood curbside with her luggage at Honolulu International, and as Jordan approached, he was sure he could see steam coming from her ears.

"Where were you? Mom said you left home hours ago."

Jordan thought quickly about what to say. It had been the first nice day of Christmas break, so Jordan left a few hours early to squeeze in some solo flying time. But he wasn't about to let Julie know the truth. "I, uh, decided to do some Christmas shopping on the way."

"And the mall was so exciting you couldn't answer your phone?"

"I left it in the car," he said. At least that part was true.

Jordan put her suitcases into the back of the rusted out Tercel. He reached up to pull down the hatch, and the back door broke in half right under the window. It dangled there, barely connected by a thin strip of rust. While Julie laughed hysterically, Jordan gingerly fitted the door into place and pushed gently until it latched. "How are we going to get my bags out?" Julie asked when she finally quit laughing enough to talk.

Jordan shrugged. "Fold down the seats and pull them out the front doors, I guess."

They got in the car, and Julie screamed as a cockroach ran across the strip of plywood covering the floorboard. "You still don't have a girlfriend, do you." It was a statement, rather than a question.

"No," said Jordan, annoyed by her accusatory tone.

Looking around her, Julie said, "Yeah, I can see why. You oughta consider getting a new car."

As they began driving, Julie reached between the front seats and pulled out something thin and dark. "What's this?"

Jordan looked over, and to his horror saw she was holding his pilot's log book. "It's nothing. Here, give it back."

But Julie pulled the book out of his reach, and her eyes grew wide as she looked through the log. "These entries are from this year. This one's from today!"

"Give me that," he said again. But Julie kept the book out of his reach, and the car next to them honked as Jordan nearly swerved into the other lane.

Julie's mouth dropped open. "You were late to get me because you were flying. You got your pilot's license."

"No, I didn't. Not yet." Jordan sighed. "I got my solo endorsement, so I can practice by myself now."

"Wow. I'm impressed. Did Mom freak out or what?'

"No! Mom doesn't know." Jordan managed to snatch the book away. "And you can't tell her, either."

"Oh, really?" Julie's look of surprised turned to one of conspiratorial glee. "And how are you going to stop me?" Julie asked.

"Do you need me to make a list? If you say one word to anybody, I'll start by telling Mom the story of Paka and the Zippy's chili, and then . . ."

"Okay. Okay. Your secret's safe. But still—after all these years, I finally have some dirt on you!"

When they reached La'ie and drove in front of the PCC, Julie said, "You know, I never thought I'd say this, but I really want to go to the PCC while I'm home."

"I thought you said you never wanted to go there again after you quit working at Gateway," Jordan said.

"I know, I know," said Julie. "It's just that it's been four months since I've seen a shirtless Samoan. I bet Noelani can get us tickets."

Jordan was not excited about going, but Julie and Rebecca really didn't give him a choice. He took comfort in the fact that they would only be going through the villages.

"Jordan's little heart was broken by a hula girl who dances in the night show," Rebecca explained to Julie, which made Jordan's ears burn.

They walked through the park, enjoying a rare December day with only partly cloudy skies and not even a hint of rain in the air. Julie made the most of playing tourist, mispronouncing every Polynesian word she could find and asking absolutely moronic questions of the befuddled tour guides. However, anyone paying attention to the group would know they were not strangers to La'ie, as they couldn't go more than five minutes without meeting someone they knew.

Jordan led his little posse of sisters into one of the huts in the Hawaiian village and suddenly found himself face to face with Kehau. She was dressed in a red and yellow costume, standing at the *poi* bowl and offering samples to the tourists. Jordan caught his breath. Despite all his effort to get over her, his heart ached at the sight of her. Kehau smiled at him uneasily. "Hi, Jordan."

"Hi," he said, trying to pretend seeing her didn't bother him. "So, you're, uh, working in the villages now?"

"Yeah, just over the break. They let us take extra hours during Christmas and over the summer, so . . ." Her voice trailed off into an uncomfortable silence.

"So, you're not going home for Christmas?" he asked, trying to keep the conversation going and ignoring the urge to run away.

"Just for a couple of days. I really need to stay here and work as much as I can right now." The uncomfortable silence returned. This girl had such an effect on Jordan, and he didn't really understand it. She had rejected him—wounded him—and it hurt to stand there talking to her. But he couldn't pull himself away.

"Excuse us." Julie's voice interrupted the silence. "We need to leave. Jordan is going to buy everyone ice cream, so we really need to go."

"Bye," Jordan said as Julie pulled him out of the hut. "It was good to see you again."

Once they were safely out of the Hawaiian village, Jordan asked, "What did you do that for?"

"Oh my goodness, Jordan. I wasn't sure we were going to get you away from that girl before your head exploded."

Jordan started to protest, but Julie cut him off. "Jordan, you need some serious help, and it looks like I got here just in time."

The day after Christmas, Julie was already awake when Jordan stumbled out of his room. He couldn't remember that ever happening before in his life. She had the newspaper spread out on the table next to her laptop and was busy taking notes.

"There you are. I thought you'd never get up."

"It's not even seven o'clock yet," he protested.

"Yeah, well today's a big day, and we've got a lot of ground to cover. Hurry up and get your shower—you'll have to eat in the car."

Jordan stared at her dumbly.

"Go on, clean yourself up!" she insisted. "There's, like, fifteen cars you need to look at."

Jordan sighed. "Yes, I need a new car," he said, his voice a low whisper. "But if I take any money out of my account, Mom's gonna freak. She always does."

But just then, Beth walked in and looked over Julie's shoulder. "That one would probably work," she said, pointing at Julie's computer screen.

"You think so?" Julie asked, copying the information into her notebook.

Jordan's mouth hung open in disbelief. "You really do need a new car, honey," his mom said before returning her attention to the screen.

"Okay," Jordan said. "Well, let me call my friend, Chad. He's got cars." But Chad didn't answer when Jordan called, so he left a message. He tried again after his shower, but with the same results.

"He's probably still asleep, like every other sane person," Jordan said after the third try.

Jordan and Julie climbed into the Tercel, and Jordan drove past Chad's house. It was quiet, as was most of the town, and Jordan noticed fewer cars out front than he expected. *Maybe there's too many to park by the house*, he thought.

"Is Chad the guy who sold you this blue thing?" Julie asked.

"Yes."

"Then I say forget him. There's nothing here cool enough for the New Jordan."

"Wait, what do you mean, 'New Jordan?'"

"You're getting a makeover, bro. And it's starting with your car. By the time we're done here, the girls will be all over you, and you won't have time to worry about Mahana or whatever her name is."

Jordan frowned but said nothing and drove toward the highway. Just as he began to turn, a scream of blue streaked past and darted ahead of them. "Hey, now. Maybe you should look at getting a motorcycle."

"I'm not getting a motorcycle," Jordan said, speaking louder than he meant to.

"Oh, c'mon! It would be cool. You could use some cool."

"You know something? Spencer told me what he pays for insurance. I don't need that kind of cool."

Traffic slowed to a crawl as they drove down the northwest coast. Sunset Beach, Pipeline, Waimea Bay—all of the famous surf spots were pounding with huge, tourist-stopping waves under a steel-gray winter sky. As they inched along, Jordan asked, "How'd you do it?"

"Do what?"

"Get Mom to agree to this car thing?" Julie's face flushed, and a knot formed in Jordan's stomach. "Julie, what did you do?"

His sister shrugged, and a half smile formed on her lips. "I told her you would never find a *haole* girlfriend unless you had a decent set of wheels."

"What?" Jordan said, a mixture of anger and disgust rising inside him. "That is just wrong. I can't believe you told her that. You, especially."

"Yeah, I know. It was a bit hypocritical," Julie said, grinning. "But it worked, didn't it?"

Jordan was still fuming when they stopped at a place in Haleiwa, where Julie had Jordan look at an old orange VW Thing. Julie had picked it out because it was a convertible but decided it was ugly when she saw it in person. Jordan thought it had a lot of class and character, but the engine barely ran, and there was too much body work needed for the price being asked.

They looked at a Celica that was way too expensive ("What did you think my price range was, anyway?" asked Jordan), a Miata with a rotten roof and moldy seats, and a convertible Beetle that actually lost a fender when Jordan closed the door. Finally they came to some housing near Hickam Air Force Base, where an airman about to be transferred was selling a red convertible Mustang. The car was old, but not old enough to be a classic, and it had undoubtedly spun around the island way too many times in its former life as a tourist rental.

However, the car was clean, if not perfect, and everything worked. Julie had grown impatient because Jordan hadn't made offers on any of the previous wrecks, so after a successful test drive he felt he had to at least pretend to try to buy the car. Still believing he could get a good deal from Chad, he decided to lead off with a very low offer. Jordan expected the airman to balk, but he was highly motivated to sell and countered Jordan's offer with one just a couple of hundred dollars higher. Julie was ecstatic. Jordan experienced a mixture of guilt at having taken advantage of a desperate serviceman and excitement at getting the new car at a good price. After a quick trip to the bank for a cashier's check, Jordan signed the papers and was handed the key to his Mustang.

As he put the key into the ignition, a large drop of water hit Jordan squarely on the top of his head. That drop was soon joined by another, and then two more, and it was all Jordan could do to get the top up before the heavens opened in a mighty downpour that would last for over a week.

He soon had a case of buyer's remorse as only a new convertible in the rain can provide.

fourteen

Jordan walked out of the dressing room wearing yet another set of clothes as his makeover continued for the rest of Christmas break.

"What about these?" he asked.

"Now those I like," Julie said.

"Good. Finally. Let's get these and go." Jordan moved uncomfortably in the starched jeans and plain black T-shirt. After the car shopping adventure, Julie and Rebecca had persuaded Jordan to take numerous shopping trips, where they dressed him up like a Ken doll and spent way too much money.

"You can't be finished yet! We've only been to half of the mall."

Jordan went back into the changing room. "Look—we spent all of yesterday at Pearlridge, two days at Ala Moana, and I've seen about all of Windward Mall I can take."

"You'll thank me for this some day, you know." Julie continued browsing the racks, picking up a couple of new shirts.

"Yeah, well it won't be today." Jordan emerged from the dressing room, took the shirts from Julie and returned them to the rack. "Even Rebecca had enough sense to quit after Pearlridge. I'm broke, my feet hurt, and I'm ready to go."

"Wimp."

They were just leaving Macy's when Todd and his friends spotted them. "Hey, Jordan! Julie!" Todd called from across the mall.

Jordan looked up and waved. "C'mon. Let's go say hi. Just for a second."

He expected Julie to grumble about this, but instead of running away from Todd, she now appeared to want to run after him. "Hi, Todd," she said, giving him a big hug and kiss on the cheek, and then doing the same to each of his friends.

"Hey—guess what! Jordan's almost a pilot now."

A jolt of panic shot through Jordan, and he elbowed his sister hard. But Todd just smiled. "Yeah, I know. He's been hogging The Bomb, and I've had to start work on my complex endorsement in the Bonanza. But, shh," he said, putting his finger to his lips. "I think it's supposed to be a secret." Todd turned to Jordan and winked. "Dude, you've got to learn to fly the Bonanza."

Jordan smiled weakly. "I've got to finish up my private first. If it ever stops raining."

"It will, don't worry. But I can't complain—I've gotten quite a bit of actual IFR PIC this week." Turning to Julie, he added, "Your brother's VFR only so he can't fly in IMC."

"Okay, hold it. If you're going to start spelling everything, I'm outta here."

"Yeah, sorry," said Todd. "VFR just means Jordan can only fly when the weather's nice and he can see out the window. I'm learning to fly by instruments, and actually flying in the soup is a lot different than pretending."

Julie nodded, clearly not understanding a thing Todd had just said.

"So, how long are you home for?" Todd asked.

"Just until tomorrow," replied Julie. "Then it's back to the frozen north of Chicago. I've spent the whole week shopping with my brother, and I want to do something special for my last night here. Do you have any ideas?" she asked.

"We were going to go watch that new movie, *Midnight Passage*."

"Oh, I want to see that!" said Julie.

"Well, why don't you come with us?" Todd asked, looking first at Julie and then Jordan.

"I will," Julie replied quickly. "But Jordan needs to go home. He's tired."

Suddenly, Jordan had gone from Man of the Hour to fifth wheel.

"Yeah, I'd better get going," he agreed. "It's good to see you guys. And remember, Julie, you've got an early flight tomorrow."

"Oh, yeah, right. Like I won't be able to sleep on the plane. There's nothing else to do between here and Chicago. Last time the movie didn't even work. Go on, beat it. Oh, and here, take my stuff for me." She handed him her bags of spoils.

"Nice," said Jordan. He took her things, gave her a hug, waved to the guys, and headed toward the door.

He walked through the mall, hoping the rain had stopped, or at least slowed down. But the crowd gathered at the entrance next to the food court told him the downpour was still going strong. When he finally got to where he could see through the glass doors, he saw a black sky and rain falling in torrents. He joined the group of people watching for a break in the storm. A couple of young local guys pulled their jacket hoods over their heads and, slippers in hand, made a run for it. They were soaked through before they reached the first car.

Jordan absentmindedly scanned the crowd and recognized a familiar face. Chad's girlfriend, Heather, was standing alone, glancing anxiously between her watch and the downpour outside. He slipped through the crowd and approached her.

"Heather, hi," he said.

She looked up, and it took her a second to place him. Once she did, she gave him a broad smile. "Oh, hi! It's Jordan, right?"

"Yeah," he said, returning her smile. "So, are you waiting for Chad?"

Her smile turned to a scowl. "No. I'm here by myself. Alone, on the bus, in a rainstorm, returning the Christmas present I got for Chad but didn't give him because he left me to go to Provo for his other girlfriend, and now I find out they already got married and . . ." Her voice began to choke, and she looked down.

"Oh, wow," Jordan said. "That's a bummer." Then he suddenly caught the full meaning of what she said. "So, wait—Chad's gone? He's coming back, though, right?" A twinge of panic started just behind his ribs.

Heather forced an angry smile. "Nope. They're headed off on some backpacking trip around Europe. I was just a little filler to take up time until she got back from South America. And I guess she knew all about me but didn't care. At least that's what Chad said, although I doubt I can believe anything he told me ever again."

"Oh, man." Jordan's panic blossomed as he realized the money he'd given Chad—the money Chad had promised to nearly double—was gone. Jordan stood in stunned silence for a minute, feeling sick.

"I can't believe I let him use me like that," she said. Jordan suddenly felt an affinity with Heather. He looked at her more closely now. She was probably a foot shorter than he was and slightly built. Her wavy brown hair was pulled back in a ponytail, and although she had forgone her usual makeup routine, she was still quite attractive. And here he was, a white knight ready to rescue her, fresh from Julie's makeover with just enough confidence to try to make a move.

"Well, you shouldn't be taking the bus in this weather. I've got my car. Do you want a ride home?"

"That would be great," she said, putting her hand on his arm.

"I'm parked kind of far out, but I have an umbrella. Do you want to wait and see if it slows down any, or should we make a break for it?"

"Oh, please—I just want to get out of here. I've been waiting for half an hour, and I don't think it's ever going to let up."

They worked their way through the crowd and out the single doors. Standing under the shallow overhang, Jordan put up his umbrella and took his keys from his pocket. Heather slipped off her sandals, and Jordan put his arm around her, pulling her close. "Ready?"

She nodded, and together they ran.

Heather squealed as they splashed their way through deep, cold puddles, the rain soaking their legs and backs. Jordan pulled her closer, trying to keep them both under the umbrella. He felt her warm at his side and smelled apricot in her hair. They loped along together like two kids in a three-legged race.

Whatever dryness Jordan had managed to preserve for himself under the umbrella was surrendered as he helped Heather into the car. She leaned across the seat and unlocked his door as he hurried around to the other side. He had a hard time climbing in with his bags and struggled to get the umbrella down, and once he did they sat for a minute and laughed at the absurdity of the situation.

"Okay, let's go," said Jordan.

The rain pounded around them, obscuring visibility and filling the roads with deep, rushing water. Jordan concentrated hard on driving, the rain striking loudly on the fabric roof.

Although it was still late afternoon, the thick, heavy clouds made it look like dusk. They puttered out of Kaneohe, down the hill, and up toward Temple Valley, where the rain finally slowed to a mere downpour.

"You sure did a lot of shopping today," Heather observed.

"Oh, that's not all mine. Some of that's my sister's. We ran into some friends of hers at the mall, and she decided it would be more fun to go and see *Midnight Passage* than come home with me."

"*Midnight Passage*? I heard that was really good," said Heather.

"Yeah, so did I," said Jordan. "Hey, do you want to go see it?"

Heather shrugged, smiling broadly. "Yeah, sure."

Jordan turned right at the light next to the Temple Valley shopping center and drove toward the theaters to see if *Midnight Passage* was playing. "There's a show starting in about thirty minutes. What do you think?"

Heather nodded. "Let's do it."

They huddled together under the umbrella, Jordan again noticing her warmth against him. Brimming with confidence, he put his arm back around her after they were safely inside the door. The theater was starting to fill up, but they still had quite a few seats to choose from, and Jordan led Heather toward some a little behind the middle.

He sat down on her left and put his right arm around her. Heather snuggled in close, and he reached across with his left hand to hold hers, which she eagerly accepted. All of this sudden success both confused and excited Jordan and allowed him to almost ignore the sick sensation he felt when he thought about Chad and his money.

After the movie, when they arrived back at Heather's off-campus house, the rain was still pouring hard, and neither of them was in any hurry to get out of the car. They sat for a minute, holding hands. Heather looked at Jordan expectantly, and it didn't take long for Jordan to convince himself that a kiss was his for the taking. He put his hand behind her head and pulled her toward him. She met his lips eagerly, and to the sound of pounding rain and splashing cars, Jordan took from her every kiss he had dreamed of but never before received, and willingly she gave.

When Jordan arrived home, he walked quietly through the front door. The living room was dark, but he could make out the shape of someone sitting in the La-Z-Boy. "Hi, Mom," he said quietly. "Sorry I'm so late."

The figure in the chair stirred, and a sleepy voice said, "Hey, I'm not your mother, lover boy."

"Julie? What are you doing out here?"

"I had to wait up so I could get all of the juicy details. Plus, you have my stuff."

"What juicy details?" Jordan asked, wondering what Julie knew.

"Don't give me that. You were so wrapped up with that girl in the theater I thought she'd have to be surgically removed."

"But how . . ." Jordan stammered.

"We missed the show at Windward, so we caught the one at Temple Valley. I was sitting just two rows behind you," she said. "I've been home for an hour, so I know something happened. C'mon. Spill it."

Jordan smiled in spite of himself and sat down on the couch. He told her about meeting Heather at the mall and deciding to take her to the movie. "Then I took her to her house over on Moana Street, and we just sat in the car and talked for a while."

"Yeah, uh-huh. Right," Julie said. "Somehow I don't think all you did was talk."

"Well, mostly," said Jordan.

"Yeah, I thought so. So, is she a good kisser?"

"Like I'm going to tell you."

"Oh, fine. Be that way. After all, it's only because of me that you had the hot car and cool clothes to be a real babe magnet. But if you don't want to tell me about it, that's fine. I see how you are."

"Okay, so if you must know," Jordan started, and then continued in hushed tones, "yeah, she's a pretty good kisser." Not that he had much to compare her against, but he enjoyed locking lips with Heather and was looking forward to having another chance.

"Good. Serves ya right. No need to thank me—just doing my job. Now if you'll give me my stuff, I'm off to bed."

fifteen

Jordan awoke the next morning to the sound of water dripping from the roof into large puddles that had accumulated under the eaves, and the previous night's events came flooding back to him. The sweet memory of his evening with Heather contrasted sharply to the sick feeling he got when he thought of the money he had given to Chad.

Chad gets the money, Jordan gets the girl. He sat up and held his head in his hands. Staring at the floor, Jordan realized that he'd lost not only the money but also the trust his mother had grudgingly given him. He closed his eyes tightly, as if he could shut out the reality of his financial failure.

What was he going to tell his mom?

His predicament still weighed heavy on his mind when Jordan arrived at Pua's that afternoon, wearing some of the new clothes from his makeover shopping spree. "Well, look who's all dressed up today," said Malia. "The all new Jordan MacDonald, now open for business."

Amber concurred with cat calls. The gloom started to lift from Jordan as he blushed and couldn't help but smile.

"Not only is he open for business, I believe he's already had his first customer," said Lani, not bothering to look up from her flowers.

Jordan looked at Lani, eyes wide. What did she know?

"Ooh, Lani. Tell us more," said Amber.

"Well, it seems a certain red car was parked at the house across the street last night for quite some time."

"And who lives at the house across the street from you?" Malia asked.

"Girls," Lani said. "Pretty girls. About five or six of them."

"I see. And which one of those girls were you visiting, Jordan?"

"That's none of your business," he said, trying to keep a grin from spreading across his bright red face.

"So, did you have a good time last night?" Amber asked.

"Good enough," Jordan replied.

"Well, then," said Malia, walking toward the refer. "I think you need to send flowers. Little bouquet or big bouquet?"

"Neither," said Jordan.

"Lani, what do you think?"

"Malia, Jordan's date is none of our business, even if he was parked there in the rain for a full forty-two minutes before anyone got out of his car."

"Really? Oh, better send the big one then."

"No, Malia, I'm not sending any flowers."

"No worries," said Malia. "This one's on me."

"Pay up front this time, dear," said Lani.

"Okay, fine." Malia reached for her purse, fished inside, and then slapped a couple of bills on the counter. "Now, what am I writing on this card?"

"I'll write the card, thank you," said Jordan as he tried to take it from her.

Malia held the card out of reach "No, way. Your handwriting stinks. Now, how about . . ."

"How about 'Thanks for a great evening. Can't wait to see you tonight,'" Jordan said, not wanting to hear Malia's version.

She smiled and said, "Tonight? What are you doing tonight?"

"We're going to some 'last day before school starts' party with her friends."

"Meeting the friends already?" Amber asked. "Sounds serious."

"Shut up." Jordan blushed.

As Malia wrote on the card, Amber waved a little envelope. "And what do we write on here?"

Jordan bit his lips, trying to suppress the inevitable grin, but quickly admitted defeat. "Heather Martin." His face burned hotter than he ever thought possible.

Malia looked up from the card, her brow furrowed. But Amber's eyes grew wide. "Heather Martin?" she repeated, and then quickly wrote the name on the envelope

"Isn't she that one guy's girlfriend?" Malia asked, taking the envelope from Amber and slipping the card inside.

"She was," Jordan said, cringing at the mention of Chad.

"I don't think I ever met her, though. Have you?"

Amber nodded. "Oh, yeah. She's a cutie—way to go, Jordan!"

Malia stuck the card onto the pick nestled among the daisies. "Awesome. I can't wait to meet her." She walked to the lock box and took out the keys to the van.

"Hey, no. Wait. You're not delivering those." Jordan reached for the keys, but Malia held them away.

"Well, you sure can't do it—conflict of interest."

"But . . . Lani!" Jordan protested.

Still focused on her arrangement, Lani said, "Malia, I need you here to help with all these orders." Jordan again reached for the keys, but Lani continued. "Make sure you're back by ten thirty."

With that, Malia stuck out her tongue at Jordan and practically skipped through the door.

Jordan puttered around the shop, anxiously awaiting Malia's return. His phone rang, and his heart jumped into his throat—it was Heather.

"Oh, Jordan, I just got the flowers. They're beautiful. Thank you so much."

Jordan blushed, and Amber giggled. "You're welcome," Jordan said. "So, um, what time should I pick you up?"

"Six?"

"Okay," said Jordan. "Six it is."

After nine solid days of downpour, Jordan had begun to wonder if he would ever see the sun again, but the rain had been slowing all throughout the day, and a few rays of sunlight broke through the clouds just as Jordan and Heather arrived at the beach house. A small bonfire of wet driftwood smoked heavily on the sand, and nearby a couple of mismatched grills cooked steaks, burgers, and hot dogs. They ran into Heather's former roommate Erin, who had gotten married over the Christmas break and was now living in the Temple View Apartments.

"It's like a rabbit warren in there—kids and toys everywhere," Erin said.

"Where's Trey?" Heather asked.

Erin rolled her eyes and scowled. "He and his buddies just had to go to the reef and get some fish."

Heather and Erin began the process of catching up, and Jordan wandered around until he found himself in a one-sided conversation with a kid who had a serious lisp and a strong desire to talk politics. He managed to break free when a small commotion started near Heather and Erin.

Erin's husband, Trey, had returned with a bucket half full of fish he and his buddies had speared out by the reef and a bloody T-shirt wrapped around his hand. "No, seriously. It was a shark about this big," he said, holding his hands four feet apart. Behind him, his fishing companions shook their heads and indicated a much smaller fish. Erin seemed split between sympathy and irritation, but eventually sympathy won out, and she took Trey inside to nurse his hand while his fish waited for their turn on the grill.

The early colors of sunset touched the broken clouds dancing across the sky, and Jordan put his arms around Heather as they waited for the food. When dinner was finally served, Jordan and Heather sat on a log overlooking the ocean. Heather had some of Trey's fish, but Jordan opted for a burger.

"Oh, you've got to try some of this," she said. She gave Jordan a bite, and it tasted like fish. "Isn't that good?" she asked.

"I guess. I've never cared much for seafood."

"What? How can you live in Hawai'i and not like seafood?"

Jordan just shrugged and returned to his burger.

As the sun set and the stars began to appear, Jordan looked forward to taking a moonlit stroll on the beach with Heather. He'd long fantasized about taking a walk on the beach with a beautiful girl in the moonlight and sharing a kiss along the shore, waves crashing in the background. It looked like he would finally get his chance.

He waited until the moon rose above the horizon. Although no longer full, it would still provide a fine romantic backdrop. But before he could suggest the walk to Heather, another of her roommates appeared in crisis. Jordan didn't catch the whole story, but the tears and repeated reference to "that jerk" told him all he needed to know.

"I'm sorry, Jordan," Heather said. "I really need to talk to Megan for a minute."

The minute turned into an hour, and Jordan ended up sitting alone for the rest of the party.

As things began to wind down, Jordan still held out hope that he'd get his walk on the beach with Heather. But instead, he took Megan and Heather back to their house. Heather was so concerned about Megan that Jordan almost didn't get a good-night kiss at all.

"Wait," he said, as they dashed for the door. "Can we get together tomorrow?"

"Um, yeah. Seven, maybe." She came back and gave him a quick peck, and then she was off.

"Yeah, okay. Seven," he muttered to himself as he watched the girls go into the house.

The next night, however, as Jordan walked Heather to her door after their date, he felt his golden opportunity with her was slipping away. She let him take her hand, but her grip was weak, though not nearly as weak as the way she returned his kiss.

"What's wrong?" Jordan asked.

"Nothing," she said, not meeting his eyes.

"It's my mother, isn't it?" Jordan said. Heather's revelation that she'd met his mom that day had been bothering him all night.

"Oh, no. You're mom's great. It's just . . ." She sighed, and then looked up at him. "I'm tired." She gave his hand a light squeeze, kissed him again quickly, and said, "Thanks for tonight."

Jordan stood on the small cement porch for a moment after Heather slipped through the door and then walked slowly back to his car.

Parking on the street in front of his house, Jordan saw his mom through the large picture window, sitting in her chair with a book. He'd been sure to tell her about Heather but hadn't felt the time was right for making introductions. He hadn't anticipated the two of them meeting on their own. After taking a deep breath and exhaling quickly, Jordan made his way into the house.

"Alas, Romeo returneth." Beth set her book in her lap and smiled teasingly at Jordan. "So, how was your date?"

At the sight of her smile, Jordan felt his shoulders relax. "It was good," he said. "Heather told me the two of you met today."

"I did. Elissa introduced us."

Jordan cocked his head. "Who's Elissa?"

Beth raised her eyebrows. "Elissa—our student secretary with the long brown hair."

"Oh, is that her name?" His mom scowled, and Jordan shrugged his shoulders. "I didn't know. She barely even acknowledges me."

Beth rolled her eyes. "Anyway, we had quite a long talk. I have to tell you, Jordan—I really like Heather. Do me a favor and don't mess up with this one."

The memory of his less-than-stellar date came rushing back to Jordan, and he forced himself to smile. "I'll try not to, Mom."

sixteen

The following morning, as the engine of The Bomb droned on, Jordan found it hard to concentrate on his flight. With the weather finally clear for the first time in weeks, Jordan had immediately scheduled a training flight. To do so, however, he had to miss the first day of his winter semester classes. Prior to taking flying lessons, he had never cut a single class, and now he was skipping the whole first day.

But the guilt of flying while he should have been in class barely even registered with him. Jordan's thoughts were focused on Heather. It felt like she was slipping away from him, just as Kehau had. The fact that his mother actually liked Heather would only make his failure that much worse.

Jordan's thoughts were interrupted by a sudden, drastic change in the sound of the plane. Instead of a healthy hum, the engine had slowed to near idle, and the horizon line shot above the windshield as the plane's nose dropped toward the ocean. A quick jolt of panic grabbed Jordan. Why isn't Roach doing anything? Jordan looked at Roach, who stared back impassively.

"You've just suffered a catastrophic engine failure. What are you going to do?"

It took Jordan just a second to realize what had happened. This was a test, a simulated engine failure. "Fly the plane," he muttered to himself, quickly stabilizing their descent. Had he been paying attention like he should have, he would have known where the nearest airport was, but he needed to take precious time and regain his bearings. The island of Lanai lay ahead in the distance. To their left, the island of Molokai loomed large, and Jordan made the decision to turn toward the nearer island, even though the airport sat far inland. An off-field landing would be preferable to ditching in the sea.

At the thought of a water landing, Jordan reached up and touched the life jacket that he and his instructor both wore. He found the requirement for inter-island flight disconcerting at first, but now fully appreciated its wisdom.

Jordan checked his altitude, looked ahead at the island, and felt the panic return. They had been flying at four thousand feet when the engine "failed," but they were now at only twenty-two-hundred and descending quickly. Jordan pulled back on the yoke gently, slowing their descent, but in the process, he also reduced their forward airspeed.

The ocean rose quickly to meet the plane, while the island remained in the distance, out of reach. Jordan looked at Roach, who raised his eyebrows but said nothing. Finally, when the ocean was just a few hundred feet below them, Roach spoke. "In five minutes, you're fish food. My plane."

Roach shoved the throttle open and the plane began climbing away from the sea. Fifteen agonizing minutes later, they sat parked on the tarmac of the Molokai airport.

"Okay. What happened up there?"

Jordan gave the answer just as he had rehearsed it in his mind. "The engine failed, and we didn't have enough altitude to make it to land."

"No!" Roach said. "We had plenty of altitude when the engine died. So what happened?"

"I don't know," Jordan muttered.

"What?" Roach said, the calm gone from his voice.

"I don't know what happened."

"Of course you don't know what happened. You weren't paying attention, and by the time you figured out what was going on, you lost over fifteen hundred feet, which would have been more than enough to get you safely on the runway." Jordan hung his head, and

Roach sighed. "Listen, MacDonald. People think flying is dangerous, but really it's not. It isn't any more dangerous that just about
anything else you can do. But it is unforgiving. You cannot afford
to let down your guard, not even for a minute. Do you understand?"

Jordan nodded and managed a weak "Yes."

"Good. Now what was the other thing you did wrong up there?"

Jordan looked and knit his brow. "I, uh . . ."

"You don't know, do you?"

"No, I guess not."

"You didn't even try to troubleshoot the problem, and you didn't
ask for any help—you just let things fall apart around you. It's okay to
ask questions when you get in trouble. You need to use your resources
whenever there's a problem like this. Now, you sit here and think
about that for a minute. I'll be right back." Roach popped the door
and climbed out.

As Roach hurried toward the general aviation services building,
Jordan thought about the advice he'd just been given and decided
using all of his resources was just what he needed to do.

The next morning, he put his plan into action. "Amber," he said
softly, leaning in to the tall blonde's ear. "Do you think Lani would
let you come to the airport with me today?"

Amber set down the strand of red carnations she had been
stringing and gave Jordan a questioning look. After a second, she
raised her eyebrows. "Date three didn't go so well?" Jordan wrinkled
his nose slightly and shook his head. Amber pursed her lips then said,
"We're pretty slow today. I'll see what I can do."

She began interrogating Jordan as soon as he eased the van onto
Kamehameha Highway. "Okay. So, what's going on?"

"Well," Jordan started out, but paused to think. "I'm not really
sure."

"Mom getting in the way again?"

"Oh, no. Nothing like that." Jordan let out a quick laugh. "No,
actually my mother has given Heather her blessing."

"That's good. So what, then? You had a date a couple of nights
ago, right? What happened?"

Jordan shrugged his shoulders. "I don't know. I mean, nothing
bad happened or anything. It's just, well, afterwards . . ."

Jordan floundered for the words, but Amber seemed to have a

pretty good idea. "Let me guess—she seemed distracted and the good-night kiss was weak, right?"

"Well, yeah. That's pretty much it. But how did you . . ."

"Classic bored girl behavior. What did you do for your date, anyway?"

"I wanted to go for a walk on the beach, but the wind was too strong so we went bowling instead."

Amber scowled. "Just the two of you?"

"Yeah," Jordan said. "And the pin machine kept breaking down."

Amber scrunched her eyebrows. "That's not good. Besides, you really need a group for bowling to be fun." She bit her lip and thought for a while. Jordan steered the van around Kahana bay, past the lava formation that looked like a crouching lion, and was all the way to Ka'a'awa Elementary before Amber finally spoke again.

"I'd say you've probably still got a chance to make this relationship work. You made a great impression on your first date—obviously. But the next two left her a little underwhelmed. So this coming date needs to really impress her. You need to knock this one out of the park. Hit her with full-scale 'shock and awe.'"

"Okay," said Jordan. "So how do I do that? You got any ideas?"

"Oh, yeah, baby. I'm made of ideas."

For the next half hour, Amber peppered Jordan with questions about Heather—her likes, dislikes, friends, family, classes—everything. Jordan found he didn't know the answers to most of them, but Amber was surprisingly insightful, and Jordan decided to trust her intuition.

When they reached the airport, they loaded the large white flower boxes into the van and began the long trip back to La'ie. As soon as Jordan was cruising comfortably along the freeway, Amber spoke up.

"Here's the deal. I think, based on what you told me, this girl is just feeling bored. You picked her up on the rebound, but now she's starting to drift away. So what you need to do is give her an entire day and treat her like a princess: feed her, pamper her, take her to the beach, treat her to a nice dinner, take her to a show—not a movie, but a live show—down in Waikiki. And if you really want this girl, you can't be afraid to spend a little money."

"Um, okay," Jordan said hesitantly. "It's just, I'm not sure where I'm going to find a whole day for a date."

"Well, what are you doing on Martin Luther King Day?" The smugness in Amber's voice showed she had anticipated this objection.

"I dunno," Jordan said, but he smiled, thinking for the first time that this idea might actually work.

"There you go," said Amber. "No classes, and I know at least Pua's will be closed. I would think the lab would be closed too. So what you need to do is get her to clear her calendar for next Monday and then really show her a good time."

The rest of the drive, Jordan and Amber came up with ideas for specific activities. On his way to the computer lab, Jordan stopped by the writing center with a half-dozen roses for Heather. She was alone in the room and seemed excited to see him, which came as a relief. "Hi," she said, smiling at the flowers. "What are these for?"

"These are to let you know that you have been selected to spend an amazing, incredible day with yours truly."

"Really?" she said, lifting her eyebrows.

"Really," he said. "Whatever plans you've made for next Monday, cancel them. You and I are going to have an unforgettable day."

Heather smiled. "Oh, that's perfect. All the girls in my house want to hike to some bunker up in the mountains, and now I have an excuse not to go."

She took Jordan by the elbow and led him to a table just out of sight of the door. "Set those here," she said. And then she kissed him, long and slow.

seventeen

"So, what is this place?" Heather asked as they drove up to La'aloa Aviation at the start of their big date adventure.

"You'll see," said Jordan, pulling into a parking space next to Todd and his friend Ashley. When initially planning this date, Jordan had wished he could fly Heather around the island, but he was still at least a month away from getting his pilot's license, due in part to the excessive rain. But then he thought to ask Todd to fly them and offered to pay for the rental. Jordan was overjoyed when Todd agreed and relieved when Todd insisted on paying half.

"Hey, boys and girls," said Todd as they climbed out of Jordan's car. "Are we ready for a little aerial tour?"

Heather looked at Jordan, her eyes wide with excitement and concern. Jordan smiled at her. "How about it? Are you ready?" Heather didn't look ready, but after glancing at both Todd and Ashley, she seemed to get a shot of confidence and nodded.

"Jordan should have his license next month. Then he can fly you himself." Jordan shot Todd a look of mixed shock and panic. "Oh, sorry," said Todd. "That's still a secret, isn't it?"

Jordan swallowed hard. "Um, no. Not from Heather, anyway." He smiled weakly.

"You're going to be a pilot? Why didn't you tell me?" she said, clearly impressed.

"I haven't told anyone. Except Todd. I can't risk word getting back to my mom." As soon as he said the words, Jordan regretted them. But she didn't seem fazed by what he'd said.

Jordan and Heather squeezed into the back seat of The Bomb. He wrapped one arm over her shoulder and used his free hand to hold hers. The layer of overcast clouds was high enough for a visual flight, but as they lifted into the sky, the little plane bounced roughly in the unstable atmosphere. Jordan hoped that the air would smooth out as they climbed, but instead it got even worse—like riding a dirt road on a four-wheeler with bad shocks. Jordan looked at Heather, and his worst fears were confirmed. Instead of enjoying the flight, her eyes were clamped shut tight, and the color had drained from her face. Jordan reached into the seat pocket in front of him, but it was empty. Checking the pocket in front of Heather's seat, he found what he was looking for—an airsick bag.

"Todd, do you think it's going to smooth out any?" he asked.

"Um, maybe. Let's go a little farther and see what the air is like over the ocean."

But Heather didn't make it to the ocean. Her eyes got large, and Jordan saw her begin to gag. Quickly he opened the bag, and handed it to her just in time. The sound of Heather retching, in addition to the turbulent ride, was nearly enough to push Jordan's queasy stomach over the edge.

"Todd, I think you'd better get us back down. Sorry."

If Todd was disappointed, he didn't let on. He simply called the tower, which was fortunately able to accommodate their immediate return to the airport. Unfortunately, Heather managed to be sick again before the wheels hit the ground.

Jordan helped Heather to the pilot's lounge at La'aloa, where a can of ginger ale helped her color return to normal. A light rain began to fall, and Todd said, "Well, I guess we'll have to try this again another time."

"No," Heather said. "No way. I am never, ever going up in one of those things again. Ever."

"Ah, she'll get over it," Todd said to Jordan quietly.

"No, I won't," Heather insisted.

"I'm really sorry," Jordan said. "I didn't realize you got airsick."

"I never have before, but this . . ." she said, waving a hand toward The Bomb and shaking her head.

After an uncomfortable pause, Ashley asked, "So, what else do you have planned for today?"

"Well, ah," Jordan started, looking out at the rain. "I had thought we might spend some time at the beach, but that doesn't look very likely now. So, um, we could always go to a museum or something." Heather gave Jordan a withering look. "Or not. Maybe a movie? I don't know."

Jordan had hoped to reveal each activity one at a time, but the look on Heather's face told him he'd better lay out the complete itinerary before she cancelled the whole thing. "I was planning on flying to take most of the morning, and spending the afternoon at the beach, which is why I had you bring your swimsuit. Then back to La'ie to clean up before we go to the Outrigger for the Society of Seven dinner show."

"Oooh," Ashley said. "S. O. S. That's a fun show. You know, we should go to the mall and have you pick out a new dress for that."

"Whoa, wait," Todd said. "Dress shopping at the mall? Count me out."

But Jordan noticed Heather's face light up at the suggestion. "Yeah, that might work," he said. "We can pick up pizza for lunch or something . . ."

"Ugh! Don't mention food!"

Four hours later, Jordan and Heather made their way through the crowded walkways of the Ala Moana shopping center, arms wrapped around each other. Jordan had been to the giant, upscale mall at the edge of Waikiki at least a hundred times, but in all of his visits he had never been inside so many women's clothing stores. As the only male in his family, he'd been dragged into quite a few of the shops, but he always did his best to escape to one of the more interesting retail outlets. However, as Heather worked her way from the smallest specialty boutique to the large anchor stores, picking through rack after rack of dresses, Jordan didn't have the slightest desire to leave.

It only took a little shopping before the gloom completely left Heather's face, and she had smiled coyly at him as she modeled dress after dress, taking pictures with her phone and adding notes about her favorites. Watching her try on shoes was far less interesting, but Heather compensated by being increasingly affectionate—hanging on his arm between shops, rubbing his shoulders when he craned his neck, and stealing quick kisses between the racks.

Once Heather finally made her decision, they re-entered a small shop near the center of the mall, and she took the brightly-colored floral print dress from the rack. Holding it in front of herself, she scowled slightly, and Jordan saw her shoulders droop just a little. The dress wasn't exactly ugly, but Jordan didn't really like it, either.

He had hoped Heather would get the simple black knit dress that looked to be tailor made for her. That one seemed to be Heather's favorite, too, but when combined with the shoes she had picked to go with it, the total was well outside her budget.

As they stood in a short line to buy the floral dress, Jordan had an idea. After doing a quick calculation in his head, he put his hands on Heather's shoulders and leaned her body back against him. Whispering in her ear, he said, "Put this thing back, and let's go get that black dress. My treat."

Heather turned quickly to face him, her eyes wide. Then she grabbed his hand and pulled him from the store, tossing the rejected dress haphazardly onto a rack of swimsuits.

During the hours they had been at the mall, the rain had stopped, the clouds had broken, and patches of blue sky peeked through, as if their shopping trip had lifted the spirits of the entire world. "So, what do you think?" he said as they took their spoils back toward the car. "Are you still up for a trip to the beach?"

"Oh, yeah," she replied.

Heather told Jordan where to find a beach with decent changing rooms, and he waited patiently outside for her. There were several hundred people along the wide strip of sand; a rather light crowd for Waikiki. Jordan heard the changing room door open, and caught his breath. He had come to admire Heather's form as she tried on various dresses, but none of them showed it quite the same as the bikini she now wore. It was actually fairly modest as bikinis go, but it showed off more of her soft, slender figure than Jordan was expecting.

More enticing than the smooth lines of her tan body was the look she gave as she walked toward him. It was one of acceptance—ownership, even. She was looking at him, coming toward him, claiming him as her own, and the feeling was intoxicating.

The thrill only increased as Heather applied sunscreen to his back, and when he rubbed lotion on her back and shoulders he felt a tremendous sense of accomplishment. For the first time in his life, he was in a relationship that was going somewhere.

When the lotion finally disappeared into Heather's skin, Jordan eased her back so she leaned against his chest. She nestled in, and he wrapped his arms around her. Despite the sun peeking through the clouds high overhead, the January breeze blowing off the ocean was just a little cool, and the warmth of her body felt nice in his arms. Jordan nuzzled her ear with his nose. "You smell like apricot. Which is so much better than lavender or freesia, if you ask me." Heather looked at him funny, and Jordan said, "That's from . . ."

"I know where it's from. I just didn't expect you to be a *Twilight* fan." She elbowed him playfully and then nestled back against his chest.

"I'm sorry the flight this morning was such a disaster," he said. "Once I get my license, I'll wait for the perfect day and fly you around the island."

Heather sighed softly and then said, "I'm not sure I want you taking flying lessons any more."

"What? Why not?"

"Because, it takes up so much of your time." She turned to face him. "Time we could be spending together instead." She twisted around as far as she could and kissed him. Jordan leaned forward, cradled her in his arms, and returned her kiss. They sat wrapped together, talking and kissing, until it was time to leave.

When they got to the car, Jordan said, "Hey, I know—let's put the top down."

"Oh, no. Please don't."

"Why not? They invented convertibles for days like this."

"No, Jordan, don't. It'll just mess up my hair."

Jordan expected her to crack a smile and tell him she was kidding, but she didn't. So he left the top up.

They held hands all the way back to La'ie, and Jordan dropped Heather off at her house, returning ninety minutes later to pick her up. She was stunning, with her hair pulled up into a loose, elegant bun. She wore bright red lipstick and that black dress. While he hadn't been a big fan of the shoes she had picked, he had to admit they looked great with the rest of the outfit.

Jordan wore his missionary suit, but instead of a white shirt and tie he had on the black T-shirt Julie had insisted he buy for just such an occasion. He hadn't been all that interested in the shirt at the time, but he had to admit that the look was pretty sweet.

Dinner went extremely well, as did the show. After Jordan returned Heather to her house with a proper good-night, he went home wearing a large grin on his face. Still too wound up to sleep, he sat down to send an email to Julie. He knew she'd be pleased. Glancing through his unread messages, he saw one from Facebook, telling him that Heather had added him as her boyfriend and asking him to confirm. Jordan felt as though he had just won the lottery. For the first time in his life he had a girlfriend, and now it was official.

eighteen

A couple of weeks later, Jordan found himself alone in Pua's. Amber had classes on Tuesday mornings, and Lani had to run to the bank. Malia was supposed to be there but hadn't made it in yet. He was straightening the bouquets in the front display case when he heard the bell on the door. Assuming it was Malia, he said, "It's about time you got here." But when he turned to look, he found Kehau.

She smiled at him and said, "Hi, Jordan. How have you been?"

Jordan stood, a bit surprised to see her there. They hadn't talked at all since the day he saw her in the Hawaiian village. "Pretty good. How about you?"

"Oh, not too bad," she said, shrugging her shoulders. "I heard about you and Heather—good for you." Kehau clasped her hands in front of her and rocked onto the balls of her feet. "I don't really know her, but she seems nice."

"Yeah, it doesn't take long for news to travel around this place, does it?"

Kehau smiled again. "No, it doesn't. Are those for her?" she asked.

Jordan looked down at the small orchid and carnation bouquets he held in his hands. He had just been straightening the case, but the idea of giving flowers suddenly seemed like a good one. "Uh, yeah. These are for Heather," he said, indicating the flowers in his left hand. "And these are for my mom." Jordan raised the bouquet on the right.

"Flowers for your mother? That's really sweet," Kehau said.

Just then the bell on the door sounded again, and Malia stormed in. "One of these days I'm going to kill my brother," she said. "Hi, Kehau—what are you doing here?"

Kehau glanced quickly at Jordan and then back at Malia. "I need to talk to you."

It took Jordan only a moment to realize Kehau hoped for a private conversation, so he snatched a couple of generic cards and said, "I need to go fill out some tags for these. Good to see you again, Kehau."

She smiled at him. "You too."

Walking back into the workshop, Jordan wondered just what to write on the little cards. His motivation for sending the flowers was primarily the guilt he felt at sneaking off to complete his flight training behind his mother's back, and now Heather's as well.

He'd always considered himself an honest person, and lying to his mother was killing him. And with Heather in on his secret, the odds of him being found out went up dramatically. Maybe he should just come clean and tell her the truth.

Jordan collected the other morning deliveries and walked toward the front of the store when the sound of Malia talking in a loud whisper stopped him. He waited, not wanting to interrupt their conversation, and heard Malia exclaim, "That two-timing jerk!"

In an instant, Jordan realized she must be talking about Scott. He took a step back and tried to listen to more of the conversation, but just then the bell on the door sounded, and he heard Lani's voice. "Good morning, Malia. Hello, Kehau."

"Hi," the girls said together, and he knew he wasn't going to get the rest of the story.

Jordan made the morning deliveries, saving his mom's for last. He knew Heather would be in class, so he had one of her housemates put the flowers in her room and then drove slowly to campus. He turned onto Big Circle—the road was actually more of a rounded rectangle encircling the library, McKay building, and Aloha Center—and began looking for a parking spot. The spaces that flanked the road were full all the way from the library to the business department offices at the back of the campus, so Jordan turned toward the dorms and parked between Hale 3 and the tennis courts. Taking the flowers from the seat next to him, he walked past the Health Center and around the corner toward his mom's office. His anxiety at confessing about his flight training grew with each step.

The School of Business occupied a small, low building across Big Circle from the McKay Auditorium, and as Jordan approached, he quickened his pace, anxious to get this over with and hopeful that doing so would cause a weight to be lifted from his conscience.

Pausing at the front door, he took a calming breath and entered. As he walked past the front desk, Elissa, the student receptionist, smiled at him and said, "Hi, Jordan." This caught him off guard. She'd been at the desk since the start of the school year and had always regarded him with indifference when he'd come to visit his mother. Why, all of a sudden, were they on friendly terms?

The answer suddenly occurred to Jordan—Elissa was Heather's friend. As Sister MacDonald's son, he'd been a nobody, but now he was Heather's boyfriend, and apparently that counted for something.

Jordan returned her greeting and made his way through the open door into Beth's office. "Hey, Mom."

"Well, hi, Jordan. What are you up to this morning?"

Jordan shrugged his shoulders. "Just finishing up the morning deliveries. Here—these are for you."

Jordan smiled at the look of surprise on his mother's face. "For me? What's this all about?"

"Oh, I just wanted to let you know I was thinking about you."

"Well, thank you," she said, taking the bouquet. "It's been a long time since anyone's sent me flowers."

"You're welcome," he said. Beth looked expectantly at him, apparently sensing there was something more behind the gesture. Jordan took a breath and began just as he had rehearsed. "Do you remember that summer before my mission, when I was working with Dad in Texas?"

Beth's eyes narrowed. "Yes."

"Well, while I was there, he . . . I started taking flying lessons." Jordan expected a look of shock, but instead he saw his mother's face harden ever so slightly, and her cheeks and neck began to darken. He took another breath and continued, "Well, anyway, I—"

"No, stop right there!" Beth cut him off. "Whatever it is you're about to say, just forget it—I don't want to hear it."

"But . . ."

"No! That's enough. This topic is closed. End of conversation. I don't want to hear another word about this again. Do you understand me?"

All of Jordan's anxiety congealed in his gut and sat there. He looked down. "Sure."

"And Jordan?" his mother called after him as he turned to walk away.

"Yeah?"

Her face softened and her voice returned to normal. "Thanks for the flowers. They really are very nice."

A light rain fell on Jordan as he walked back to the van, head hung low, trying to figure out what to do. The obvious answer was for him to give up and stop his lessons. But he couldn't stand the thought of quitting when he was so close, and this had meant so much to his father that Jordan felt he owed it to him to finish. Besides—he really enjoyed flying. And he'd already paid for the flight hours.

By the time he pulled in at Pua's, he had made up his mind. He would finish his lessons, get his ticket, use any remaining flight hours, and then hang up his wings for good.

In the days to come, the weather remained unsettled, as was typical during mid-winter in La'ie. It took over a week before the skies finally looked like they would cooperate for Jordan's solo cross-country. The long, bumpy flight across the ocean to Molokai and Lanai and back seemed to take forever, a fact he shared with Roach once he was finally on the ground.

Roach just grinned at Jordan as he plopped onto one of the couches, closed his eyes, and willed his stomach to calm down. "Flying The Bomb interisland is always too slow. Now, if you want to fly in this weather, what you need is the Bonanza. On a day like today, you just put on a little oxygen and let the turbo take you up over the clouds. Almost twice as fast, and much more comfortable."

"And twice as expensive," Jordan replied.

"At least," Roach said with a smile.

The flight went longer than Jordan had planned, and he missed one of his classes. He knew he needed to get back but couldn't quite get himself to move. As he sat in the lounge, trying to regain his composure, his phone rang. On the other end was Heather, sounding more than a little annoyed.

"Where are you?" she asked.

Jordan sighed. "Things took a little longer than I expected this morning, but I'm just leaving." He pulled himself off the couch but had to steady himself on the coffee table. Roach laughed.

"That means I'm not going to see you until after you're done working."

"I'm sorry, hon," said Jordan. "I'll meet you in the library after my shift is over. Just right inside the lobby."

Jordan hoped that would be good enough. After the day he'd had, some quality time with Heather sounded pretty good.

nineteen

As Jordan waited for Heather in the foyer of the school library, he eyed the portrait of Joseph F. Smith, sixth president of the LDS church, and the man for whom the library was named. Though Jordan had seen this picture probably hundreds of times, he found himself studying it as though he had never seen it before.

While admiring the lifelike quality of the portrait and trying to pick out the individual brush strokes, he saw someone approach him from behind out of the corner of his eye. As he turned, expecting to find Heather, he was surprised to see Kehau looking at him quizzically.

"You're sure studying that picture closely," she said with an amused smile.

Jordan's ears flushed at being caught in his decidedly nerdy examination of the portrait.

"He taught my family the gospel," Kehau said, indicating the portrait of President Smith.

"Really?" asked Jordan, hoping to induce a conversation.

"Mm-hmm. He was a missionary here in Hawai'i for four years, starting when he was fifteen. One of the people he taught was my great-great-grandfather."

Jordan expected Kehau to share the story of her grandfather, but her eyes suddenly looked over Jordan's shoulder with a hint of alarm. Jordan turned to see Heather approaching.

"There you are," she said coolly, her face in a forced smile. She wrapped her arms possessively around Jordan's waist and said, "I need to be careful not to leave you waiting so long."

Completely ignoring Kehau, Heather pulled Jordan toward the main library section. His conversation with Kehau had been perfectly innocent, yet Jordan felt a little pang of guilt at enjoying her company as much as he did. Still, he didn't quite understand Heather's reaction, and her behavior embarrassed him.

"Hey, it was good talking to you," he said, waving to Kehau over his shoulder.

Kehau returned his wave and smile, though she certainly looked rather put-off by Heather's brusque behavior. They went upstairs, and Heather led Jordan to a small study table in a back corner. "Who was that?" Heather asked when they were settled.

"Just a friend," Jordan replied. He expected Heather to grill him about Kehau, but she let it go at that. Instead, she took out a book and began reading, but every few minutes they were interrupted by groups of students walking past.

Finally Heather announced, "I can't concentrate with all this. Let's go." And without waiting for a reply, she shoved her book in her bag and stood up. Jordan quickly followed her lead, and they walked out. Jordan had parked in one of the spaces behind the library, and mercifully the rain had slowed to a light drizzle. Jordan let Heather into the car and then walked around and climbed in. Putting the key in the ignition he asked, "Where to?"

She leaned over, grabbed his hand to stop him from turning the key, and said, "Right here is fine." She took his face in her hands and pulled him close, kissing him hard. He was hers, and she seemed to be making sure there was no doubt in his mind.

In a humid environment, it doesn't take much for condensation to form on cold glass, and as a result Jordan's car was thoroughly fogged when campus security knocked on his window.

■ ■ ■

Jordan slinked into work the next morning, hoping that his little incident with security the previous night hadn't made it through the gossip channel yet. After a quick chorus of greetings, the girls all went back to their flowers, and Jordan started sweeping out the walk-in fridge, relieved that his embarrassment from the night before remained a secret. With Valentine's Day fast approaching, the girls were hard at work getting small arrangements of roses ready to go in the display, and even Jordan began stringing leis once his other tasks were done. After several minutes, Malia tilted her head and asked, "Jordan, can you come do something with my neck?"

"Yeah, sure." The bell on the shop door rang as Jordan set down his strand of flowers and began rubbing at the base of Malia's skull. He quickly found a knot in the muscles and began working it out with his thumb. Malia grimaced and moaned slightly, and soon the knot started to relax.

Jordan felt a hand slip around his waist, causing him to jump. Turning quickly, he found himself face to face with Heather. Although the neck rub had been perfectly innocent, Heather's icy smile combined with his own surprise at seeing her sent a wave of guilt over him. He stopped abruptly and felt the blood rush to his ears. "Oh, Heather. Hi."

"Hi," she said, wrapping her arms around him possessively just as she had the night before. "I can't seem to leave you alone for a minute." The other girls all stopped their work, sensing the sudden rise in tension.

He put his arm around her and gave her a hug. "So, to what do we owe this pleasure?" he asked.

"I had a feeling I should come in and check on you. And from the looks of it, I was right."

"What? Oh, this? That was just, um, she had a crick in her neck."

"Yeah, sure," Heather said. "So why don't I meet you tonight after work?" She continued in a whisper loud enough for all to hear: "We'll see if we can fog your windows enough to attract campus security again." With that, Heather slapped Jordan on the behind and strode out the door.

Jordan watched her leave and then turned to face the girls. Amber's mouth was hanging slightly open, and Malia stood with her arms folded, one eyebrow cocked. Even Lani had stopped work on her large arrangement and eyed Jordan curiously. "Well," she said. "It looks like someone is a little possessive. Good luck, Jordan."

Later that night, Jordan returned home after his shift in the lab to find his mother waiting for him. She sat in her chair, arms crossed and mouth pinched tight. A knot formed in his stomach when he saw the look in her eyes.

"I had a very interesting talk with Heather this evening."

The hair on Jordan's neck tingled, and he struggled to keep his voice steady. "Really? What about?"

"Oh, lots of things."

Jordan immediately thought of his flight training and the practical flying test he had just scheduled—the last step to becoming a pilot. Stealing a glance at his mother's eyes, he tried to discern the level of her anger but had to quickly look down. "Mom, I—I'm sorry."

"You're sorry. Jordan, do you have any idea how this makes me feel? How Heather feels? It's one thing to think you can keep me in the dark, to hide your big, bad secrets." She raised her arm and gestured aimlessly into the room. "I'm hurt, Jordan—hurt and disappointed. But that's not what really upsets me."

Jordan cast her a tentative look as she continued. "I just can't believe, with someone as lovely Heather in your life, you would still find it necessary to flirt with every girl you can find."

Jordan scrunched his eyebrows. "What?"

"Don't play dumb with me, mister. I heard about you, hands all over the girls at the shop. And last night with that Kehau girl? What are you thinking, Jordan?"

His muscles tensed defensively. "We were talking about Kehau's grandfather's baptism—that's all. And today, Malia had a crick in her neck. I give all the girls neck rubs all the time."

Beth's jaw dropped. "So the fact that this happens 'all the time' is somehow supposed to make it okay? Jordan, I raised you better than that. Now, if you can't keep your hands to yourself, you just might want to consider moving yourself away from that temptation."

It took Jordan a second to figure out what she was trying to say. "You mean quit Pua's?"

Beth refolded her arms. "If that's what it takes."

Jordan sighed and shook his head. "No, that's not—it won't happen again." With his head bowed, Jordan took a step toward his room.

"Wait—I'm not done with you yet. Heather and I had one other discussion tonight."

Jordan tensed again. "About what?"

Beth cocked her head and pursed her lips tightly, and the blood drained from Jordan's face. Then she raised her eyebrows and said, "We had a nice, lively discussion about your 'investment' with her ex-boyfriend Chad."

Jordan lowered his head. After a moment, he raised it again and said, "You were right—it was a stupid move. I should have listened to you."

"And you need to listen to me now, Jordan. I'm your mother, and I know what I'm talking about."

twenty

Jordan sat in The Bomb, waiting for the FAA examiner seated next to him to start the practical flying test. It had taken a dedicated effort to sneak away to the airport, as Heather had been keeping a very close eye on Jordan after the flower shop neck rub incident.

He felt tremendous guilt at the necessary deception, but he only had to pass this test and then he would be done. He had completed all of the required flights, flown more than enough hours, and passed the written test with a ninety-four percent. He just couldn't bring himself to quit when the goal was so close at hand.

"So, how have you liked flying my plane?" Burl asked. Burl was an older man, probably in his late sixties. Age spots and thin wispy white hair covered his otherwise bald head, and he wore a dour expression that Jordan quickly learned was just a front.

"Um, okay. This is your plane?"

"Well, it was. I bought her new the spring of sixty-eight. This whole operation was mine at one time."

"What happened?" Jordan asked.

"Well, some friends of mine and I have had this regular Saturday night poker game going since probably before you were born. This one night about five years ago, my mechanic was on a roll, and he ended up winning this plane."

"Roach?" Jordan asked.

"Yep. Over the last few years, he either won or bought the whole outfit." Then with a smile, he added, "It was getting to be a bit much for me, if you know what I mean."

Burl's easy demeanor helped Jordan relax enough to perform pretty well on all of his flight maneuvers, and he only made one small mistake talking to the tower. But his landings just didn't work. The examiner had him try three times, and Jordan bounced seriously on all of them, and once had to abort and go around.

After the last landing, Burl had him taxi back to La'aloa and park. He sat in the passenger seat, his lips pursed and shaking his head. Jordan didn't dare move or speak, waiting for Burl to say something first. He had a sinking feeling in the pit of his stomach—he had failed.

Burl turned, squinted his eyes, and studied Jordan, tapping his pen against his pursed lips. "Start the engine," he said. "Let's take one more trip around the pattern."

Jordan's heart jumped. He was getting a second chance. Nervous energy shot through him, and he determined to get it right. But just as he was about the start the engine, he heard Roach's voice in the back of his mind. "Just relax, MacDonald. You bounce when you're tense."

Jordan pulled his hand back from the starter button, looked at Burl, and said, "Just a second." He closed his eyes, took a deep breath, and said a quick but heartfelt prayer that he'd be able to relax and do his best.

After one more deep breath he started the plane, and with everything else blocked from his mind, began to taxi. He still found himself fighting off tension and anxiety, but with another quick prayer, the calm returned.

The taxi, take off, and flight through the pattern all proceeded without incident, as Jordan knew they would. Lining the airplane on the runway for his final approach, Jordan fought for control of his emotions and kept himself calm through the exertion of sheer will. He brought the engine back to idle, and the plane seemed to hang motionless in the air for just a moment. The stall horn sounded just seconds before the main gear gently touched on the large white numbers, and a slight forward motion on the yoke brought the nose wheel softly to the ground. A choir of angels sang in Jordan's head, and he failed to keep a grin from spreading across his face.

"Congratulations, Mr. MacDonald. You are now the nation's newest pilot."

twenty-one

The next few days were torture for Jordan. Excitement and pride at finally getting his pilot's license filled his mind, and yet he couldn't share his good news with anyone but Todd and Julie. He almost broke down and told Malia one afternoon as the two of them drove north to the Turtle Bay Resort with a large order in the back of the van. Three separate sections Lani had worked on for the last two days needed to be joined to make one large arrangement. At the last minute, Lani had been unable to go, so she quickly gave Malia instructions on setting it up.

The flowers were a centerpiece for a board meeting being held in a large formal conference room at the hotel, and the resort represented a big account for the shop. Being entrusted with such a significant responsibility made Jordan nervous, especially since Lani wasn't with them.

They drove up alongside the golf course, past a security station, and beyond a cluster of condos to the main hotel itself. Situated on a little peninsula, every room of the Turtle Bay hotel looked out to a view of the ocean, which churned with choppy gray waves that day.

Jordan had a difficult time finding a parking spot, and the nearest spots were far from the main entrance. He thought of the large collection of flowers in the back and knew there was no way the two of them could carry everything in one trip. "Why don't I drop you and the flowers off at the main entrance. I'll go park and then run back to help."

Malia looked back at their cargo. "Good idea," she said. "I wondered how we were going to get all those flowers in there."

They pulled under the large overhang and began unloading flowers into the open-air lobby. All of a sudden, Malia said, "Hey, Jordan. Why not just have the valet park the van?"

Before Jordan could raise an objection, the air was rent by an ear splitting whistle. "Hey, you! Valet! Over here!" A small, dark-haired man in a loud pink aloha shirt ran toward them, and Jordan handed him the keys to the van. He turned around to find Malia dragging a golden luggage cart toward their stack of flowers, a tall slender porter hurrying along after her. "Here, look at this, Jordan. Put everything on here."

Jordan smiled and obediently began loading the flowers. They easily found the conference room, and Jordan lined up the three rectangular blocks of foam bristling with proteas, bird-of-paradises, anthuriums, and gingers. He then unpacked the rest of the flowers and greenery, and Malia began filling in the voids, merging the three separate arrangements into one. Like a surgeon's assistant, Jordan handed her flowers as she called for them: Delicate sprays of white dendrobium orchids; broad, glossy ti leaves; and thin, delicate palms.

"Jordan—hand me one of those flowers."

Jordan looked around, confused. "Which flower?"

"The red one. Anthurium." Malia grinned.

Jordan picked up one of the blood-red blooms and handed the flower to Malia.

"I love anthuriums," she said as she deftly placed it in the arrangement. "I'm going to have thousands of them at my wedding." She stopped and looked at Jordan. "Only ninety-seven more days."

Jordan shook his head. "You're really going to do it, aren't you? You've waited for him his whole mission, and you're really going to get married."

"Yes," Malia replied. "Why does everyone always seem so surprised by that?"

"Because it usually doesn't happen, that's why. When I went into the Missionary Training Center, there were eleven other missionaries going to Oregon at the same time. I was the only one who didn't have a girlfriend. Sixteen months later at our mission conference, not one of those girls was waiting any longer."

"Oh, wow," she said. "Well, lucky thing you didn't have anyone to break up with you then, huh?"

"Ha! Yeah, right. I knew the odds were against having a girl-friend make it the whole two years, but it still bothered me that I was the only one who didn't have one. It was like there was something wrong with me."

"No," she said. "Besides, you've managed to find yourself a girl-friend now, right?"

"Well, yeah," Jordan replied.

"You don't sound very excited about it. Is there already trouble in paradise?"

"No," Jordan replied. "No, everything's fine. It's just . . ." His voice trailed off, and he tried again to put his finger on it. "I don't know. I just thought things would be different, you know?"

Malia didn't know, and the expression on her face showed it. "It's like she's trying to run my life."

"Really? How?"

"Well, she was all upset about my flying lessons, and . . ." Jordan stopped suddenly, but the damage was done.

"Flying lessons? You're not . . ." Malia's eyes widened in sudden understanding. "Wait—that's where you go sometimes in the morn-ing, isn't it? You're going to be a pilot? That is so cool."

"Yeah, it's cool, but you can't tell anyone."

"What, this is some big secret?"

Jordan fidgeted with a piece of fern. "Kind of. My mom would explode if she found out."

"Your mom doesn't know?"

"Nobody knows. Except Todd Jameson, Julie, Heather, and now you. I just passed my check ride, so I finally have my license. But Heather doesn't want me flying."

"Did she say why?"

"She said it takes away from our time together."

Malia shrugged. "Well, sometimes you have to do what it takes to keep your lady happy."

"I know. And I will because I hate trying to hide it from her."

"What? It's not that bad, is it? I mean, it's just flying, right? C'mon. Show your woman a little respect."

Jordan sighed. "She wants me to quit Pua's, too."

Malia whipped her head around. "What? You can't quit Pua's. We need you. Why does she want you to quit?"

"You remember the other day when she came in, and I was rubbing your neck?"

"Yeah? Oh, don't tell me she's jealous of that!" But Jordan's look confirmed that she was. Malia was suddenly riled up. "Oh, that's just ridiculous. Jordan, you gotta do something about that girl of yours. How can she be jealous of a neck rub? It's not like she owns you or anything. Honestly, I don't know what you see in her, other than she's got a pulse and was real quick to get all kissy with you—"

Malia's tirade was cut short when her cell phone rang. "Oh, wait. That's Lani's ring," she said as she dug around in her purse. Putting the phone to her ear, she said, "Hi, Lani. Everything's going great— we're almost pau. What's up?"

Jordan watched Malia as her eyebrows came together. "What? You're kidding me!" Malia's mouth hung open, and there was danger in her eyes. "You're going to charge them for this, right?" She looked at Jordan and shook her head. "Good. So, what are we supposed to do with all of this?" Malia said, gesturing around the room.

A knot formed in Jordan's stomach as he realized their work was about to be undone. Malia scowled at Lani's answer, and then said, "No, no, we'll think of something. See you in about an hour." She hung up the phone and shook her head again. "Well, it seems our friends at the Hui Ka'ulua Foundation have rescheduled their board meeting at the last minute, and they don't need these flowers after all."

"So what now?" Jordan asked.

"Back to the shop, I guess."

It took them only a couple of minutes to pack up the extra flowers, and Malia spoke just as they were finishing. "Help me see if we can get this on the cart in one piece. I'll be danged if I'm going to let all that work go to waste."

twenty-two

Working together, Jordan and Malia managed to gently lift the long, unstable arrangement from the table to the cart, and from the cart to the back of the van. "Okay, where to?" Jordan asked as he slid behind the wheel.

"To the hospital," Malia said.

Jordan drove to the old Kahuku hospital, and he pulled into a parking space. "Where are we going to take this?"

"I don't know yet," said Malia, shoving her way out of the van. "*Hele mai*," she said, urging Jordan to come along.

Malia led Jordan to a small row of offices and through a door marked, "Financial Director." Sitting at a desk piled high with papers, Jordan recognized Sister Boyce, wife of the TV studio guy at BYU—Hawaii. Malia introduced her to Jordan. "Sister Boyce was the best young women's president ever," she said, causing Sister Boyce to smile. Malia then explained the predicament with the flowers.

"Do you have any place where you could use them?" Malia asked.

Sister Boyce's eyes twinkled. "I think we can come up with something."

By the time Jordan and Malia left, the grand floral centerpiece sat proudly at the hospital's entrance, nearly overwhelming the small reception area. "Are you sure Lani will be okay with us giving them those flowers?"

Malia shrugged. "She said to just throw them away. Hui Ka'ulua already paid for them, and if they want to change their meeting at the last minute, that's their problem." Then with a smile she added, "It's a nice gift to the hospital, don't you think?"

■ ■ ■

Later that week, the excitement of getting his license proved too much to keep to himself, and Jordan finally confided in Brandon, offering to take him for a flight as his first passenger. Brandon insisted on bringing Stacie along, and with the two of them sandwiched together in the back of the plane, Jordan felt something like an air taxi pilot. Even with an ice-filled cooler strapped into the front passenger's seat, the plane's center of gravity sat uncomfortably far back, although it was still well inside the limits.

Jordan flew them over Mililani and up toward La'ie, slightly annoyed that neither one seemed interested in looking out the window. Why did they bother coming if they're just going to sit in back and talk? But as La'ie came into view, he noticed them paying more attention to their surroundings. Brandon asked, "Jordan, can you circle around the temple a few times?"

"Yeah, sure." Jordan set up a banking turn, with the wing pointed directly at the temple. As he began the second turn, he felt a sudden, unexpected shift in weight behind him. Whipping his head around, he saw Brandon with his knees on the floor between the seats. Both he and Stacie had their headphones off, and Brandon held his face near Stacie's ear.

What on earth? Jordan's thoughts were shattered as Stacie suddenly screamed and the tail began to bounce violently. Quickly Jordan righted the plane, adding power to start climbing, and saying a quick prayer as he verified attitude, altitude, and airspeed. The bouncing ended as suddenly as it had begun, and Jordan turned back around to make sure his passengers were okay. Both Brandon and Stacie still had their headsets off, and it looked like Stacie was crying. *Great. My first passengers, and I've scared them to death.* But just then Stacie began hopping up and down in her seat, bouncing the whole plane as she did so.

Jordan tapped Brandon on the shoulder and raised his eyebrows questioningly. Brandon's giant grin grew even larger, and he lifted Stacie's hand to show Jordan a diamond ring.

Jordan smiled back, gave Brandon a thumbs-up, and did his best to ignore his passengers for the rest of the flight.

Back on the ground, Jordan waited until Stacie was in the restroom before pulling Brandon aside. "Hey, Brandon," he said in a low voice. "Why didn't you tell me what you had planned?"

Brandon grinned at Jordan. "I thought it was best to keep it a surprise."

Jordan didn't grin back. "Yeah, well, see the problem is any airborne proposal like that is kind of supposed to have prior FAA approval." Brandon's smile faded and his face turned ashen. Jordan bit his lip for as long as he dared before allowing a huge smile to fill his face. "Just kidding, man. Congratulations."

"You dog!" Both the color and grin returned to Brandon's face, and he punched Jordan hard in the shoulder.

twenty-three

"Jordan is a pilot now Maybe he can fly us."

Jordan looked up in alarm. Malia stood talking to Kehau in the front of the shop, but none of the other girls were there. Still, he cleared his throat and shot Malia a warning glance.

"Oh, relax. Kehau's not gonna tell anyone." Malia whispered loudly to Kehau, "His mommy and his wifey don't want him flying, so it's all a big secret." Jordan glared at her. Malia continued loudly. "Yeah, it's so sad. Jordan has to leave us too."

"Really?" Kehau asked. "Where are you going, Jordan?"

"Nowhere," he said, gently bumping Malia's behind with the handle of his broom as he swept.

"It seems that somebody is jealous of all us beautiful girls here at Pua's, and she's making him quit."

Jordan could feel his ears turning red. "She's not making me quit."

"You know," continued Malia. "It's a shame that girl has Jordan on such a tight leash. I'm sure he'd fly us to Tutu's party in his little plane, but he's grounded."

"I'm not grounded. Heather doesn't want me to fly, but that doesn't mean I can't."

"Oh, really?" asked Malia. "Just like how she doesn't want you working here, but that doesn't mean you can't?" He suddenly regretted confiding in Malia. The fact that he was thinking about quitting the flower shop to make Heather happy was starting to sound a bit weak.

"When is this big party?"

Kehau said, "No, Jordan. Malia is just joking—aren't you, Malia?"

"Who me? I don't joke. Tutu's birthday is next Saturday at noon, and Kehau really wants to go." Kehau elbowed Malia hard. "I think it would be fun too."

Jordan pulled out his phone and looked at the calendar. He could probably pull it off on a Saturday. He worked the late shift in the lab, and before that, he and Heather were going to dinner with her friends Erin and Trey, but he could easily make it back in time. "Your grandmother's on the Big Island?"

"Yup. So what do you think? Are you gonna do it?"

"Malia, you're such a pig! I can't believe you're doing this. Jordan, she's just kidding, really." But Jordan wasn't listening. He had made his way to the shop's computer and was checking the schedule for The Bomb. It was available, and a large grin split Jordan's face. Before he could talk himself out of it, he scheduled the aircraft for the entire day.

"There, the plane's reserved. We're all set for next Saturday."

"What?" Kehau said. "Wait—how much does it cost to rent the plane?"

"Less than three round-trip tickets on an airline."

"Jordan, that's too much. I can't let you do this."

"Too late. Besides, I think it'll be fun. I've always wanted to fly to the Big Island, and here's my chance. Plus, I had to buy my flight hours in a block, and I still have some to use up."

Malia slapped him playfully on the shoulder. "Way to go, Jordan. Stand up for yourself. Be the man. Wear the pants. You tell that girl not to mess with you."

Jordan smiled, but he knew he wasn't really standing up for himself—in his mind he was already trying to figure out a cover story to tell Heather and his mom so he could fly without them knowing.

twenty-four

Jordan loaded his flight bag into the trunk of his Mustang and put the top down, hoping the cool morning air would help wake him. The town was still except for the sound of his car as Jordan motored toward Malia's house, where Kehau had spent the night because of their early departure. He felt a mix of excitement at the prospect of flying all the way to the Big Island, and apprehension over the cover story he'd fed his mom and Heather. The fact that he would be flying with two beautiful girls added to his guilt, but he reminded himself that he was just the pilot—nothing more.

He cut the engine as he approached Malia's home and coasted into the driveway. The door opened, and Kehau walked out alone. "Jordan, I was just going to call you. We need to cancel."

Jordan's heart sank. "Why? Is something wrong?"

"Malia was sick all night—throwing up and everything."

"Oh no. Is she okay?" Jordan asked.

"Yeah, she's doing better now. We ate at one of the shrimp trucks last night, and I think she got some that was bad. She says she feels better now, but she's wiped out."

Jordan tried to hide his disappointment. "Is there anything I can do?" he asked, knowing there probably wasn't.

Just then the door opened again, and Malia came out. She was wrapped in a thin white kimono, her hair a wild tangle. "Kehau, you go. I'll be fine. You two go already."

"No," Kehau said. "I can't. It costs too much money for Jordan just to fly me."

Jordan was torn between disappointment and relief at the thought of cancelling the trip. He wrestled with his feelings until his desire to fly finally won out. "Kehau, listen. I have a plane reserved for the whole day and a flight plan filed from Honolulu to Kamuela. I need to use these hours sooner or later, so I'm going. You're more than welcome to come with me."

Kehau bit her lip. "See?" Malia prompted. "You go. I'll be fine. Just go."

"Okay, okay, already," said Kehau, allowing herself a smile. "I'll be just a few minutes."

"Great. I'll wait right here."

Jordan sat in the car looking up at the stars and listening to the roar of the surf in the distance. A tingle of excitement ran up the back of his neck. He was really going to do this flight. Roach had given him the spare key to The Bomb the day before, and Jordan checked his pocket, making sure he remembered to bring it.

Kehau returned about ten minutes later, wearing a black sweater over a blue aloha shirt and light tan pants. Jordan got out, opened her door, took her small bag, and put it into the back. Returning to his seat, he started the car and pressed a switch. The car's black canvas top began to move into place.

"Oh," said Kehau with a hint of disappointment.

"What?"

She shook her head. "Nothing." But he saw her glance at the car top before turning away.

Jordan hadn't even thought to ask Kehau if she wanted him to put the top up. He just assumed she would, given the fuss Heather always made about the wind and her hair. "Do you want me to leave the top down?"

Kehau smiled and said, "If you want to."

Jordan lowered the top back into place as Kehau pulled her hair into an elastic band, and together they drove toward the airport.

Driving on the highway with the top down made conversation difficult, so they drove toward town in the silence of rushing wind. The sky brightened while they drove, with the sun just creeping above Diamond Head when they arrived at the airport. Jordan took their bags and said, "The plane's over here." Kehau fidgeted with her hands as he walked her across the tarmac toward the little blue Cessna. Even at this early hour, the rumble of commercial jets on the other side of the airport was regular and frequent, and occasionally they heard another piston plane take off as well.

Approaching The Bomb, Jordan fished the key from his pocket. "Well, here she is. She may not look like much, but Roach keeps her in top mechanical condition." Jordan repeated this statement to reassure himself as much as Kehau. He started to tell her the plane's nickname, but thought better of it. "You said you've been in a small plane before, right?"

"Um, yeah," said Kehau. "But nothing this small." Her eyes were larger than Jordan had ever seen them, and he figured he'd better start working to reassure her.

"Well, don't think about it as a small plane. It's a lot like being in a car with wings." Jordan smiled at her and willed her to smile back at him, which she did weakly. "Now, I'm going to go around and make sure everything is okay, and then we'll get in. All right?"

Kehau nodded, and Jordan proceeded with the preflight inspection. As he walked around The Blue Bomb, he noticed someone coming toward them. He motioned to the man and said, "There's Roach. I'm surprised he's here this early."

Aware that he was undoubtedly being scrutinized now, Jordan continued his inspection with increased precision. "Still planning on going to the Big Island this morning?" Roach asked as he approached.

Jordan nodded and smiled. "Yes, sir."

"What time do you think you'll be back?"

Jordan did the math in his head. "We were planning on leaving at three o'clock." He looked at Kehau. "That's enough time, right?"

Kehau seemed startled to be suddenly included in the conversation. "Um, yeah, I think so. I mean, the party starts at noon, so that should be fine."

"Oh, I'm sorry," said Jordan, realizing he'd failed to make introductions. "Kehau, this is Roach. Roach, Kehau Pulakaumaka." Roach was reaching out to take her hand when he paused. Jordan saw his eyes narrow slightly.

"Pulakaumaka?" he asked quietly. Roach looked as though he wanted to say something else to her but just shook her hand. "Okay, well, you two have a good flight." Another pause. "Just the two of you?"

"Yeah. The other girl got some bad shrimp."

Roach grunted in understanding. "As long as you're back here by five, you should be okay. It might get a little bumpy after that—there's that front blowing through this evening."

Jordan nodded. "Yes, sir."

"Good. You be careful, all right?"

Jordan nodded again.

As Jordan finished the preflight inspection, Kehau called her brother to give him their updated schedule. "No. Not Hilo, and not Kona. That little airport by Kamuela. Yes, right. About a hour and a half."

As Jordan helped Kehau into the plane, he was afraid the life jacket would completely unnerve her, but after the initial surprise, she took it in stride. He gave the preflight briefing and hoped that his professional delivery would instill confidence.

He glanced at her as they sat at the end of the taxiway, awaiting their clearance. The look on her face was just short of terrified, and Jordan was disappointed he hadn't been able to reassure her. "You know what? Maybe we should have a quick prayer."

She glanced at him and nodded. They bowed their heads, and Jordan offered a short invocation. Kehau's face had relaxed slightly by the time he finished, and he smiled at her one last time before putting his mind to the task of flying the airplane.

Jordan gently pushed in the throttle, and the little plane buzzed to life. His take-off and departure were probably the smoothest he had ever done, but experiencing them through the lens of Kehau's trepidation, he noticed every little bump, jerk, and dip. The morning's busy airspace left him no time to dwell on his mistakes, though. The controllers routed him over Honolulu so he would be out of the way of incoming airline traffic, and he had to keep track of two other planes and a tour helicopter. As they flew over Waikiki, Jordan finally felt he could relax enough to check on his passenger.

Kehau sat with her face to the window, and Jordan reached over to gently touch her arm. She turned, and to his great relief, she wore a giant grin. "So, what do you think?" he asked her.

She looked back out the window, and her voice crackled through his headset. "Oh, it's amazing."

Jordan dialed in the heading that would take them straight over the island of Lanai, and then tuned in to the navigation radio. When they were well out over the ocean, he asked Kehau "So, are you ready for your turn to fly?"

Kehau knit her brow, and he gestured at the controls. Her eyes grew wide, and she shook her head. "Oh, no," she said.

Jordan smiled. "Here—look. It's easy. Just take the yoke, and put your feet on the pedals. Don't worry, I won't let go. But put your hands on so you can feel what I'm doing."

She started to reach for the yoke, but hesitated, looking back at Jordan. He nodded at her reassuringly, and she gingerly took hold of the squat rectangular wheel.

"There you go. Good. Now, just watch what I do with the controls and feel how the plane moves. Okay?"

She nodded.

"Turn the yoke to bank the wings, like this. Then push in to go down, pull back to climb, and use the pedals to control the yaw." He demonstrated as he explained, feeling the tail move side to side as he pushed the pedals. "Now you try. I'll keep my hands right here, I promise. I won't let you do anything wrong."

When she was done trying each axis of control, she still seemed hesitant and unsure, but she didn't let go of the yoke, so Jordan decided to put her to work. "See this instrument here?" he said, pointing at a round gauge with two lines running horizontally. "That's the localizer. It's tuned in to a radio near the Lanai airport. Now, all you have to do is keep this needle lined up with that one, and we'll pass right over the top of it. Which is what we want."

He had her make the slow and small corrections that would keep them headed on the right course. "I'll take care of altitude for now. You just work on keeping the needle lined up."

They flew south of Molokai, straight toward the island of Lanai. Ahead and to the left, Maui's Haleakala rose high above the ocean. When the long dark shape of the Big Island appeared on the horizon, Jordan pulled out his chart and set the second navigation radio. "I just entered the frequency for the Upolu Point VOR," he said to Kehau, indicating on his chart the point on the northwest corner of the Big Island. "In about an hour, we'll be fairly close, about here, and we'll come around to the south of the point and pick up the

Kamuela VOR, which will take us straight in to the airport."

Kehau followed his finger as he traced it along the map. "Um," she said, looking at Jordan, and then shook her head and looked back at the map.

"What is it?" Jordan asked.

"Never mind," she replied.

"No, what? Do you want to fly over your house or something? Because we can, no problem." From the look on her face, Jordan thought he had hit the mark.

But Kehau surprised him by saying, "Can we fly around Upolu to the north? I'd love to see Waipio Valley from the air." Kehau traced the route with her finger.

"Yeah, sure," said Jordan, although he didn't know just where Waipio Valley was. He found a small town named Waipio marked on the map, and he was sure the valley would be close to it.

As they reached Lanai, Kehau let go of the yoke so she could look out at the rugged landscape and little plantation town. When they were back over the open water again, she rolled up her sweater and used it for a pillow as she leaned against the window and closed her eyes.

"What? Don't you want to drive anymore?" Jordan teased.

"No, thanks," she said with a smile. "Just wake me up before we get to the Big Island."

"Well, at least you've relaxed enough to sleep. I'll take that as a compliment." Kehau's smile widened, but her eyes remained closed.

twenty-five

As they neared the Big Island, Jordan got an updated weather briefing for Kamuela. Kehau stirred at the sound coming through the headset, and a huge grin stole across her face when she saw the Big Island large in the windscreen.

"Did you sleep well?" She stretched and nodded. Jordan smiled over at her. "Good."

Kehau stared out the window, soaking in the view. They passed around to the lush, green windward side of Kohala Mountain, and Jordan was struck by the stark contrast between it and the dry, brown leeward side. A few small towns dotting the northern coast soon gave way to thick green cliffs that seemed to plunge straight down into the ocean. Then a break in the cliffs appeared, revealing a wide valley with steep green walls that stood nearly vertical on either side. "Look! There it is!" said Kehau. Seeing her excitement, Jordan decided to circle the valley for her before continuing on to the airport.

Kehau gazed out of the window, slowly shaking her head and holding her hand to her mouth. The valley was truly spectacular, but Jordan thought there must be more to explaining the depth of Kehau's reaction. Kehau watched until the valley was out of sight and then turned and smiled at Jordan. "Thank you. That's probably my favorite place in the world. I go there whenever I have a problem to work through. Well, I used to anyway. Thanks again."

Jordan smiled at her "Hey, no problem." He soon intercepted the radial that would lead them to Kamuela airport. The landing was not one of his best, but heeding Roach's advice, he didn't apologize.

The Kamuela airport was little more than a strip of asphalt with a few buildings off to the side, but there were some transient tie-downs that Jordan could use. Several gliders sat tucked off to one side, along with a couple of twin-engine planes from the smaller interisland airline, and a few other single engine planes.

Jordan taxied to a spot next to a sleek new Cirrus and stopped. "Well, here we are," he said. He slipped out of the plane and hurried to help Kehau. Then he began gathering his stuff. Jordan saw some movement out of the corner of his eye and looked up to see a large, rough-looking man with black matted hair and dirt-crusted clothes approaching the plane. The man called out, "Hey!" and quickened his pace toward them.

Heart racing, Jordan moved to put himself in front of Kehau, but before he could make it around the plane, Kehau looked up and yelled, "Maleko!" She ran over and wrapped the man in a hug.

Maleko held out a large, calloused hand to Jordan. "And this must be Scott."

Kehau's face reddened. "Uh, no. Maleko, this is my friend Jordan," she said. "Jordan, this is my brother, Maleko." Jordan heard her add under her breath, "I'm not seeing Scott anymore."

Maleko stepped back and surveyed the plane. "So, you flew this thing all the way from O'ahu, huh?" There was admiration in his eye.

Jordan smiled. "Yeah."

"Cool. Okay, let's get you guys home. This is gonna be one good surprise."

The three of them piled into Maleko's old Ford truck, with Kehau in the middle. The truck, which was dark brown and covered in a healthy layer of red dirt, sped along the thin ribbon of highway before turning off onto a small, winding side road.

"So, are you making Mom and Dad crazy yet?" Kehau asked.

"Try the other way around. Sheesh! I forgot how *lolo* those guys are. I should have enough for my own place in a few months."

"Do you still like your job?"

"I love it. It's the best job I ever had."

"What kind of work do you do?" Jordan asked.

"Ah'm a cowboy," Maleko said in a decent Texas drawl, which

made Kehau laugh. Jordan had forgotten how much he loved that laugh.

"Maleko's a *paniolo* over at Parker Ranch," Kehau said.

So Maleko really was a cowboy. Now it was Jordan's turn to be impressed. "Cool," he said.

Maleko turned down a road that led into a quiet neighborhood. The houses were old plantation style wood-frame homes, and the yards were well kept with large trees and the heady aroma of flowers mixed with the faint smell of wood smoke. The dozen cars surrounding the Pulakaumaka's house made it easy to spot. The house itself sported a fairly recent coat of light blue paint and had obviously been added to several times over the years.

They entered the house, and Jordan felt quite out of place as everyone fawned over Kehau and hardly noticed him. But then Kehau introduced Jordan, and he was suddenly the center of attention, which he found even more disconcerting. Kehau's mother, Hina, was a tall, stately woman with long black hair streaked with silver and pulled in a ponytail that hung to her waist. Kehau's father, Joe, had a broad, round face and a rounder belly. His white hair and beard gave him the look of a Hawaiian Santa Claus, complete with a friendly grin and a twinkle in his eye.

Soon the welcoming was over, and everyone set back to work. It was clearly going to be a big party—even with just those getting ready, the house nearly burst with people. Jordan did his best to simply stay out of the way.

A woman who looked like an older, heavier version of Kehau came in through the back door. "Mom," she called over the din. "Mom!

"Nani," Kehau said, running to the woman and pulling her into a hug.

"Kehau, I didn't know you were coming."

"Yeah, it was kind of a surprise. This is my friend, Jordan. He's a pilot, and he flew me."

"Oh," she said, looking appraisingly at Jordan. "Well, it's good to meet you."

Hina worked her way through the crowd and put her hand on Nani's shoulder. "What is it? Is everything all right?"

Nani shook her head and frowned. "Junior Boy cut his foot. We gotta take him to the doctor. I was just getting ready to make the *pani popo*, but I'm not gonna have time now."

"That's okay, don't worry about it," she said, patting Nani's back. "You take care of my grandson. Tutu can do without *pani popo* for one year."

"I have everything all ready, if someone else wants to make it. It's just . . ."

"No, I need everyone to stick with what they're already doing. We'll be okay."

Nani and her mom hugged, and Nani turned to go when Jordan spoke up. "Um, Kehau and I aren't doing anything. We can help."

Nani, Kehau, and their mom all looked at each other with wide eyes, and Jordan wondered what he had said wrong. Maleko walked by and said, "Kehau cook? What you trying to do? Kill everybody?"

Kehau slapped him hard on the shoulder as he passed. "Shut up," she said. She turned to Jordan and whispered above the noise, "I don't know anything about making *pani popo*."

"Don't worry," he said. "I can make it. It's really not that hard."

Nani cleared her throat. "Look, if you want to make it, that's fine. Go ahead. But I really need to go. Love you, Mom," she said, hugging her mother again before walking out the door.

Kehau looked at Jordan and motioned him outside. "Do you really think you can make *pani popo*?" In her eyes he saw mixed skepticism and hope, and he smiled.

"Not a problem. I've made it a lot."

"Okay, then. Let's go." Kehau walked to the door and yelled, "Mom, we're going to Nani's."

Jordan and Kehau walked three doors down, and he quickly assessed the situation. Various ingredients sat out on the old Formica table in the small but tidy kitchen.

"Here's an apron," he said, taking it from where it hung on the back of a chair. "It might be good if we can find another—this can get messy." Kehau dug around in a few drawers until she came up with one and put it on.

She turned around, and Jordan saw that it said, "Kiss Da Chef." For a split second he imagined himself doing just that. But he quickly blocked the mental image, reminding himself he already had a girlfriend—and a jealous one at that.

128

"So, you've never made *pani popo* before?" Jordan asked as he organized the ingredients.

"No," she said. "I'm a lousy cook."

"You can't be all that bad," said Jordan, as he began measuring warm water into a large mixing bowl.

"Yes, I can. But mostly I just don't like it."

"Well, let's see what we can do about that."

Jordan set to work, ignoring Nani's recipe and mixing from memory. He directed Kehau in measuring the dry ingredients for the rolls while he took care of the yeast. Nani didn't have a mixer like his mom's, so he ended up preparing the dough by hand. Kehau watched him intently, and once he got the bread at the consistency he wanted, he showed her how to knead, folding the dough in half again and again, turning it every couple of times. She started hesitantly, but soon began working with an impressive strength and vigor.

"See? We'll turn you into a proper chef in no time." Kehau smiled in response, and Jordan set to work on the second batch. Soon six pans of sweet rolls were rising in the warm kitchen, and Jordan said, "We've got about a half hour before we need to make the coconut sauce. What should we do?"

He was enjoying his time alone with Kehau, so his heart sank a little when she said, "Let's go back and see how everyone else is doing." Walking back to her parents' house, Jordan found himself confused about his feelings for her. It was becoming more and more clear that his attraction to her had never really gone away. He had simply buried it when she began dating Scott. Keeping that attraction buried was proving to be a challenge.

Kehau's family was a very social bunch, and Jordan enjoyed sitting back for a while and listening to them update each other on everything. When Kehau's grandmother arrived, Jordan was introduced. "Tutu, this is my friend, Jordan MacDonald." Tutu was a little hard of hearing, and Kehau did the introduction several times. A few minutes later, Jordan heard Tutu say, "That's Kehau's friend. He works at McDonald's, I guess. I don't know."

When half an hour had passed, they returned to Nani's. Jordan mixed up the coconut milk pudding, and Kehau poured it over the bread. Twenty minutes later, Jordan pulled the first two pans from the oven and set them on the counter. "Oh, yeah. That's how it's done," he said, admiring the golden brown rolls. He put the second batch in the oven and then took two bowls from the cupboard.

"What are you doing?" Kehau asked, as he filled the bowls with *pani popo*. "Those are supposed to be for the party."

"Quality control," he said, handing one of the bowls to Kehau. "Chef's prerogative."

As they ate the sweet, sticky rolls, the front door opened, and they both jumped like children caught stealing cookies. "Wow, it smells good in here," Nani said as she came into the kitchen, followed by her husband, Ben, who carried their young, injured son. Nani pulled a roll from the pan and bit off the bottom. Her eyebrows furrowed. "You didn't use my recipe?"

"Uh, no," Jordan said, feeling his cheeks flush.

Nani took another bite and nodded her head. "These are good. Give me yours before you go."

Soon it was time for the party back at Kehau's parents' house, and the confusion from earlier turned to near pandemonium. With Kehau being the youngest of eleven kids, there was no small crowd of people in attendance. She tried to introduce Jordan to everyone as they arrived but was soon deep in conversation with cousins and nieces and nephews, and Jordan quickly found himself on his own. Every room was packed, and Jordan sought refuge outside. Plumeria and pandanus trees bordered the modest back yard, with a large cluster of banana plants and a few guava bushes growing along one edge. Gingers, anthuriums, and bird-of-paradises joined countless other flowers Jordan didn't recognize. He found a spot on a large lava rock, out of the way of the growing crowd, and contentedly watched the family celebrate together.

He started from his observations when he heard his name. "Jordan, there you are." Kehau made her way through the crowd. "What are you doing all the way out here? Are you okay?"

Jordan smiled. "Yeah, I'm fine. Just enjoying the show from the sidelines."

Kehau looked back at the talking, laughing throng. "I guess we can be a little much, huh? Sorry."

"No, it's fine. I'm having a good time watching. It's not every day a family this size gets together without someone calling the cops."

Kehau laughed. "No need. There's three policemen here right now. Well, two policemen and one police woman."

Just then, Jordan's phone beeped, indicating a voice mail. He looked at the display and saw that he'd missed three calls, all from La'aloa. "How did that happen?" He tried to get his message, but the call failed.

"Cell service can be kind of spotty here," offered Kehau. "Do you need to call somebody?"

"Yeah," said Jordan.

"Come inside and use my parents' phone." Jordan grew concerned as he followed Kehau into the house. Roach couldn't have good news. Jordan looked at his watch—two o'clock. They weren't scheduled to leave for another hour.

Kehau led Jordan back to her parents' bedroom where there was a phone surrounded by a little bit of quiet. He picked up the receiver and dialed Roach's number. "Hi, this is Jordan," he said as soon as Roach answered.

"So you haven't left yet?" Roach sounded disappointed.

"No, not yet. Why? Is the storm coming sooner?"

"Oh, yeah. It's moving much quicker than originally forecast, and it's bringing a lot of rain with it. The system's supposed to be here in a couple of hours."

Jordan's pulse raced. "Fine. I'll go get Kehau and we'll leave now."

"No, it's too late. If you leave now, that puts you here at the same time as the storm. You're going to have to wait it out."

Jordan felt a sudden surge of panic. "Well, what time is the storm supposed to be there? I really need to get home this afternoon."

"Look, MacDonald. It's too late. Now if you packed your flight bag like I taught you, you have everything you need to spend the night."

"But . . ."

"And don't forget, it's Saturday—poker night. We're starting early on account of the weather. If you even think of trying to beat the storm, there will be two FAA examiners right here in the office. They'll have to arm wrestle to see who gets to yank your license."

Jordan was undeterred. If he didn't get home, he was going to be in trouble much deeper than the FAA could dish out. As if reading his thoughts, Roach added somberly, "And if that's not enough to stop you, think of your pretty little friend. Think of her parents, and what would happen to them when the Coast Guard has to fish you two up off the bottom of the ocean."

Jordan's eyes were drawn to a picture of the whole Pulakaumaka clan on the wall above the bed. He looked at Kehau, and then at her parents and all of her brothers and sisters, and he knew that Roach was right. He couldn't risk flying ahead of the storm. He was going to have to stay the night and take the consequences, whatever they might be.

twenty-six

Jordan stood in the room for a few minutes, not quite knowing what to do next. The party was still going in full swing outside, and he heard Kehau's distinctive laugh. He smiled weakly. At least he wouldn't have to drag her away from her family. But what was he going to do about his mom and Heather? The thought made him sick to his stomach.

He glanced absently around the room, trying to think. His eyes came to rest on a framed picture of a praying child hanging on the wall. He thought about kneeling right there and offering a prayer for help but quickly dismissed the thought. The prompting persisted, though, and he knelt beside the bed, his hands folded on top of the beautiful hand-made Hawaiian quilt.

He prayed silently, explaining his situation to the Lord. However, when he got to the part about asking for help, he couldn't do it. Instead, all he could think was, *It's your own fault you're in this mess, you know. If you were honest with your mom and Heather, there wouldn't be any problem.* Jordan took a breath and then continued his prayer. Admitting his guilt and responsibility for his problem, he asked for help—help to get out of this situation, help to know what to do. As he closed his prayer, he realized there wasn't anything he could do but call his mom and Heather and let them know where he was. He imagined their reaction, and, fearing what they would say, he tried to formulate a half-truth that would keep him out of trouble.

Then he scolded himself—half-truths weren't going to cut it any-more. He needed to be honest.

He was still kneeling by the bed when he heard the door open. Glancing up, he saw Kehau, who looked understandably concerned. "Jordan, is everything okay?"

He stood to meet her as she walked into the room. "The storm came in faster than the forecast. We're not going to make it back tonight." Kehau's look of concern deepened, and he tried to reassure her. "It's supposed to blow through pretty quickly. We'll be able to fly back tomorrow morning."

Kehau thought for a moment. "Well, I think we can probably find you some extra clothes. My brothers aren't as tall as you, but . . ."

Jordan cut her off. "No, I've got a change of clothes in my flight bag. That's not the problem."

"Well, what's wrong then?"

Jordan sighed. "The problem is, my mom and Heather don't know I'm here." He looked down at his hands. "I told them I was helping a friend move. My mom doesn't even know I'm a pilot."

"Oh." Kehau's apparent disappointment made Jordan's embar-rassment even worse. "Well, I'm sure you'll think of something. I'll leave you alone so you can call them."

When she had closed the door, Jordan decided to phone the lab first to let them know he wouldn't be in for his late shift that night. He left a message on Hisaishi's cell, telling him he would explain more on Monday.

He took a moment to build his courage before calling his mother. He dialed her number, and the phone rang five times before drop-ping him to voice mail.

"Hi, Mom. It's me. Hey, um," Jordan's mind scrambled to figure out just what to say. "I probably should have told you that the friend I'm helping is actually on the Big Island, and . . ." Jordan thought for a second, trying to find just the right words. "They've cancelled our flight back and rescheduled us for the morning. I don't have very good cell reception here, but don't worry about me. I've got a place to stay, and I'll see you tomorrow morning."

He hung up the phone. Although he started with every intention of confessing his pilot status to his mom, he didn't feel doing it over voice mail was right.

He picked up the phone and dialed again, hoping he might get Heather's voice mail, too. "Hello?" No such luck.

"Heather, hi. It's me, Jordan."

"Hi, Jordan. Is everything okay?" Jordan thought he was keeping his voice cool and level, but somehow Heather seemed to sense his tension.

"Um, yeah. Hey, listen. About dinner with Trey and Erin tonight . . ." Jordan hesitated for a moment. "I'm not going to be able to make it."

"Oh, no, Jordan. Why? What's wrong?" Heather sounded concerned rather than angry, and Jordan hoped to keep it that way.

"Well, a friend of mine needed to come to the Big Island today," Jordan said, carefully choosing his words so as not to reveal he'd been flying with Kehau. "So we flew over this morning, and we were hoping to get back this afternoon, but there's a storm coming, and it's just not safe to fly back. I'm really sorry."

Jordan grew nervous as silence filled the line. Then Heather finally spoke. "Where did you say you are?"

"Um, I'm on the Big Island. Look, I know you don't really like me flying, but—" There was a click on the line, and Jordan didn't get a chance to finish.

The party continued for hours, lasting much longer than Tutu, who fell asleep sitting up on the couch. Once the rain began, though, most people decided it was time to leave, and soon only a few of the Pulakaumaka family remained.

Tutu woke up when Maleko brought out his guitar. Sitting next to her, he began to play. Soon the only noise in the house was the rhythmic beating of heavy rain on the roof and the melancholy sound of Maleko's slack-key guitar. Kehau's parents nestled close, arms around each other, as did Nani and Ben, with Junior Boy sleeping soundly on Ben's lap.

Kehau sat on the other side of her grandmother. There was room next to her, and Jordan had a sudden urge to move beside her and pull her close. Was it the music, or the rain, or the fact that he was frustrated with Heather? Whatever it was, he knew he still had feelings for Kehau, and soon those feelings were too strong to ignore. He quietly walked out onto the *lanai*, hoping distance would provide some respite.

He stood and watched the rain fall, listened to the soothing music, and thought back to the day he first met Kehau. He wondered if there were anything he could have done differently that would have made their relationship work.

Jordan heard the door open and felt Kehau move next to him. The urge to pull her close nearly overwhelmed him, and he quickly folded his arms.

"Are you okay?" she asked.

Jordan nodded weakly and then shrugged his shoulders. "I don't know. It's just . . ." He let his words trail off. What could he say? He believed the only reason Kehau had let the wall between them come down was because he was safely in a relationship with someone else. If he acknowledged his feelings for her, it would simply drive her away again. And at least her friendship was better than nothing, right?

Besides, he had an obligation to Heather.

They stood together in silence for several minutes, a cool evening breeze filling the night with the cleansing aroma of rain. The screen door opened and closed behind them, and they both turned. Joe approached with two small plates. "I thought it was only right for the expert bakers to get the last of the *pani popo*."

Jordan started to refuse, still full nearly to the point of pain, but then he followed Kehau's lead and took the plate. "Thank you," he said. Leaning against the railing, he began eating.

Then Joe said, "Kehau tells me you sometimes go by the name '*Pono*.'" Jordan looked over at Kehau, and even in the dim light he could see her face flush. "That's a very powerful name. Do you know what it means?"

"It means 'good' or 'righteous,'" Jordan said. Joe nodded, and Jordan shrugged his shoulders. "It's just a name some of the guys I used to work with gave me."

"Oh?" Joe raised his eyebrows, compelling Jordan to continue.

Jordan grimaced uncomfortably. "It's nothing, really. It's just . . . Well, during one summer when I was in high school, I went to Kauai with a bunch of other guys to work construction. And some of us were LDS—not all, but most, really. Anyway, the church was a couple of miles away, and after a few weeks I was the only one going on Sunday. I tried getting the other guys to go, but they wouldn't.

And one guy . . ." Jordan decided not to mention Scott by name, but looking at Kehau he saw she understood. " . . . said to me 'Why you always gotta be so *pono*.' And it kind of stuck."

Joe nodded. "That's quite the compliment your friend gave you."

"Hmm," Jordan said. "I don't think he meant it as a compliment."

"No matter. He saw in you goodness, righteousness, honesty. And even if those things didn't impress him, the fact that he saw them and talked about them reflects highly on you."

Joe's words hit Jordan hard, and he lowered his head. Here Joe was complimenting him on his righteousness and honesty, when it had been a string of lies that had brought Jordan to their home in the first place.

twenty-seven

The storm passed in the night, and morning broke cool and clear. After an uneasy night's sleep, Jordan rose before dawn, packed his bag, and waited somewhat impatiently for everyone else to come to life. He called in to flight services for a weather briefing, and it came back just as he had expected: CAVU—ceiling and visibility unlimited. Why couldn't the clear weather have come the day before?

Hina fed everyone a classic Hawaiian breakfast of eggs, rice, and Spam, which Maleko and Kehau both smothered in catsup.

Sitting at the table eating, Jordan's mind reeled with everything that had gone wrong since getting stuck in Kohala. He tried to figure out some way of keeping his mind off his troubles, but the only idea he had—watching Kehau—just made things worse.

As they ate, Kehau's dad came to the table with a large, well-worn album. Hesitantly he handed the book to Jordan. "Since you're a pilot, I thought you might like to see some of these." Jordan opened the book and saw it contained photos from Joe's Air Force days.

"I was an aircraft mechanic in Vietnam. This plane here is the OV-10 Bronco," Joe said, pointing at a twin engine plane with a double tail and large glass canopy. "The first time I saw one, I thought it was the strangest plane I'd ever seen."

Jordan looked at the picture and had to agree. The plane sat at a forward angle and looked as though it were ready to spring to action when just sitting on the ground. "They used 'em to look for targets on the ground, and when the observer found something, he'd shoot a smoke flare at it. Then the boys in the Phantoms would come and bomb it." As he continued through the album, Jordan saw fewer pictures of planes and more of people. In one, Joe stood with his arm around a large black man. Jordan noticed their name tags. Pulakaumaka nearly filled the patch. The other man's was only five letters—Roach.

Jordan studied the face closely. "This guy here—Roach. I'm pretty sure he's my flight instructor."

He looked at Joe, expecting to see surprise. But instead, Joe's mouth curled into a sad smile, and Jordan saw him exchange a glance with Hina.

Joe reached slowly for the album. "I should let you go—you've got a long flight ahead." He smiled at Jordan. "We'll look at the rest of these the next time."

Once the breakfast table was cleared, hugs were passed around, and then Maleko drove Jordan and Kehau back to the airport. Jordan did a quick preflight inspection, relieved to see that the plane had weathered the storm without any trouble, and soon they were soaring out over the ocean.

Kehau was much more comfortable with the flight back, but Jordan didn't feel like talking. All of the pleasure he should have gotten from flying interisland with a beautiful girl on a picture-perfect day was drowned out by a sense of overwhelming guilt and dread.

Jordan had screwed up big time, and the closer he got to Honolulu, the worse the anxiety became. They flew on in silence, and Jordan couldn't help but wonder how he had managed to get himself into such a predicament. He had always been a generally truthful person, and yet here he was, living a lie that was unraveling all around him.

As he flew back, he found himself unconsciously adjusting the throttle as two parts of his brain fought for control. The practical part kept pushing the throttle open, hurrying toward home. Then the emotional part would pull it back out again, slowing the plane in an effort to delay their arrival and the inevitable trouble that awaited.

As he approached the controlled airspace around Honolulu International, he forced himself to focus on flying the airplane, and although the landing was rather graceless, nobody lost any fillings.

Jordan taxied toward La'aloa, his heart beating faster with every foot of asphalt that passed. Turning around the edge of the hangar, Jordan saw a couple of women standing outside, facing the other way.

As the plane inched toward them, one of the women turned, and Jordan recognized it was Heather. His heart leapt to his throat as he saw Heather's eyes narrow, looking not at him but Kehau. The other woman turned, clapped a hand to her mouth, and Jordan's anxiety turned to dread. Heather had brought his mom.

The blood drained from Jordan's head, and his hands began to shake. In his panic, he thought of turning around and taking off again. But the thought left as quickly as it came. Even if running away would somehow solve the problem, he had no fuel to run with.

Jordan forced himself to go through the shut-down checklist and then went through it twice. But he was just stalling, and he knew it. "Oh, man," he muttered. "This is not going to be good."

He popped his door, took a breath, and pushed his way out of the plane, where he was accosted by the two angriest women he'd ever seen.

"I can't believe—"

"I should have known—"

"—after I expressly forbid—"

"—flying off with this little trollop—"

"—sneaking around behind my back—"

"—lie to me, lie to your mother—"

"—proving to me that you can't be trusted—"

"—time for this, but not for me—"

The women were showing no sign of slowing down when they were suddenly cut off by the sound of another, louder plane rounding the end of the hangar. The gold and white Bonanza taxied to a stop next to The Blue Bomb. Roach cut the engine and climbed out. The crowd behind The Bomb remained silent as he approached. Jordan expected him to stop and wondered if he should make introductions. But instead of stopping he simply said, "Meet me in my office when you're done here, MacDonald," and continued by.

Once Roach was a dozen paces away, Heather picked up again. "I've had about enough of you and your little games, Jordan. You and I are going to have a long talk when you get home, and you're going to get your priorities straight or we're through! Do you understand me?"

And without waiting for an answer, she turned and stormed toward her car.

Beth, who had begun crying almost as soon as she quit yelling, wiped a tear and said in a quavering voice, "I don't even know who you are anymore."

Jordan watched her walk away, thoroughly disappointed in himself.

"Well, I've never been called a 'trollop' before." Jordan turned quickly, having almost forgotten about Kehau. Realizing that she had witnessed the whole spectacle was yet another humiliating blow. "I'm not even sure I know what it means, but I get the feeling I'm supposed to be offended." Her face was artificially calm, which only made things worse. He walked toward her and put out his hand to take her bag, but she made no move to give it to him.

"Um, I need to go talk to Roach. This will just take a second. Why don't you come wait inside?"

Kehau took a seat on the old black couch, and Jordan knocked on Roach's open door as he entered.

"Close the door and sit down." Roach's voice was quiet. Nervously Jordan complied. Before Roach could begin, however, his cell phone rang. Roach looked at the caller ID and swore. "I need to take this. It will only be a minute—wait here." Roach answered the call and said, "Hello," on his way out the door.

Jordan stared around the room nervously, his eyes quickly settling on the photo on the wall. He remembered the pictures Joe had shown him that morning, and his curiosity soon overcame his apprehension. He stood and walked closer to the photograph, and a quick glance confirmed what he had suspected. Jordan poked his head out of the office door. Roach was outside the hangar, still cursing loudly at the phone.

"Kehau," he called. She looked up and he motioned for her to come in the office. Reluctantly she did so, and he showed her the photo on Roach's wall. "Look at that picture—that's your dad. He showed me one just like it this morning."

Kehau looked at the picture more closely. "It is," she said. "But—"

Her thought was interrupted by Roach's return. He saw them both looking at the picture and froze. After several awkward seconds, Jordan said, "That's Kehau's father in this picture with you."

"Really?" said Roach without the slightest hint of surprise. "Listen, uh, something has come up. Let's—let's do this another time." He motioned them out the door. Confused but grateful for the break, Jordan and Kehau took their exit.

Walking back to the car, Jordan said, "Roach didn't seem too excited to find out who your father is. I wonder what's up."

Kehau shook her head, looking equally puzzled. "I don't know."

twenty-eight

After letting Kehau off at her dorm, Jordan tried to call Heather, but his call went straight to voice mail. *Fair enough*, he thought. "Heather, hey. I really messed up. I'm sorry. I, uh, I hope you can find it in your heart to forgive me and work through this. I guess I'll try back later."

Jordan drove slowly through town, wishing fervently he could wake himself and find the whole rotten situation was just a bad dream. When he arrived at his house, Beth stood on the small cement porch, arms folded. Her eyes bored into him as he approached, and Jordan couldn't return her gaze. "Well?" she demanded.

"Mom, I'm sorry."

"You're sorry? That's it? After everything you've done today, that's the best you can come up with? You're sorry?"

Jordan's gaze dropped to his feet. "Mom—"

"Don't 'Mom' me. Of all the stupid, irresponsible, disrespectful things I've seen coming from my children, this is by far the worst. I have never been so disappointed in anyone as I am in you right now, Jordan Daniel MacDonald."

Jordan's face tightened. "I tried to tell you, but you wouldn't listen." The words came out louder than he intended. "But you know what? I'm glad I did it. Flying is important to me because it was important to Dad."

Jordan lowered his shoulder and took a step toward the door, but his mother stepped back, blocking his path. "This isn't about you and your father and those stupid little planes. Believe me, I'm plenty mad about that. But the real problem here is you and that girl."

Jordan raised his eyebrows. "What? Kehau?"

"Yes—Kehau. I never did like her."

Out of the corner of his eye, Jordan noticed the neighbor across the street standing by her front window. Recognizing this argument was drawing an audience caused him to hesitate but only for a moment. "The reason you don't like Kehau is because she isn't white."

Beth's jaw fell. "You're accusing me of prejudice?"

"Yes, I am, and I dare you to deny it." Jordan pushed past her and into the house. He'd made it halfway across the living room when Beth's hand clamped onto his wrist. She pulled his arm, forcing him to turn and face her.

"As far as race is concerned, you know that I have always been color-blind. This has nothing to do with the color of anybody's skin. I didn't like that girl from the beginning because whenever you got in trouble, she was right there in the middle of it. And now, because of her, you've broken the heart of one of the sweetest girls I've ever known."

Jordan lowered his head, and Beth put her hands on his shoulders. "I don't care what you have to do—you make things right with Heather."

The anger Jordan had felt just moments before dissolved into guilt. "Okay."

He skulked into his room and set his flight bag on his bed. Not knowing what else to do, he checked his computer, fearing Heather might have rescinded his status as her boyfriend on Facebook. Once reassured that she hadn't officially dumped him yet, he did a quick Google search on "how to grovel." The advice basically amounted to showering the girl with gifts and favors and apologies.

Now what? He needed a peace offering. Flowers would be a good gesture, but since it was Sunday afternoon, Pua's was closed. What he really needed was something like chocolate *haupia* pie. If it weren't Sunday, he'd drive around to Ted's in Haleiwa and pick one up. The more he thought, though, the more his situation resembled an ox in the mire, and within ten minutes of the initial thought, Jordan was puttering along the highway behind several dozen motorcycles on their weekly club ride around the island. Traffic approaching Sunset Beach slowed to a crawl as locals and tourists alike took to the beaches on the beautiful post-storm day. Ted's was packed as well, but to Jordan's relief they still had a couple of the coconut chocolate desserts in the cooler.

Jordan sat in front of Heather's house, the pie on the passenger seat, and dialed Heather's number. Again he was sent instantly to voice mail. Jordan hung up without leaving a message, and after a moment's thought, sent her a text: *Ted's* haupia *pie out front.*

He took the pie, walked to the small cement porch, and waited. After a minute, he began to think that she wasn't home. Or perhaps she was so angry even chocolate *haupia* pie couldn't fix it. But as Jordan was about to turn and leave, the door opened, and Heather walked out.

"What's this?" she said quietly, looking at the pie.

It's a high-fructose bribe to make you take me back, Jordan thought. "It's an apology."

The corners of her mouth pulled into a pouty frown, and Heather stared intently at the pie, unwilling to even look at Jordan. "Heather, look. I made a mistake. A big mistake. And I'm sorry." Jordan glanced at Heather. Her eyes were still on the pie, and she kept her arms folded firmly across her chest, but her mouth softened ever so slightly.

"It was wrong for me to go flying yesterday. So, so wrong. But Heather, I promise you, nothing happened." Heather's looked up at Jordan, and her eyes flashed. "I went because it was an excuse to go flying. A . . . a reason to fly to the Big Island, which is something I've always wanted to do."

Heather's lips tightened again, and she looked down. This wasn't going quite the way Jordan had hoped. He put his free hand on her shoulder and said, "Heather, please. I'm sorry, and I want to make this right. Please," he said as she looked up at him again, "tell me how to make things right."

Heather's mouth softened, and the tenseness in her shoulders appeared to melt away. "How do you make this right?" she said. "I need to be able to trust you, Jordan. That's how you make it right. Show me I can trust you. Show me that you respect me enough to quit that stupid job of yours and not just say you'll do it sometime, but really quit. Now."

Jordan's stomach tightened, but he had seen this coming. He closed his eyes and nodded, lips pursed. Then he said, "Okay. Tomorrow I'll let Lani know I need to quit."

"And promise me one thing," she said, putting her arms around Jordan's waist and resting her head on his chest. "Promise me that you'll never talk to that girl again. And no more flying."

"That's two things," Jordan said, hoping to avoid agreeing to this impossible demand.

"Jordan, promise me," she said, pulling him tightly to her. "Please, I need you to promise."

twenty-nine

As Jordan held Heather close, he wondered why it was so hard to agree. Then in the back of his mind, he heard Malia's words—"I don't know what you see in her, other than she's got a pulse and was real quick to get all kissy." Was that all there was to his relationship with Heather? Of course not. She was his girlfriend. She allowed herself to be his, which was something no other girl had ever done before. Plus, his mother liked her—something Jordan didn't think would ever happen. And if he didn't agree, he would lose her.

But what if he did lose Heather? He'd managed to win her over—he could win over someone else, couldn't he? Maybe. Maybe not. It was a chance Jordan couldn't afford to take.

He took a deep breath and nodded his head. "I promise."

■ ■ ■

Arriving at the shop just after opening the next morning, Jordan was disappointed to see both Malia and Amber already hard at work. He had hoped to catch Lani alone so he could deliver the bad news without an audience. Lani was nowhere to be seen, though, and Jordan hoped she was just in the walk-in cooler.

The girls looked up when the door opened. "Wow, you're here early today," Amber said. Then her eyes opened wide. "Oh, no. You're not here to quit, are you?"

Jordan pinched his lips together and nodded.

"I'm telling you, Jordan, that girl's not worth it," said Malia as she jammed carnations onto a long, thin needle. "All I know is she just better not ever get in my way,"

"It's okay, Malia," said Jordan. "I messed up. This is my fault, and I have to deal with it." Malia shot him a look, but before she could begin arguing he asked, "Is Lani in the refer?"

"No, she said she'd be about fifteen minutes late," said Amber. "So, any minute."

As if on cue, the bell on the shop door rang and Lani walked in.

"Hi, Jordan. I assume I know why you're here?"

"Lani, I'm really sorry."

"Well, I suppose we all knew it was coming." She flung her heavy purse from her shoulder and set it on the counter with a thud. "But no worries," she said with a weak smile. "I talked to a gal this morning who can start any time. We'd like to keep you around as long as we can, but if you have to quit today . . ."

"I'd probably better," said Jordan, relieved to have an easy out.

"That's fine," said Lani. She held out her arms and wrapped Jordan in a tight hug.

When she released him, he was surprised to see tears streaking down Malia and Amber's cheeks, but as he felt his own eyes sting, he began to laugh. "You guys! It's not like you'll never see me again." He grabbed Malia in a hug. "I'll still be around."

"Yeah, but it won't be the same," said Malia, refusing to release Jordan from her embrace. When her grip finally slackened, Jordan started to pull away, but Malia quickly caught him by his head and kissed him full on the mouth. After several seconds, she let go and looked at the door. "There. Did she see that? No? Better try again."

As she reached for him, Jordan laughed and held her away. "Stop. What would Robert say?"

"He'd say 'Kiss 'im again!' My boyfriend's not some insecure little whiner baby." She gave Jordan another kiss, but much quicker the second time.

He turned and hugged Amber, who said, "If Malia gets a kiss, so do I." She put her hands on either side of his head and kissed him too.

Jordan feared his trip to the computer lab would be much less enjoyable. Apprehension grew in his gut like an angry badger as he approached the computer building. Remembering the emphasis

Hisaishi placed on reliability, Jordan couldn't help feeling he would probably be fired.

"We need to have a talk," Hisaishi said as Jordan walked into the building. He led the way to a small classroom, ushered Jordan inside, and closed the door behind them. "Your message said you would explain Monday why you missed work. Explain."

Jordan recounted the story of his flight to the Big Island, trying to keep his voice from trembling. As he spoke, he watched Hisaishi for any kind of hint as to what his fate would be, but the big man's face was unreadable.

When Jordan finally finished, he stared at his hands and waited for Hisaishi's reply. "Well, Jordan. Shelly was here all alone Saturday night, and she was not happy. But weather is something we cannot control, and I am glad you're safe. I will not fire you as I had planned, but give you probation. Next time you think you might have a problem getting to work, I want you to arrange someone to cover your shift if you cannot make it."

Sweet relief washed over Jordan, and he looked up at Hisaishi and smiled. "Yes, sir. I'll make sure and do that. Thank you."

That Tuesday morning, Jordan sat next to Heather during the school's weekly devotional. The speaker announced that his talk would "discuss the important principal of integrity."

Heather nudged him in the ribs and raised her eyebrows in a look that said, "Listen up—this talk is for you."

While the speaker gave the usual stories and examples about honesty and telling the truth, he also talked a great deal about how integrity relates to personal direction. "Each of you, my young brothers and sisters, needs to decide who you are and what you stand for in life. We must all have the personal integrity to be true to ourselves as well as others, to speak out against evil and injustice wherever we find it in the world. And we must stand strong against the tide of popular opinion, a tide that would sweep us off our feet and carry us away if we let it.

"Beware of the forces that would threaten your integrity. Know who you are and what you stand for, and remain steadfast in the defense of what is right. That is true integrity."

These words hit Jordan hard, and he thought about them many times the rest of the week. What did he stand for? Did he stand for anything? Or was he letting those around him determine his course in life? As he thought about these questions, he wasn't sure he liked the answers.

Jordan was still pondering the integrity devotional that Saturday, when he took Heather to a student film and video festival. Heather had been taking communications classes, and some of her friends were presenting their work. Spencer, the crazy guy with the motorcycle, had a film about a bunch of tourists standing around a rumbling volcanic crater about to explode.

When the films were finished, Heather led Jordan toward a small cluster of students hanging out in front of the McKay building on the low wall near the little circle. Cool night air carried laughter from the group gathered around Spencer, whose video had won an award. He leaned against his motorcycle and talked about the production of his winning project.

"That sounds like so much fun," said a bubbly brunette as she fawned over Spencer.

"It is. You should try it. Brother Boyce is doing an intro to video class this spring," he said.

"Jordan," said Heather, "let's sign up for that."

Jordan shrugged his shoulders. "Okay."

Spencer continued his steady stream of bravado, and Jordan had nearly tuned him out when a snide comment caught his attention. "I had to do this one project with Spacey Stacie. Man, she is the biggest weirdo."

The brunette wrinkled her nose. "No way. I heard she's marrying that oaf from the computer lab." Jordan's throat tightened.

"Oh, I know. Their kids are going to be completely messed up."

The others laughed, even Heather. But Jordan didn't. He felt sick in the pit of his stomach. The words of the previous week's devotional came back to him again. Integrity is neither easy nor popular, but it is essential. Jordan was being tested, and he needed to rise to the challenge.

Coolly, and in a steady voice, he said, "You know, guys, I consider both Brandon and Stacie friends, and I'd appreciate it if you didn't talk about them like that." The words sounded like something from a corny seminary video, and Jordan felt stupid saying them. But he also felt a tremendous sense of pride at having spoken up.

He waited for Spencer to say something witty and spiteful, but instead, Spencer considered him for a minute and just said, "Nah, sorry, man. It's cool."

The group went quiet, and Jordan could tell they felt he was out of line, but he didn't care. "Hey," he said in his most animated voice. "I'm hungry. Who wants to go get something to eat?"

A few people muttered softly, a few others shook their heads, but most just looked away. "Okay, well, I'll see you guys later." He began walking, and noticed he was alone. "Heather? Are you coming?"

"Um, yeah," she said, glancing at Spencer and the group before slowly following him.

Together they walked past the large stone sundial and up the sidewalk into the Aloha Center, where Jordan led the way to the Seasider snack bar. The small crowd ahead of them gave Jordan a minute to look at his options. Although the night was still young, the grill and specialty bars had closed up for the evening. Aside from the ready-made refrigerator case, the only real option was ice cream. Jordan looked at the dozen or so flavors before deciding. "I think I'll have the tin roof sundae," he said to the girl behind the counter. He turned to Heather. "What do you want?"

Heather stood with her arms folded, glaring at the freezer case. "Nothing."

Her sour expression didn't ease as she slipped across from him into one of the bright red vinyl booths that lined the dining room. "So, what's up?" Jordan asked between licks. Heather pursed her lips and looked away. He had a pretty good idea what was going on, but he felt the need to push the issue. "What? Where's that beautiful smile I like so much?"

She turned and looked at him, her head lowered so her eyes tilted up contemptuously. "I don't know why you had to get all over their case. They were just having a little fun."

Jordan continued licking his ice cream without pausing. "Oh, I know. Just like I'm sure they're having a little fun at my expense right now." He shrugged. "But that doesn't make it right, and it would have been just as wrong for me sit back and say nothing. I needed to stick up for my friends. It's all part of 'having integrity.'" *Part of being pono*, he thought.

Heather's rolled her eyes. "Oh, yeah. You're the model of integrity."

Jordan shrugged and willed himself to stay calm. "I'm trying," he said. "My integrity suffered a serious lapse last week, and it almost cost me my girlfriend. I can't let anything like that happen again, now can I?"

Heather narrowed her eyes and looked away, but her shoulders relaxed, and when Jordan reached across the table to take her hand, she didn't refuse. Yet he'd gained a feeling of empowerment by standing up to Spencer and, in a way, standing up to Heather. And he liked it.

---

thirty

Heather and Jordan drove in silence to the Temple View Apartments, which made up the school's married student housing and found a parking space several buildings away from Trey and Erin's place. Walking through the TVA hallways at dinnertime was like going through a miniature world food fest. Fried chicken, curry, and teriyaki mingled with a dozen other deliciously indistinguishable smells. With windows and doors open to catch the cool evening breezes, the languages and aromas of a dozen lands floated in the air.

The smell of tomato and basil grew strong as they approached the Webbers' door. Trey welcomed the two of them into their small, sparsely furnished apartment, kissing Heather's cheek as they entered. "Good to see you again," he said.

Erin was just adding the finishing touches to the spread on the small square table that had been moved to the middle of the tiny living room. She quickly gave Jordan and Heather hugs. "Oh, I'm so glad you guys could finally make it," she said.

"How are you two?" Heather asked. "And how's the baby?"

Erin smiled, unconsciously touching her tummy. "All three of us are doing fine, thank you. And how about you two?" she asked.

"I think we're okay now," Heather said, giving Jordan a sideways glance.

When dinner was done and the plates cleared, Jordan helped Trey move the table from the middle of the room to its home against the wall dividing the living area from the bedroom. Then they all sat down on the mismatched rattan furniture. A neighbor came to the door to ask Trey for some help, and Jordan quickly grew bored as Heather and Erin continued their conversation. Glancing around the room, he noticed a digital photo frame sitting on the small side table next to him. The frame cycled through a variety of pictures, including many underwater shots of bright, colorful fish and scuba divers.

The photos had just begun to repeat when the door opened. "Sorry about that," said Trey, taking his place next to Erin. "Kimo and the guys are going out to the reef tonight, and he was having some problems with his regulator."

"You two do a lot of diving, it looks like," said Jordan, pointing at the digital photo frame.

"Oh, no!" said Erin. "Not me—that's Trey's thing. No way would you get me down there."

Trey smiled. "I can't even get Erin to try a snorkel and mask. But no worries. I bring back fish and pictures for her."

Jordan tried to understand why their situation surprised him so much and realized it was because it was so different from his and Heather's. He suddenly sensed an opening and was determined to take it. "So, it doesn't bother you that he goes diving without you?"

Jordan knew he'd connected by the look that passed between Erin and her husband. "I get scared sometimes when he's gone, but I know how much he enjoys it. I wouldn't want to come between him and something he loves so much."

Trey pulled her close, kissed her forehead, and said, "Now that's a great woman right there."

"Besides," Erin added, "I'm friends with all of the other diver's wives, and we can get away with so much when they're gone."

It wasn't long before Jordan caught Erin yawning. "Hey, listen. I appreciate you guys having us over tonight. We really need to let you get back to your lives, though."

"Pfft, yeah," said Erin. "Such exciting lives here. We'll probably just go straight to bed."

Jordan and Heather said their farewells, and an uncomfortable silence fell as they walked back to the car. Jordan knew what he needed to do and said a quick prayer he wouldn't blow it.

He helped Heather into the car, and then got in himself. He put the keys in the ignition, but before starting the engine, Jordan braced himself and said, "Maybe I'll see if Trey will take me diving the next time he goes."

"Don't even think about it," Heather shot back.

"Why not?" said Jordan, forcing down the fear rising in his throat. "I think it would be fun."

"You know what?" said Heather. "I can't believe you are even suggesting this right now. You're already on such thin ice it's not even funny."

"Oh, I see," said Jordan. "So the things I want aren't important."

Heather looked up at him, her face flushed and eyes burning. "I thought we had an understanding, Jordan. I thought you were going to make this relationship work. I thought you cared about me."

Jordan took a deep breath, trying to formulate his reply. "Heather, I do care about you." His mind raced. What was he supposed to say? How could he make this all come out right? He was finally in a relationship that looked like it was going somewhere, one his mother approved of, and he didn't want to fail yet again. "I just think that . . ." He trailed off, unsure of what to say. Then he finally said what was really on his mind. "Heather, I really like you a lot. I like spending time with you. I want us to keep doing things together, and I really am looking forward to taking this video class with you. But flying is important to me. And working at the flower shop is important to me. And I want you to be okay with those things."

"No, Jordan, I'm not okay with those things. There's no way I'm going to let you go back to work in that little shop with all those hussies flirting with you and asking for back rubs. And you know how I feel about you flying. No, Jordan. No way."

Jordan stared out the windshield for a moment, building the courage to say what he'd been thinking for the last hour. "I'm not asking for your permission."

"What?" barked Heather.

Still not looking at her, Jordan said. "I'm not asking for your permission. I don't need it. These are my decisions to make, not yours. I don't want to lose you, Heather, but I don't want to lose me, either." He paused and then added with finality, "I'm sorry."

They sat in silence, and Jordan waited for an explosion that never came.

Without a word, Heather flung herself out the car door, slamming it shut behind her. Watching her walk away, Jordan began to panic. What had he done? Here was the first real girlfriend he'd ever had. And now he had driven her away. He wanted to call to her, chase after her, and take everything back. But he knew he couldn't. He had already made his decision, and if he went crawling to her now, things would only be worse. He had to let her go.

Waiting until Heather was almost out of sight, Jordan started the car and drove slowly so he could keep an eye on her as she walked. For the most part, La'ie was a very safe place, but it wasn't perfect and, in spite of the fact that she had just left him—or perhaps because of it—Jordan felt responsible for Heather's safety. He kept back just far enough, and he only lost her once—when she took the dark footpath between Naniloa Loop and Moana Street. Jordan sped down to Kulanui and looped back around, holding his breath until he saw Heather emerge from the shortcut and cross the street into her house.

Again he felt the sudden urge to go to the door, grovel at her feet, and beg her to take him back. But he fought against the impulse to undo what he had done and instead began driving—farther and farther from Heather and his troubles. Before he knew it, Jordan had driven all the way around the island, trying to sort out his thoughts and feelings.

By the time he returned home late that evening, he was convinced he had made the right choice. His sense of loss over Heather was overshadowed by a new feeling—one of strength.

Walking into the living room, he was met by his mother, sitting in her chair with her book. "Is everything all right?" she asked, her voice a mixture of displeasure and concern. "How was your date with Heather?"

"Well, she left me, if that tells you anything."

Beth's eyebrows furrowed. "What happened?"

"Well, I told her that I . . ." Jordan paused for a moment, and then continued. "That I was going to try to get my job back at the flower shop." Jordan hadn't planned on confronting his mother about flying that night, but the words pressed against his mind until he finally let them escape. "And I'm going to keep flying."

Again, Jordan waited for an explosion that wasn't coming. Instead, Beth spoke in a quietly ominous voice. "As long as you live in my house, you will follow my rules. And as of right now, those rules strictly forbid anyone from flying in an airplane, ever. Do I make myself clear?"

Jordan fought the urge to smile. He almost asked if his mom planned to take a boat the next time she went to the mainland, but instead, he simply replied, "Perfectly clear." Beth had just given him the answer he needed. "Now if you'll excuse me, I need to go find some boxes."

The next day Jordan arrived at the flower shop early in the morning. Deep down he hoped that Amber and Malia would be there to greet him, and maybe give a repeat performance of their good-bye, but only Lani was in.

"Jordan, it's good to see you," she said, barely looking up from her work. "How have you been?"

"Good, thanks. How's everything here?"

"Ugh, same as always. But we miss you." Lani lowered her voice and tipped her head toward him. "Lindsay's not nearly as good as you, though. And too short to give a proper back rub."

Jordan smiled, stepped behind Lani, and began working the tight muscles in her neck with his fingers. "Oh, that's wonderful. Thank you."

"You're welcome. And actually, the reason I came this morning is because, well . . ." Jordan took a second to choose his words. "There are no longer any barriers to my working here."

Lani nodded. "I wondered about that, the way she stormed into the house and all." Jordan flushed slightly at the thought of Lani watching the whole affair from across the street.

The bell on the door rang, and Malia's voice called out "Jordan! You're back!" He turned to face her, and she grabbed him in a bear hug, but made no move to kiss him. "Let me guess," she said. "You broke up with that girl, and Lani fired Lindsay, and you're coming back, right?"

"I'm not going to fire Lindsay, Malia. Please stop already."

"Oh, Jordan. She's awful. It's like . . ." But just then the door sounded, and in schlumped a gangly girl with short, light brown hair and a flowing, earth-colored dress. From the way Malia scrunched her face and crossed her eyes at him, he understood this to be Lindsay.

"Hi," she said, flopping her way to the back of the store and into the refer.

"She seems okay," Jordan said, but Malia just tilted her head and shook it. Jordan smiled. "Well, you did get the other part of the story right."

Malia looked confused. "What part of the story?"

"The part where I broke up with Heather." Malia's mouth dropped open. "Er, well, she broke up with me, anyway. And you got the part right where I'm hoping there's a way I can come back."

Malia squealed and hugged him again. "Oh, please, Lani. Please, please, please."

Lani shook her head. "Oh, I'd love to, Jordan. Believe me, I would. But right now . . ." The door to the refer opened and Lani paused for a moment. "Right now that's just not possible."

"I bet I could make it possible," Malia said softly, glaring at Lindsay as she walked past.

"Hey," Jordan said, "I'm back in the air, too. Maybe we can get you your flight now."

"Oh, that's awesome, Jordan. And your mom's good with that?"

"No, not really." Jordan gave her a mischievous little half-smile. "She said I could never get into another airplane as long as I was living under her roof."

"And so . . ." Malia raised her eyebrows expectantly.

"So now I just need to find another place to live."

Malia's mouth opened wide. "You're moving out? You go, Jordan!"

"Where are you moving to?" Lani asked.

"I don't know yet. I just started looking."

"Well, my brother just had a room open up at one of his houses— Hale Honu, I think. Do you want me to ask him about it?"

"Yeah," said Jordan. "That would be great."

"Jordan at the Turtle House?" asked Malia, her eyes wide.

"Why? What's wrong with the Turtle House?" Jordan asked.

"Nothing," she said coyly. "I just don't picture you as being a Turtle House kind of guy, that's all."

Later that afternoon, Jordan met with Lani's brother at a house on the north side of La'ie. He noted with some disappointment that the house was directly across the street from the Sauagas'.

As he met the other residents of Hale Honu, Jordan understood what Malia had meant about being a Turtle House kind of guy. Even at a diverse campus like BYU—Hawaii, people tended to be self-segregating along cultural lines, and that extended to their choice of housing. Jordan soon saw that the other five residents of Hale Honu were all Polynesian. One of the guys was his friend Tomasi from the computer lab, however, and Jordan figured he could make it work. Besides, available housing in La'ie was very hard to come by, so he took the room and moved in the basics that very afternoon

Jordan soon found that Hale Honu was a bit of a gathering place, and that night the living room was full of people eating, talking, and laughing. Jordan knew some of the people by face and made a valiant effort to remember names but soon gave up trying to keep track of everyone. As the night wore on, the constant flow of visitors threatened to overwhelm him, and Jordan decided to excuse himself to his room.

As he walked toward the hallway, he was suddenly knocked off balance and fell to the floor, helped along by a strong pair of dark arms wrapped around his waist. He hit the carpet, and his assailant quickly flipped him on his back and pinned his shoulders.

Jordan looked up and wasn't the least bit surprised to see Scott grinning down at him, just as he had dozens of times in years past.

"Hey, *Pono*," Scott said. "I heard you were living here now. This will be just like old times working on Kauai." He ruffled Jordan's hair before letting him up.

Jordan walked back to his room, wondering if maybe Hale Honu was a mistake after all.

thirty-one

Jordan arrived early for the start of the video production class and nervously entered the school's TV studio. Cameras, cables, monitors, and microphones filled the large room, and a ton of lights hung overhead. The chairs were a mismatch of cameraman stools and guest chairs from the campus interview show. Jordan picked one of the more comfortable chairs, sitting next to a skinny Asian kid with a thick shock of unruly black hair. "So, have you done anything like this before?" Jordan asked.

"Oh, yeah. I've been doing video stuff for years." The boy had a thick Australian accent, and Jordan felt he was watching an old kung fu movie dubbed into English by the Crocodile Hunter. "I've got almost a hundred up on YouTube; some are just stupid little Lego brick films I did, but I've got a few I did in high school, and they're pretty good. What about you?"

Jordan tried to smother the inadequacy he suddenly felt. "Um, I played around with the video camera, you know. I'm Jordan Mac-Donald, by the way."

"David Cho. Nice to meet you."

"All right, everybody. Listen up." Jordan turned his attention to Brother Boyce and noticed Heather sitting next to Spencer on a small couch. "This class is going to be a little different than anything I've done before. I know some of you have a lot of experience, some next to none. That's okay. Part of the reason for doing this class is to help me with my doctoral dissertation. It's a win-win situation—you get to learn, and I get to study how you learn. We'll start by doing a single project as a whole class, and then we'll break up into groups and work on a series of smaller projects to give each of you a chance to learn the different jobs involved."

Brother Boyce spent the remainder of the hour going over some of the basics they would need, and by the time the class finished, Jordan felt a sense of excitement about what lay ahead. As he walked out of the studio, Jordan noticed Heather standing next to Spencer and his motorcycle. She pulled Spencer's helmet over her head, and something inside Jordan twisted in a knot.

"So," he said approaching her. "You won't ride in a convertible with the top down because you're afraid it will mess up your hair, yet you're not worried about wearing a motorcycle helmet?"

"Helmet head is much easier to brush out. And besides," she said, turning to face him, "some rides are more worth it than others." With that, she slapped the visor down and climbed on the back of Spencer's bike.

Watching them ride away, Jordan was determined not to let Heather's relationship with Spencer get to him. In fact, the more he thought about it, the more he decided the two of them were a perfect match.

His post-Heather recovery was further helped when he discovered Kehau in his Old Testament class, and she seemed genuinely glad when he sat down next to her. During the lecture Jordan's thoughts kept wandering to the girl sitting beside him, and he could hardly wait until class ended so he could strike up a conversation with her.

"So, how have you been?" he asked, as they walked along the covered walkways of the McKay building.

"Pretty good. And you?"

Jordan shrugged. "Not too bad."

"I heard about Heather. I can't help feeling that's partly my fault."

"Well, that's how things go." He gave her a smile and said, "Maybe it's for the best."

Kehau looked down, and he thought maybe she guessed at his meaning.

"So," he asked her, "anything fun and exciting going on with you?"

"No, not really. Robert's home, so I don't get to see Malia very much."

"Maybe you and I could hang out a little more, then." Jordan stopped, turning to face her. A surge of excitement ran through him at the thought of restarting his relationship with Kehau.

Instead of agreeing like he'd hoped, though, she knit her brow and bit her bottom lip. "I'm, um, I'm seeing someone now. It's Scott, actually."

"Oh," he said, trying to sound happy for her but failing miserably.

"I know," she said, her voice apologetic and a little defensive. "It's just, he asked me to give him another chance, and, you know."

"Yeah, well, second chances are good."

An uncomfortable silence settled between them for just a moment before Kehau shook her head to break it. "Anyway, I'm glad I'll get to see you twice a week, at least."

Jordan forced a smile. "Yeah, that will be good," he said, knowing full well it would be nothing but torture.

As he watched Kehau walk away, the pain of their near-miss stung far greater than anything he'd ever felt for Heather.

thirty-two

Sitting on the end of a picnic table at Malaekahana Beach Park, a few miles north of La'ie, Jordan absentmindedly played with his video camera. He was supposed to be using it to film the class's first group project, but instead he taped Whitney and another girl from the class playing frisbee while a mournful siren in the distance echoed his dejected feelings.

He thought about the difficulty he found fitting in at Hale Honu. He liked the guys, and they tolerated him well enough, but he couldn't shake the feeling that he was somehow trespassing on their territory. He'd looked for a new place to stay, but as tight as housing was in La'ie, he'd been lucky to find the room he had and wasn't likely to come across anything else until the spring term ended.

His thoughts were interrupted as the frisbee sailed in his direction. He reached out, caught it, and sent it flying back toward the wide, grassy area where the girls were playing.

"Thank you," Whitney called out to him. Jordan waved his reply and set the camera down to check his watch: one thirty. The rest of the class had been at the park since before one, but Spencer and Heather still hadn't arrived. Jordan grew increasingly frustrated, mostly because Spencer had been so insistent in reminding everyone to be on time, and now he was the one holding up production.

As the frisbee sailed toward Jordan again, Whitney sprinted to catch it. She threw to her partner and then waved to a group of girls walking over a grassy rise. "Linda. Over here."

"Hey, guys," Linda said as she approached. "Wow. Can you believe that accident?"

Whitney cast a questioning look at her companions. "What accident?"

Linda raised her eyebrows. "You don't know? There was like this big crash right over there. The highway's closed and everything."

"Really? No, we didn't."

"Yeah, we were coming back from Walmart, and traffic just stopped. We waited for, like, fifteen minutes, and a lot of cars started turning around to go the other way. We decided just to come in here and wait it out."

Well, at least that explains why Spencer and Heather are so late, Jordan thought. They should at least have called, though.

"So what happened?" Whitney asked.

"I don't know for sure, but it was bad. There were a bunch of ambulances and police cars. We saw this truck flipped over on one side, and there was a motorcycle lying in the middle of the road."

A knot suddenly formed in Jordan's gut. "What color was the motorcycle?"

The girls all turned to look at him. "I don't know. Blue, I think." His sick feeling turned to full-blown dread. Jordan jammed the video camera into the case and began running over the grassy knoll toward the parking area.

"Hey, where're you going?" David Cho asked as Jordan ran past, but Jordan kept running. Jumping into his car, he hurried down the dirt road that led to the entrance of the park. As he rounded the last bend, he saw that the La'ie-bound traffic was still stopped. He pulled to the side of the wide park entry and leapt from the car. With the camera bag slung around his chest, he ran full tilt toward the ambulance idling up the road. His heart skipped a beat when he saw Spencer's bike lying in a crumpled heap, and nearby, a figure covered in a sheet.

"Hey! Hold up!" A policeman moved to intercept Jordan as he approached the bike. Jordan stopped, winded. "I need you to go back to your car." Jordan tried to respond, but his lungs burned as he gasped for breath. He looked down at the figure ahead of him, trying to identify it.

Just then a siren blared, and the ambulance sped past.

"Who was that in the ambulance?" Jordan asked.

"I think she was the passenger on the bike," the officer said. "Sir, I need you to stay back."

"Is she going to be okay?"

The policeman shook his head. "I don't know. She got hurt pretty bad."

"Where are they taking her?" Jordan asked.

"They're going to Kahuku to try to get her stabilized."

Jordan gave a quick nod of his head. "Thanks." He turned and began running. His muscles felt like jelly, but he pushed them to carry him the rest of the way to his car. Legs and feet tingling, Jordan forced them to work the pedals. Traffic on the other side of the highway was backed up for miles, and a rusted-out minivan in the La'ie-bound lanes suddenly turned around in front of him, forcing him to slam on the breaks. Jordan cursed under his breath as the van puttered along twenty miles an hour under the speed limit.

"Hurry up, you moron!" Jordan yelled, but the minivan continued limping along. Jordan hit the steering wheel, and with a sharp exhale of breath forced himself to calm down. After a moment, his head cleared enough that he thought to call David and tell him what had happened. "The road's closed going into La'ie. I don't know how long before it'll open. I'm following the ambulance now."

Finally, Jordan reached the road leading to the hospital. He turned and sped up the hill and quickly found a spot near the emergency room. With the camera still swung over his shoulder, he hurried through the glass doors.

"Hi. I'm looking for Heather Martin. They just brought her in an ambulance."

The girl behind the desk said, "I think they're getting her ready for surgery. If you'll have a seat, someone will help you once we know what's going on."

Jordan nodded and walked toward the chairs, but he couldn't sit. A thousand volts of nervous energy forced him to pace the room. On his third circuit, he noticed a police car pull into the parking spot next to his. A tall, broad Polynesian policeman Jordan recognized from the crash scene got out and, after helping a man with a large cut on his leg out of the car, walked into the waiting room and made a beeline toward him.

"You again?" he said to Jordan. "Have a seat—I want to ask you some questions." Jordan complied, too concerned about Heather to even be nervous.

"What's your name?"

"Jordan MacDonald," he said, wringing his hands.

"Did you see what happened?"

Jordan shook his head. "No, we were back in Malaekahana. We're doing a video project for school. Heather and Spencer were supposed to be there too, but nobody knew where they were. I tried to call a bunch of times, but . . ." Jordan trailed off, imagining Heather lying on the side of the road, unconscious while her phone rang and rang. "Anyway, some people told us there was an accident with a motorcycle," Jordan's voice tightened. "I had to see if it was Heather."

The officer leaned across to an end table and grabbed a box of tissue, which he handed to Jordan.

Jordan blew his nose and took a deep breath, trying to regain his composure, but the reality of what had happened finally hit him, and he couldn't continue speaking. He sat and silently wiped his tears, which flowed freely.

The cop closed his notebook and said, "From what we can tell, it looks like your friends tried passing a line of seven or eight cars just past the egg farm road." His voice was soft and measured. "A line of cars was approaching on the La'ie-bound side, and when the rider attempted to return to his lane, his rear wheel clipped the front of a pickup. The girl was thrown onto the grassy shoulder. She got beat up pretty bad, but the helmet saved her life. The bike and rider were knocked into incoming traffic. Even if he'd been wearing a helmet, I doubt that would have saved him. I'm sorry."

Jordan wiped a tear and nodded.

"I need to get back," the officer said. "She's in good hands here. They'll take care of her."

Jordan nodded in thanks, but as soon as the policeman left, he felt ready to jump out of his skin. He hopped up and asked the girl at the window if she knew Heather's status.

"No. Sorry."

He resumed pacing, and the thought came to him that he should give Heather a blessing. But how could he get in to see her? Then he remembered Sister Boyce. Jordan walked quickly into the main section of the hospital and found her office. He explained what had happened and that he couldn't get any information. While she listened to Jordan, her husband called. "Yes, I just heard. One of your students is here. Maybe you'd better talk to him while I try to find out what's going on."

Jordan took the phone and recounted the story to Brother Boyce. The phone was silent for a minute before Brother Boyce said, "I need to be there. Do you know if the road is still closed?"

"I don't."

"Well, I'm going to try it. Here's my cell number. Call me if you hear anything."

Jordan programmed the number into his phone while waiting for Sister Boyce. When she returned, she was accompanied by a large man in scrubs with thick black hair pulled into a long, bushy ponytail.

"This is one of our nurses, Reggie Fa'alau. He's agreed to help you give the girl a blessing."

Jordan reached out and shook Reggie's hand. "How is she?" he asked.

"She's stable," Reggie said. "They're going to airlift her to Queen's. The helicopter's on its way, so we need to hurry."

Sister Boyce led them through the halls to the ER and around a curtain. Jordan caught his breath when he saw Heather. She had a tube in her mouth, and her face was badly bruised. Dried blood from a gash on her forehead matted her hair.

Jordan suddenly thought about consecrated oil for the blessing and realized he didn't have any. Fortunately, Reggie had already removed a vial from his pocket and was undoing the lid. "You want me to anoint?" he asked Jordan.

"Uh, yeah. Her name's Heather Veronica Martin."

Once Reggie was done with the anointing, Jordan reached out and gently touched his fingers to the top of Heather's head. His mind raced for what seemed like an eternity before a sudden, overwhelming feeling of peace washed over him. Jordan offered a short but powerful blessing, the words flowing easily, and he heard the helicopter as he closed the prayer.

As soon as they finished, an orderly wheeled her out, and she was gone. Jordan shook Reggie's hand and hugged Sister Boyce. "Thank you," he said. "Uh, do you know how to get to Queen's?"

As he walked to his car, a printed map in hand, Jordan called Brother Boyce. The professor was still stuck in La'ie, but he told Jordan he would turn around and meet him in Honolulu, and Jordan began driving the long way around the island to The Queen's Medical Center.

Brother Boyce was already in the waiting room when Jordan arrived. He had secured permission to visit as soon as Heather was out of surgery. As they entered the lobby outside the intensive care unit, Jordan turned off his cell phone as instructed by a sign on the door. They waited for hours, but eventually Jordan and Brother Boyce were allowed to see her. When they arrived at Heather's bed, Jordan saw that she wasn't conscious, and she looked bad, but the doctors said she was through the worst and was expected to make a full, if long and difficult, recovery.

"We intend to keep her sedated for at least another twenty-four hours to give her body a chance to heal." They were allowed to give her another blessing, with Jordan anointing this time and Brother Boyce repeating Jordan's earlier promise of healing. Throughout the blessing, Jordan struggled to keep his breathing steady, but he allowed the tears to pour from his eyes, feeling a strong sense of relief.

After the blessing, Brother Boyce talked to Heather's surgeon for a few minutes. "I have to hand it to the doctors at Kahuku. If they hadn't been there to patch her up, I'm pretty sure she never would have made it here. It scares me to think what would happen if those little country hospitals ever close."

As they walked toward the main lobby, Brother Boyce suggested Jordan go home.

"I don't know if I feel good leaving her here alone," said Jordan.

Brother Boyce smiled. "She's not going to be alone, Jordan. I've already talked to her bishop, and he'll be here within the hour. I'll wait until then. He contacted her parents, and they're flying in from Idaho. They should be here sometime tomorrow."

"Maybe I'll wait here with you," Jordan said.

"There's nothing you can do here tonight, Jordan. Go home and get some rest. You look terrible. I'll call you if anything changes."

Jordan finally agreed and began walking out toward the parking lot. The sun had long before gone down, and the Honolulu city lights illuminated the night sky. As Jordan arrived at his car, he remembered that he'd turned off his phone in the hospital. He quickly pulled it from his pocket and turned it on. Before he could even put it back in his jeans, the voice mail tone played. Jordan saw that he had three messages and fourteen missed calls.

A sense of doom flooded over him as he realized he had completely forgotten his shift at the computer lab. Shelly's irate voice chewed him out on the first two messages, and the third was Hisaishi, informing him he didn't need to worry about working at the lab any more.

thirty-three

The regular weekend crowd met Jordan as he walked through the front door of Hale Honu, and he took a deep breath before pressing through to his room. Fighting off the emotional and physical fatigue that weighed him down, Jordan quickly got ready for bed.

Grabbing a couple of foam earplugs from his nightstand, he rolled one into a small line and jammed it into his ear. As he started rolling the other one, there was a quick knock on his bedroom door before it opened, and Tomasi's face appeared.

"*Sole*," Tomasi said, addressing Jordan with the Samoan word for brother. "You okay?"

Jordan shook his head and looked down. "No, not really."

"That was your girlfriend in the crash, huh? The one from before?"

Jordan nodded. "Is she gonna be okay?"

Jordan shrugged. "I dunno—maybe. I hope so."

Tomasi nodded. "Me too." Tomasi raised his eyebrows and said, "You look like you need sleep. I'll go tell the guys to be quiet."

A smile stole across Jordan's face. "Thanks, Tomasi."

The next day, as soon as church finished, Jordan drove straight to the hospital. Heather was sleeping, but he was able to meet her parents, who had just arrived from Idaho, and they expressed their gratitude to him for everything he had done.

"I didn't really do anything," he said.

"You came when she needed you, and you made sure she was

170

taken care of. And you were worthy to give her a blessing," Heather's mom said, her voice catching. "I know those blessings saved her life."

The doctors wanted to keep Heather sedated for a while longer, so Jordan left for home. When he got to La'ie, he kept driving, past town and out to the accident site. Flowers and ribbons marked the site on the side of road where they crashed. Skid marks and bits of broken plastic were the only physical evidence left. Jordan pulled over and sat, taking several deep breaths as he pondered the events of the previous day.

He pulled back onto the highway, but instead of heading for home, Jordan drove toward Kahuku. He turned on the road leading up to the hospital and parked in the same spot he had used the day before. He turned off the car and sat for a moment and then got out and walked around the grounds.

Jordan thought about what Heather's surgeons at Queen's had said—about how the hospital had saved her life. He looked up at the small, old concrete building and thought about how many people must have been helped during the decades the hospital had been there, and yet it seemed every other year it was threatened with closure because of lack of funding.

The thought came to Jordan that a short documentary about the hospital might be a good topic for his video class project. He sat down on a bench in the shade of a tree and began pondering this idea. He was so engrossed in thought that the sound of his phone made him jump.

"Hi, is this Jordan?" a woman's voice asked.

"Yes, it is."

"Jordan, this is Carlene Martin—Heather's mom. I know you were just here, but Heather's awake now and she's asking to see you. Is there any way—?"

Jordan was already trotting toward his car. "I'll be there in an hour."

Heather looked better than she had the night before, but her face was still swollen and bruised. She was breathing on her own, and when she saw Jordan she began to cry.

"Oh, Jordan. I'm sorry. I'm so sorry."

Jordan hurried to her bed and held her hand. "It's okay. Shh," he said.

"Sweetie?" Carlene said, "We'll just be outside talking to the nurse."

"Okay." Once her parents were gone, Heather said, "They told me everything you did. Thank you."

"No problem," he said.

"You're a good man, Jordan." Heather looked down and fiddled with the top of her sheet. "I'm so sorry for the way I treated you. Can you forgive me?"

"Sure."

"I promise things will be different now. I don't care if you fly, and you can work anywhere you want. I just—I'm so sorry."

Jordan looked at Heather and realized she was offering to take him back. He felt an overwhelming sense of responsibility for her and struggled with what to do. He'd enjoyed having a girlfriend, and he believed things really would be different now, but a nagging feeling held him back. "Let's just wait and see what happens, okay?"

She smiled at him. "Okay." They sat in silence for a few moments, and then Heather closed her eyes. As her breathing changed, Jordan realized she had drifted off to sleep.

thirty-four

Hisaishi stared at Jordan for what seemed like hours before the scowl on his face finally softened. "This is a great tragedy for our school and, I think, for you too. I am not happy that you forget your shift. But you are good lab assistant, and students like you. That is why I think I must give you one more chance."

Jordan exhaled deeply and realized he'd been holding his breath. Relief flowed through him, and a smile stole across his face. "Thank you," he said, reaching out to shake the big man's hand.

Jordan worked extra hard throughout the week to prove himself worthy of his third chance. He was grateful for the routine of work and school, which provided a break from the nagging questions that swirled through his mind.

Jordan thought a lot about what he should do with Heather. Should he take her back? She needed him now more than ever. But did he need her? Was his hesitancy because she was battered and broken, or was there something more? Jordan found himself wrestling with these questions as he drove back toward Hale Honu. His route home took him along Naniloa Loop, and as he drove into the roundabout in front of the temple, he found himself circling several times before moving onto the small pullout.

Jordan sat for a moment, gazing across the manicured grounds to the stately white building beyond and felt an overwhelming urge go inside and attend a session. He tried to dismiss the thought, but it persisted. Remembering the peaceful spirit he'd felt in the temple before, Jordan yielded to the prompting in hopes of finding relief from the weight he carried.

The temple was only open during the mornings on Saturdays— and closed Sundays and Mondays—so Jordan raced to Hale Honu, knowing this would be his only chance for several days. One of the guys kept a schedule stuck behind a refrigerator magnet, and Jordan checked it as soon as he got to the house. He could make the next session if he hurried. If not, there were still several more after that. Jordan wanted to take his time getting ready, but he found himself pushed along by a sense of urgency he didn't quite understand.

Obeying the more convenient traffic laws and practically running through the parking lot, Jordan managed to make it in time. Once inside the temple, Jordan relaxed, feeling a peace stronger than he had ever felt during any other session. Perhaps it just seemed that way, as he had never borne such a heavy burden before, and setting it aside for a while in the temple gave him even more relief.

After the session ended, Jordan sat in a large armchair, more beautiful than comfortable, and prayed. He prayed for guidance. He prayed for direction. But all he got was peace.

Jordan was filled with an overwhelming sense that everything would work out, but when he tried to picture how in his mind, he got nothing. He had learned in the past that inspiration, when it came, was often just a confirmation of thoughts and ideas that he had already had. But he did not experience this sort of direct inspiration that morning, no matter how hard he tried. Instead, he just got peace and the sense that he needed to go. The longer he tried to wait for an answer, the more urgently he felt he should leave.

Finally heeding the promptings, he quickly changed from his temple clothes back into his shirt and tie and left the temple. He walked out the front door and down to the parking lot, but as he approached his car, he didn't feel the time was right to go home yet. So instead he walked through the gate that led to the hill behind the temple.

A curving path guided Jordan's slow, thoughtful climb toward the large, square gazebo that had been built at the top of the hill. This was a popular location for peaceful thought and reflection, so

Jordan was not surprised to see a girl sitting on the gazebo's bench. It wasn't until he had almost reached the little structure that the girl looked up and said, "Hi, Jordan."

It was Kehau. She smiled at him and pulled back a stray bit of hair the breeze had blown across her face. On her lap, the pages of her open scriptures fluttered.

Jordan returned her smile and quickened his pace. "So," he said, "what's a nice girl like you doing in a place like this?"

Her smile broadened. "Oh, the usual. You know—'search, ponder, and pray.'"

Jordan sat down next to her and looked out over the top of the temple and beyond to the sun reflecting off of the ocean. "Well, it's not Waipio Valley, but it's still a good place to take your problems." Kehau smiled shyly at Jordan's mention of her favorite place. "So, have you gotten the inspiration you were looking for?" he asked.

She looked at him thoughtfully and then said, "Yeah, I think I have." Pulling herself from her reflective state, she asked, "And what about you? What brings you to the temple this morning?"

Jordan shrugged. "The same, I guess. Trying to find some direction. Something."

"I heard about what happened to Heather. That must be so hard. How are you doing?"

Jordan stared out across the treetops of La'ie, and then looked back at Kehau. "Better, I guess." He shook his head. "This thing with Heather is just so complicated. I was hoping I could come here and get some answers."

"And did you?"

Jordan looked at Kehau, and his feelings for her surfaced more strongly then ever. He tried to push them away, reminding himself that it was Heather who needed him. But as he stared into Kehau's dark brown eyes, a warm, peaceful feeling burned inside of him, and he smiled. It was suddenly clear to him why he had been led to this spot. "Yeah, I think I have found my answer. Not the one I was expecting, but maybe something even better."

Kehau smiled broadly. "Good."

"So," he said, looking her square in the eye. "Do you have any plans for next Friday night?"

"What?" she said. "Hello—that's Malia's wedding."

"Oh, yeah," Jordan said, pretending to be surprised. "The big wedding. What time should I pick you up?"

Kehau looked at him, and then shook her head. "Jordan, no. I . . ." She looked down at her scriptures.

"What?" Jordan asked. "Scott?"

Kehau nodded.

"He isn't going to change. You know that, right?" Jordan put a hand on her shoulder. "Look, I don't know what's going on between you two, but I've known Scott for a very long time, and I think I have a pretty good idea." Jordan wasn't certain where the words were coming from, but he let them flow. "I'm sure he really does care about you, but he'll never give you his heart. Not completely."

Kehau's head dipped ever so slightly, and Jordan knew he had hit close to home. "You're very kind and very trusting, and I know you believe everyone deserves a second chance, right?"

Kehau looked up, her eyes slightly moist. She wrinkled her brow in confusion and nodded.

"Well," Jordan said, "what do you say to giving me a second chance?" He held his hand out to her. She looked at it and then up at his face for what seemed like forever.

Then her lips curled into a smile, almost involuntarily, and she said, "Okay." She reached out and took his hand, and he helped her to her feet.

"So, getting back to my question: What time should I pick you up on Friday?"

thirty-five

The day of Malia and Robert's wedding could not have been any more beautiful. Warm, blue skies gave way to a brilliant night lit by a full moon. They held their reception at Turtle Bay Resort, and the large tents set up on the lawn were filled to capacity. Anthurium bouquets covered the tables, just as Malia had wanted.

A group of musicians played traditional Hawaiian songs in one corner of the main tent, while Jordan waited in line for the luau dinner. Kehau, wearing a red floral print mu'u mu'u and the tube-rose lei Jordan had given her, flitted around the gathering, rejoining Jordan in line every few minutes only to excuse herself again so she could greet another long lost friend or relative. The tenth time Kehau did this, Jordan began to wonder if maybe it had been a mistake bringing her on a date to a wedding reception.

At the head of the tent, Robert and Malia sat at a long, raised table—six bridesmaids on one side, a half dozen groomsmen on the other. Jordan had expected Kehau to be part of the wedding party, but the betrothed had enough sisters between them to more than fill the ranks.

After Jordan and Kehau finally got their food, Kehau saw her *tutu* across the room and took Jordan to say hi. Kehau introduced him to her grandmother, who said in a loud whisper "He's much better looking than that one you brought to my birthday."

Jordan ate while Kehau talked. When his plate was empty, he sat and picked apart the crown of a pineapple while Kehau continued catching up with friends and relatives. He finally decided that if he was going to get any time with her, he would have to make it happen himself.

Kehau stood with a group of women, and though she seemed interested in the conversation she was not directly a part of it. Jordan put his hand on her shoulder and whispered in her ear, "What do you say we go for a walk on the beach?"

Surprised, Kehau started to decline, but she must have realized how bored Jordan was and took pity on him. "Okay."

She excused herself from the group, and together she and Jordan began walking out. But before they reached the exit, the band finished their number and one of the ukulele players called out over the loudspeaker, "We now have a special dance, performed by the beautiful Kehau Pulakaumaka. Kehau, are you here? There she is—over by the back."

Every eye in the room was suddenly on Kehau and Jordan. "Oh, I'm so sorry. Malia asked me to do this dance for her." She took a hold of Jordan's arm. "But I promise I'll come back as soon as it's done, okay?"

She hurried toward the table where the wedding party sat. "Ladies and Gentlemen, how about a big round of applause for Miss Kehaulani Pulakaumaka dancing 'The Hawaiian Wedding Song.'"

Jordan shook his head, disappointed at being interrupted yet again, but as Kehau took her place in front of the band and the noise of the crowd died down, he decided watching her dance the hula was an interruption he could handle.

Kehau danced with even more beauty and power than she had that night when he first watched her at the PCC. Perhaps it was the fact that he got to see her up close, or it could have been that she was dancing for close friends and family instead of strangers. Whatever the reason, her grace and elegance mesmerized him. He worked his way to the front of the tent and welcomed the opportunity to stare. Kehau's smile broadened each time their eyes met, and a chill ran up Jordan's neck. Watching her dance was magical, and Jordan found himself wanting to be with her more than ever before.

The song ended, and there was thunderous applause. Kehau bowed, slipped on her shoes, and skipped over to the head table, where she hugged Malia and Robert. She then walked quickly toward Jordan and, taking his hand, led him out away from the tents.

"I thought it was tradition for the bride to do that dance."

Kehau shrugged. "It is. But dancing's not Malia's thing. And I think she felt bad not having me in her line, so she wanted me to do something."

As they walked hand in hand around a grassy hill toward the beach, Jordan saw a figure wearing a bright orange aloha shirt standing on the path ahead of them. At first he assumed this was just a worker at the hotel, but then he heard a familiar voice say, "So what, *Pono*? Think you're some kind of tough guy now that you can take out my girlfriend?"

Jordan's heart leapt into his throat as he recognized Scott. Although he could hear the sound of people all around them, they stood in an isolated spot, and Jordan's first instinct was to pull Kehau back toward the reception where they would be safe among the crowd. While Jordan stood probably six inches taller than Scott, he knew he would be no match for Scott's strong, muscular build if this little meeting came to blows.

But he pushed that instinct aside, determined to stand his ground. Jordan was done backing down from Scott, whatever the consequence. He straightened up to his full height and looked Scott square in the eye.

Before he could speak, Kehau said, "Ex-girlfriend, Scott."

"You hear that? Kehau doesn't consider herself your girlfriend any more. She's here with me tonight." Jordan felt as though he were standing outside himself, listening to the words rather than speaking them. He saw Scott's eyes narrow and his nostrils flare, but Scott didn't say anything.

Then Jordan heard himself say "I know you have at least one other girlfriend, maybe two or three. Go spend some time with them and leave Kehau alone." As soon as those words left his lips, Jordan realized he had crossed the line. Scott's eyes flared, and his body tensed. He shifted his weight, and Jordan braced for the punch he knew was coming. But Scott backed down, cursed, and stormed away.

As he watched Scott disappear around a corner, Jordan tried to keep from shaking. He jumped as a strong hand gripped his left shoulder. Whipping around, Jordan found himself face to face with Kehau's brother, Maleko.

"Whoa—you okay?" Maleko asked.

"Yeah, I'm fine," Jordan said, visibly shaking now. "How long have you been here?"

"Pretty much the whole time," Maleko said. "You be careful, and let me know if that punk gives you any more trouble. And you—" he said, pointing at Kehau. But instead of saying anything to her, he just winked and smiled.

Jordan took Kehau's hand in his, and they walked toward the gently roaring surf. "Did you really not know Maleko was there?" she asked.

"No, I had no idea," Jordan said.

"Hm." Kehau reached across and took hold of his arm. They walked in silence to the top of the beach where they stopped to watch the moon reflecting off the dark ocean waves rolling ashore.

"You were very beautiful dancing up there tonight," Jordan said, just loud enough to be heard over the surf.

Kehau raised her shoulder and smiled shyly. "Thank you"

"You were beautiful the last time I saw you dance, but I didn't get the chance to tell you."

Kehau knit her brow. "When was this?"

"In the night show."

Kehau's eyes grew wide. "The night show?"

"Last September. I went and watched, but I couldn't find you. I thought maybe I'd come on your night off. But then a beautiful girl in a white dress took the stage and stole Mana's heart."

"Oh, no," she said, holding her hand to her mouth. "You were there that night? I'm so embarrassed now."

"Why?" Jordan asked.

"Both Kalani and Janet were out sick. My boss asked me to cover for them, and I had no idea what I was doing. I'd only practiced a few times, and I messed up so many places. Oh, it was awful! And you were there? I'm so embarrassed!" She raised her hand to her forehead and looked down.

Jordan put his hands on her shoulders and turned her gently to face him. "Hey, don't be. You did a great job that night. If you messed up, I can promise you nobody in the audience noticed." He put his finger under her chin and gently raised her head. "And Mana's heart wasn't the only one stolen that night."

Jordan leaned forward without hesitation and pressed his lips against Kehau's. She wrapped her arms around his neck and pulled him close. His heart beat faster, and he felt a rush from head to foot. Tenderly he moved his mouth over hers, and the roar of the ocean filled his ears while the sweet aroma of her tuberose lei mingled with the smell of the sea.

After a moment their kiss ended, and Kehau rested her head against Jordan's chest. Jordan kept still, not wanting to break the spell as they stood together, silent in the cool evening breeze.

When Kehau finally spoke, it was almost a whisper. "You stole my heart too, you know."

A chill ran up Jordan's spine. "Really? When?"

"That day, at Nani's, when . . ." Kehau lifted her head off of Jordan's chest, but kept it bowed, looking away and down. "When you fed me *pani popo*." She looked up at him, and when their eye's met, she failed to hold back a giggle. Soon they were both laughing, arms wrapped around each other.

Jordan leaned down and kissed her again—quickly this time. "We'd better go back," he said. "There must be a hundred cousins in there you haven't hugged yet."

"Ah," she said in mock incredulity, breaking away from him. He caught her shoulder and held her tight as they walked back to the reception. They kept their arms around each other most of the night, and Jordan was pleasantly surprised when Kehau began introducing him as her boyfriend.

They were still wrapped tightly around each other an hour and a half later when they walked out through the parking lot to Jordan's car. As he reached to open Kehau's door, he stopped and pulled back. Something wasn't right—the car sat at a funny angle. By the light of his cell phone, Jordan discovered his tires had all been slashed.

thirty-six

"**N**ice wheels," Tomasi said, pointing at Jordan's car through the front window of Hale Honu. "Where'd you get those?"

"Kehau's cousin had a spare set for his street racer. We got these changed out last night so I could drive home."

"And you really think Scott sliced your tires?" Tomasi asked.

"Who else could it be?" Jordan asked. "He's been pulling these stupid little stunts on me since the sixth grade. But this is a new low—even for him. It's gotta stop before somebody gets hurt. Hey, look," said Jordan. He pointed out the window at Scott, who stood across the street eyeing the Mustang suspiciously. "There he is. I knew he'd jump at the bait. Wish me luck."

Jordan walked out the door and called, "Wadda ya think? Pretty nice, huh?" He saw Scott jump slightly and felt a surge of confidence. He walked to where Scott stood and said, "Come with me. I've got something to show you."

Tomasi and another roommate, Seti, came outside as well and watched from the front of the house. Scott stayed put, apparently leery of a trick. "Keep up, Scott," Jordan said, his voice firm with authority. "Unless you're some kind of chicken."

Jordan's roommates began laughing and pointing at Scott. Confusion, curiosity, and humiliation led Scott to follow Jordan to the end of the street, right to the entrance of the Hukilau Cafe. Jordan opened the door. "In," he said, his face set like stone.

Jordan followed a bewildered Scott into the small, crowded dining area. The cafe was built in a corner of the old Sam's Store, with a cement floor and thin wooden walls. Small mismatched tables littered the dining room, filled as usual with a mostly local crowd.

"Two," Jordan said to the T-shirt and slipper clad hostess. Sensing the tension, she looked back and forth from Jordan to Scott and then led them to a table near two Honolulu Police officers, the police woman looking every bit as tough as her male partner. Seeing them gave Jordan added comfort. Though he doubted Scott would try anything in the restaurant, he felt confident nothing would happen now.

Jordan picked up his menu, and then motioned for Scott to do the same. "Order whatever you want. It's on me."

Still wary, Scott ordered the Hungry Hawaiian. Jordan opted for the house specialty—banana pancakes.

When the waitress had taken their orders and menus, Jordan stared hard at Scott. For a moment, he feared he would loose his nerve, but to do so now that he'd come this far would ensure the worst possible failure.

"Okay, Scott. The game's over."

Scott glared at him for a second and then without looking away, he half smiled, half sneered. "What game?" he said.

"You know what I'm talking about," said Jordan, his cool voice belying the adrenaline surging through his body. "How long have we known each other now? Ten years?" Scott didn't answer. "And you've had it out for me since day one, haven't you?" Scott continued to stare, his sneer fading to a look of passive contempt. "Tell me, Scott. What have I ever done to you?"

At that, Scott turned away uncomfortably. He looked at the door and probably would have left if it hadn't been for the large foam plate covered with food that the waitress set in front of him.

"Enjoy your breakfast," the girl said.

"Thanks. We will," replied Jordan, smiling.

When she left, Scott leaned forward onto the table. "So what? You're some kind of tough guy now? You think you can just steal my girlfriend, buy me bacon, and suddenly we're all buddy-buddy? Huh?"

Jordan had Scott's attention, and he tried not to smile. "I don't think we'll ever be 'buddy-buddy.' And as for Kehau, she's not one of your girlfriends any more."

"Oh, yeah?" Scott's voice rose, and the cops looked their way. He gave them a wary glance and lowered his voice. "We'll see about that."

"C'mon, Scott. Kehau knows you're not a one-woman man, and she's tired of it. She's too good for you."

Scott didn't agree and told Jordan as much in a rather profane way.

Jordan shook his head. "Such language—and for a returned missionary too. You know, Scott, you really should watch yourself. You never know who might be listening." Jordan reached into his pocket and pulled out a small silver disc. "Or watching."

He held the disc up for Scott to examine. "Do you know what this is? It's security video from Turtle Bay. Video showing someone doing something to my car."

"So?" Scott asked. Jordan thought he saw just a hint of concern cross Scott's face.

"So it's a crime to slash someone's tires." Jordan kept his gaze on Scott but tilted his head slightly toward the police.

"I didn't do nothin'." Scott folded his arms.

"Right. Just like you didn't put dirt in my water bottle or feed my lunch to the dogs."

"What? You're full of—"

Jordan cut him off. "That bright orange shirt of yours shows up really well on video." He held the disc up for Scott to see, and spun it around in his fingers. Scott glanced at the cops, and then back at Jordan, his face turning an ashen brown.

"What do you want?" Scott demanded.

"Leave me alone. Leave Kehau alone. Just move on, get a life, do whatever it is that you need to do—I don't care. Just leave me and Kehau out of it." Jordan held the disc out to Scott.

Scott looked at Jordan, his face full of rage. But Jordan didn't flinch. Finally Scott narrowed his eyes and said, "Fine."

Scott seized the disc and snapped it in half. He wolfed the rest of his breakfast in three large bites and left without another word. Jordan sat back in his chair. "I told you it would work," he said aloud.

Kehau appeared from behind a small wall dividing the dining room, shaking her head. "You were right. I'm impressed." She sat in the chair Scott had just vacated, looked at the broken disc, and said, "A blank CD and a guilty conscience. Amazing."

thirty-seven

The next morning as Jordan was getting ready for church, his phone rang. Recognizing Heather's number, he hesitated before answering.

"Hello?"

"Jordan—hi. How are you?" Heather asked.

"Doing okay. What's up?"

"I, um, the doctors said I'm well enough to travel, so I'll be going home on Wednesday."

"Really? That's great."

"Do you . . . ?" Heather hesitated. "Could you come down? I want to see you before I go."

"Yeah, sure." He answered quickly, though inside he was torn between his feelings of responsibility toward Heather and his new relationship with Kehau. "How about I come by later today?" he asked, knowing that a Sunday afternoon would be the easiest time to get away.

"That will be great," Heather said. "And Jordan?"

"Yeah?"

"Thanks again—for everything."

Jordan met Kehau after church, just as they had planned. He explained his intention to visit Heather. "I'm sorry," he said. "I just feel like I need to go see her."

"No, it's fine. You do need to see her before she leaves." Kehau hugged him tightly.

When Jordan arrived at the hospital, he picked up some flowers for Heather in the gift shop. As he got off the elevator and began walking toward Heather's room, he heard Heather's mother talking to her father about something. He couldn't make out the words, but she sounded just like Heather had when she'd gone off on one of her rants. When he came around the corner, he saw Heather's father, Walter, with his head bowed and shoulders slouched, much as Jordan imagined he had looked when Heather had talked down to him.

Walter's eyes lit up when he saw Jordan. "Hey, Jordan. Glad you could make it." He seemed grateful for the opportunity to pull himself from his current situation. "Did Heather tell you the news?"

"About getting to go home on Wednesday? Yeah, she did."

"Oh, those flowers are lovely," said Heather's mom. "She'll be so glad to see you."

When Jordan entered the room, Heather said, "Oh, thank you, Jordan. Set those right over here." Jordan put the flowers on the table by her bed and sat down. An uncomfortable silence threatened to fill the room, and Jordan spoke quickly to dispel it.

"So you go home on Wednesday?"

"Yeah. I get to fly on a private jet. There's this thing called Angel Flight where people donate their planes to patients flying for medical care."

"I've heard of that," Jordan said. "I think Roach does it sometimes."

Heather nodded. "Well, there's a guy who's from here but he's some kind of big shot in Silicon Valley, and he's flying us to San Jose, and then someone with a smaller plane flies us to Nevada, and then we fly in another plane to Idaho Falls."

"Wow," said Jordan. "That sounds like quite the trip."

"My doctor didn't think it was a good idea for me to be on an airliner with all those other people, but he thought I could probably do it this way. It'll take longer, but there's less chance of me getting sick." Jordan nodded his head, and the uncomfortable silence returned. This time, it was Heather who broke it. "It looks like I'll be getting into a little plane again after all." She smiled at him weakly. "So have you done much flying lately?"

Jordan looked up at her, and he thought he saw regret in her eyes. "No, not really. I'm too busy with school and work right now," he said. "The video class is really taking a lot of time."

At the mention of the class, Heather looked down, suddenly quiet, and Jordan regretted bringing it up. "Spencer's parents came by to see me a few weeks ago. They were here to—" Her voice caught, and it was high and choked when she continued. "To take him home."

A knot formed in Jordan's throat, and he reached out to take Heather's hand. After a moment or two, she wiped her eyes and looked up. "Have you started your small group productions?"

"Uh, yeah. I'm in a group with David and Anaise and Luanne. We're doing a documentary on the Kahuku Hospital."

"Interesting. Why'd you pick the hospital?"

"It was because of what one of your surgeons said. He said there was no way . . ." Jordan's voice cracked, and took a moment to regain his composure. "There was no way you would have made it without their help." Jordan looked down at their hands. "They saved your life."

When Jordan looked back up at Heather, she had tears streaming down her cheeks. "Oh, Jordan—I'm going to miss you. You will keep in touch, won't you?"

Jordan stood and gave her hand a squeeze. "Of course I will," he said. Then he leaned down and kissed Heather gently on the forehead.

thirty-eight

Tiny waves, mere inches high, lapped at steep, jagged rocks as Jordan walked past in water up to his chest. He felt the sharp ocean floor through the thick rubber soles of his borrowed water shoes and tried not to think about what was swimming around his feet. He liked the ocean, but only the nice, soft sandy bits, and Jordan wondered aloud how on earth he had let himself get into this situation. A shout and wave from Kehau several hundred feet ahead answered his question, and he smiled at the sight of her climbing up onto the rocky shore, holding a knife in one hand.

It had been several weeks since Malia's wedding, and the happiness he found with Kehau amazed him. Yet as he made his way toward her, he began to question the sanity of following her around this jagged coastline. "You're not the first guy to do something stupid for a pretty girl in a swimsuit," he said to himself. The early morning sun glittered across her sleek red one-piece, and Jordan admired her solid, athletic form as she leaned across the rocks.

"Oh, I got one!" she said, turning toward him. He climbed slowly out of the water and walked over to her, trying not to think of the blood that would surely flow if he lost his balance and fell.

"I got one," she repeated as he approached. She held out her hand to show him a squat, conical shell about an inch and a half across.

"And what's that again?" Jordan asked.

"It's *opihi*," she said. "They used to grow all over the place, but now they're rare. They're protected—you can't pick anything smaller than a quarter."

Jordan nudged the shell in her hand with his finger. "So what's it for?"

Kehau raised her eyebrows and smiled. "You eat it. Don't tell me you've never had *opihi* before." Jordan wrinkled his nose and shook his head. "Oh, c'mon. They're so good. Here—you've got to try one." Kehau held the shell tightly and pulled out a lump that looked like gray-brown bubble gum.

She offered it to Jordan, but he gently pushed her hand away and said, "No, thanks."

"Oh, c'mon," she said, but Jordan just shook his head. "Okay, fine." She popped the mollusk into her mouth. "Mmm." Kehau closed her eyes and smiled.

Jordan looked at her with a mixture of curiosity and disgust. "You got me up before sunrise on a Saturday to help you find endangered clams so you could eat them raw?"

Kehau's face fell. "Jordan, I'm sorry. It's just . . . conditions were perfect, and I heard about this place and I thought—"

"No, it's okay," Jordan said, placing his hand on her shoulder. "Don't worry about it." He tried to reassure her with a smile. "It's not what I had in mind, but, well, the company's good." He took her hand and gave it a quick squeeze, and she smiled back. "Are there any more over here?" he asked.

"No, just a few small ones."

"Well, let's go find some more."

"Are you sure?" she asked.

"Sure I'm sure. I don't have to be to work until after dinner. What could be more exciting than hunting clams among the jagged rocks with a beautiful, knife-wielding girl?"

"Oh, yeah?" she said, pointing the knife at him playfully. "Well, for your information, these are snails, not clams." She touched the tip of the blade to his chest. "And if you're going to go *opihi*-picking with me, you'd better get it right."

For the next couple of hours, they searched along the rocky coast, occasionally seeing other *opihi* pickers drawn by the unusually calm sea. Kehau kept the *opihi* they found in a small mesh bag tied around her waist, and by the time the rising tide made it impossible to walk along the ocean floor, the bag contained nine little black shells.

As they headed back toward the car, Kehau swam slowly so Jordan could keep up, but he wasn't used to spending so much time in the water, and his strength was fading quickly. "Swim over here. I think it's shallow enough that you can take a break," she said.

"No, don't worry. I'll be fine," he said, but Kehau ignored him and made her way into a little cove among the rocks. Jordan followed, and found the water came to his chest when he stood. Kehau stood next to him, and he wrapped his arms around her and kissed the top of her head. He leaned down to kiss her lips, but all he got was a quick peck. She pulled back and gave him a mischievous smile.

"What, that's all?" he asked.

"Yup, that's it. If you want more, you'll need to close your eyes first."

Jordan felt pretty sure he knew her game but decided to play along by closing his eyes and shutting his lips tightly between his teeth. He waited for her to try to force the cold, wet snail into his mouth, but she didn't. Instead, he felt the soft, moist warmth of her lips as she pulled herself up out of the water and kissed him. Jordan opened his eyes in surprise.

The kiss was quick but powerful. Jordan shivered, and the hair on his neck stood on end. "Did you like that?" she asked quietly.

All he could say was, "Yeah."

"Would you like another?" she asked.

Jordan raised his eyebrows. "Sure."

"Okay," she said, smiling. "Close your eyes."

Jordan complied, and she kissed him again. And again. Each kiss a little longer, a little firmer, and a little more open. But as Jordan moved forward to meet her kiss yet again, she pulled back and quickly slipped an *opihi* into his mouth. Before Jordan could react, she took his head in both hands and clamped her lips onto his. He struggled for just a second, but quickly gave in, and the longer they kissed, the more he decided he liked the taste.

After an eternity that ended much too soon, Kehau let go of Jordan and backed away. "So," she said in a quietly triumphant voice. "How was it?"

Jordan cocked his head and gave her a wry smile. "I'm not sure. I think I'd better try another one."

She smiled, placed another *opihi* in his mouth, and kissed him.

thirty-nine

Gingerly, Kehau dabbed a baking soda paste on Jordan's red, swollen eyelid. Still dressed in his swimsuit, he lay on the couch at Hale Honu, his body covered in angry, scarlet welts. "I really think we should call your mom. She'll probably have some ideas." Kehau's face furrowed with concern.

He had adamantly refused this suggestion twenty minutes earlier, but his humility grew right along with the hives covering his body. "Yeah, I guess," said Jordan, feeling the uncomfortable thickness of his fat upper lip. He closed his eyes and tried to ignore the burning, itching sensation covering his body. He pointed weakly to the end table where his cell phone lay, and Kehau made the call. Jordan felt a sense of foreboding. Knowing his mother's feelings about Kehau, he feared what might happen when she arrived.

"She said you need an antihistamine. Do you guys have any Benadryl around here?" Kehau asked quietly, brushing back his hair. Jordan liked having Kehau nurse him, yet he also felt embarrassed at needing her help—especially if he looked half as bad as he felt.

"Mmm, there may be some in the bathroom. I don't know. Look, you don't have to stay. My mom will be here soon, and . . ."

Kehau cut him off. "No, I want to. Shh." She pressed a finger to his lips, and then bravely ventured down the hall of the otherwise empty house. A car pulled into the driveway, and Jordan looked up, expecting to see his mother.

Instead, it was Robert and Malia. "Hey Jordan," Malia yelled as they approached the screen door. "Is Auntie here?"

"Yeah," he said, motioning for them to come in.

"Oh, my goodness! Kehau, what happened to Jordan?" Malia asked.

"It looks like he's allergic to *opihi*," Kehau said as she came back into the room. "And there's nothing in the bathroom but five kinds of hair gel and an expired bottle of Tylenol."

"Oh, wow. Does it hurt?" she asked Kehau.

"Yes, it hurts," Jordan said, annoyed at being discussed rather than talked to.

"I had a companion who looked like that after he ate *umbu*. Like a Brazil plum," Robert said

"What happened?" Malia asked.

Robert shrugged. "After a week it went away."

"Oh, wow. A week?" said Malia.

Jordan wanted to ask her if she and Robert had a reason for coming other than to add insult to his injury, but Malia beat him to it. "Oh, Kehau. This came for you to my mom's house." She handed Kehau an envelope and shrugged. "From Vegas."

Kehau caught her breath but quickly recovered. "Oh, thanks. I'll have to see what that is." She set the envelope down, her face impassive. But Jordan noticed her hand was shaking.

She turned to Malia and said, "Thanks for bringing that by. That was very nice. Um, I'd better see if I can help Jordan some more." She hugged them both and ushered them out the door. When she came back inside, she picked up the letter and looked at it. Her brow furrowed, and she bit her lip.

"What is it?" Jordan asked.

Kehau shook her head and opened her mouth to speak and then bit her lip again.

She sat on the edge of the couch, and Jordan pulled himself up to give her some room. The dull itch that covered his skin flared into screaming pain to protest his movement, but Jordan ignored it, more concerned about Kehau and this mysterious envelope.

Kehau shook her head and let out an exasperated sigh. "It's probably nothing, it's . . ." She drew both lips in between her teeth and fingered the envelope. Then looking up at Jordan she said, "Do you remember that day behind the temple?"

Jordan nodded. "Well," she started, seeming unsure of how to continue. "Okay. I have always wanted to go on a mission. But money-wise, I just didn't see how I could. I mean, my parents paid for my brothers to go, but they're retired now, and I'm only making enough just for school, and there's no way to save, really. And everyone else has their own families, and . . ."

She turned the envelope around in her hand again, staring at it. "Anyway, about a month ago, this sister in our ward was giving a talk about her mission experiences, and I just felt so strongly that I needed to go, and . . ." She exhaled quietly before continuing. "And I thought of my dad's cousin." She looked up at Jordan. "His cousin lives in Vegas and is doing pretty well. But they're not active in the church anymore, and I didn't . . . I couldn't ask them for money. But the Spirit just kept telling me over and over to ask them, and so that day you saw me at the temple, I finally decided to write to them and ask if they would help me pay for my mission."

Jordan looked at the envelope. "And this is their answer?"

"I guess," she said. "I didn't expect them to write back so soon, and I didn't know if I'd still be in school, and I don't want my dad to know so I used my sister's address, and . . ." She looked at the envelope, which was becoming increasingly wrinkled from her constant handling.

Jordan wasn't sure what to feel. He could tell this was important to Kehau, but things were just starting to get going between them. A mission would ruin everything.

"Well, you probably better open it before you wear the envelope away."

Kehau laughed nervously and then slid her finger under the flap. She looked up at Jordan, and he saw both fear and hope in her eyes. He nodded at her, and she unfolded the paper.

Jordan watched her intently for any sign of the letter's content. At first he took comfort in her furrowed brow, but when she raised her hand to her mouth his heart jumped. Her face contorted and tears filled her eyes as she looked up at Jordan. "They said yes."

She lunged forward and hugged him tightly around the neck, sending a searing pain all over his skin. But the physical sting was nothing compared to the ache he felt inside.

She pulled back and looked into his eyes. Tears streamed down her cheeks, and she smiled at him. "They said yes! Isn't that great?"

The question was like cold water in his face. "Yeah, wonderful," he said, hoping that his grimace might be mistaken for a smile because of his heavy, misshapen mouth.

She sat up and quickly regained her composure, looking back at the letter. As she continued to read, her brow furrowed again. "What is it?" Jordan asked.

Kehau tilted her head and frowned slightly. "It's not as much as I need, but they're willing to pay part," she said, the smile returning to her face.

Jordan lay back and closed his eyes. After a minute, Kehau asked, "Jordan? What's wrong?" She brushed his hair back, but Jordan didn't answer. How could he tell her that the thing that was making her so happy was making him miserable? So he just looked up at her, took her hand, and gave her a weak smile. He hated himself for hoping she wouldn't find the rest of the money, but he hated the thought of losing her even more.

He could tell his silence bothered her, but before she could ask anything else, Beth came through the front door. "I figured something like this would happen one of these days," she said, her voice full of sympathy. "Your grandmother used to get hives, and I knew it was only a matter of time before one of you kids had a problem." She stopped when she saw the extent of Jordan's reaction. "My goodness, Jordan. How many of those things did you eat?"

Jordan shrugged. "A half-dozen, maybe."

"A half-dozen?" his mom asked, incredulous. "You would never try any of the seafood I offered to you." She pursed her lips and, looking at Kehau, added, "I guess presentation makes all of the difference."

Jordan looked up at Kehau, and she blushed.

"Uh, yeah. That must be it," Jordan said, certain he would be blushing too if his face wasn't already so red and swollen.

Kehau had to bite her lip to keep from laughing. But after a second she said, "Jordan, I think I'm going to go back to my place so I can call my parents."

She stood up, and Jordan pointed weakly at the keys on the table. "Take my car. I'm not going anywhere."

"Oh, that's okay. I don't mind walking," she said.

"No, go ahead and take it," he insisted. Doing his best to smile, he added, "That way I can be sure you'll come back when you're done."

Beth took out an old bottle of prescription antihistamine and began to fill a measuring spoon. "Kehau, why don't you wait a minute, and I can give you a ride," she said. "There's no reason for you to come back. This stuff puts him out for hours."

Jordan's eyes opened wide in alarm, but Kehau quickly accepted.

Beth handed Jordan the medicine, which he swallowed with a grimace. "All right, *opihi* boy. Go take a quick shower and get yourself into bed before this stuff kicks in. You'll be fine once the medicine wears off. We'll wait and make sure you get down okay."

The warm shower felt good on Jordan's irritated skin, but as soon as he turned off the water, his entire body felt as though it were going to explode. He gently patted himself dry, pulled on a clean pair of shorts, and walked back to the living room. His mom and Kehau stood together, talking quietly. The conversation seemed civilized, but it stopped abruptly as soon as the women saw him. His mom shook her head and gently kissed his cheek. "Oh, my poor baby. Get some rest, and I'll be back to check on you in a few hours."

His eyes met Kehau's, and he would have kissed her had his mother not been there. Then he thought maybe she wouldn't want to kiss him anyway, as puffy and swollen as his lips were. So he simply gave her a hug and said, "Thank you."

She smiled at him, and then she and Beth left together.

He didn't want to think about what they would say to each other on the way back to campus. Then suddenly he didn't want to do anything but lie down and sleep. He barely made it to his bed before falling into a deep, black, medicated slumber.

forty

The first thing Jordan noticed the next morning was a dry, crusty taste in his mouth. He opened his eyes and saw that the room was still dark. Fumbling for his phone, he flipped it on to check the time. Four seventeen. Then he noticed the voice mail symbol at the top of the screen. Maybe it was his mom, or Kehau. But when Jordan checked his missed calls, he saw it was the lab.

A terrible sinking feeling hit him. The lab. He'd missed his Saturday evening shift. Again.

A sense of dread overshadowed him throughout the morning, and once church was over, he went to Hisaishi's apartment in TVA. He explained the situation, but Hisaishi seemed unmoved. "You and I have a meeting tomorrow morning with Dr. Maran. We'll discuss the issue then."

Jordan walked slowly from Hisaishi's apartment, no doubt in his mind that his lab assistant career was over. Climbing into his car, he pulled the door closed and sighed. What he needed was some time with Kehau to cheer him up. He knew she was probably still at lunch, but he pulled out his phone and dialed her number anyway. The call went straight to voice mail.

"Hey, it's me. Give me a call when you get this." Jordan hung up and drove slowly back to Hale Honu.

Walking through the door, he heard a commotion inside. Seti waved an empty pastry box toward Paulo. "I can't believe you ate the last *malasadas*. Why you so *fa'alotoloto*?"

White granules of sugar flew from the box and stuck in the tight curls of Paulo's thick dark hair. "I didn't know they were yours. I thought they were Jordan's."

"Oh, nice," Jordan said as he walked past the kitchen. Seti pushed the box onto Paulo's head, and Tomasi laughed hysterically. Paulo said something Jordan didn't understand, but he found the corners of his mouth creeping up in a grin anyway.

Undoing his tie, Jordan tried to keep his mind off his pending unemployment, but the only thing he could think of was Seti's *malasadas*. He'd never seen anyone get so worked up about fried dough balls. But then he remembered how much Kehau liked *malasadas*, and a plan began to form in his mind.

Anxious for a project to distract him from his troubles, Jordan popped open his computer and did a search for *malasada* recipes. He found one and quickly scribbled down the ingredients. He could sense his roommates eyeing him curiously as he did a quick inventory of the fridge and pantry. With every ingredient that appeared on his list but not in their supply, he let out a frustrated little grunt. He had no yeast, no evaporated milk, and just a tiny bit of flour. Plus, the recipe called for six eggs, and he only had one.

Jordan breathed out a heavy sigh but refused to let a lack of ingredients derail the project. He quickly dismissed the thought of making a Sunday Foodland run. Next he thought of borrowing what he lacked, but remembered that his neighbors in the community ward would all be at church. He realized there was only one place he could acquire the needed ingredients: home.

He hesitated for several moments before walking out to his car. The interaction with his mother the day before had actually been okay; maybe he could keep the momentum going.

As he approached the front door, he could see his mother and sister sitting at the end of the table that peeked out from around the kitchen wall. "Knock, knock," Jordan said as he let himself in. Rebecca stood and nearly bowled him over in a hug. Jordan stole a quick glance at his mom and relaxed when he saw that she was smiling.

"That looks better. Oh, you should have seen him yesterday—he was a mess."

"Hey, Mom? I wondered if I could borrow some things—yeast, flour, a can of milk, and some eggs."

His mother raised her eyebrows. "Doing a little baking, are we?"

"Yeah, I'm going to make some *malasadas* for—" Jordan quickly censored himself. "For some friends."

"Ah." Beth cocked her head and smiled knowingly. "And would these friends include Kehau?"

Jordan's face flushed, but he kept his mother's gaze. "Yes."

"Well, then. Have at it," she said, indicating the pantry. Relieved, Jordan got a baggie and filled it with flour.

"I had a nice conversation with Kehau yesterday," she said as he zipped the top of the bag closed. Jordan held his breath. "She's a sweet girl. I kinda like her."

Well, duh, Jordan thought as he sighed in relief. *All you had to do was give her a chance.*

Beth took a drink of water, and then set down her glass. "She'll make a fantastic missionary." Jordan's insides twisted into a knot.

"Where is she going?" Rebecca asked.

"She's not going anywhere." Jordan's words came out more forcefully than he intended. "She wants to go on a mission, but it's probably not going to happen. She doesn't have the money." He grabbed a can of milk and then headed for the kitchen.

"Oh, I don't know," his mother said. "She has some, and the Lord has a way of helping those who put their trust in him. I'm sure she'll be able to come up with the rest."

Closing the fridge door, Jordan fought down the uneasiness that grew inside. "Yeah, maybe." Although he knew his mother was right, he felt guilty at hoping Kehau wouldn't get the money and did his best to force the possibility from his mind. "Okay, that's everything—I'd better get going. Thanks, Mom."

Jordan returned to Hale Honu hoping to find Kehau there, but she wasn't. He tried calling her, but her phone went straight to voice mail again, and he disconnected without leaving a message.

Jordan tried Kehau after the dough was mixed, and again once it had finished rising the first time, but failed to get anything but her voice mail. Resisting the temptation to abandon his project and go find her, he filled a pot with oil and started dropping in balls of dough.

When the first batch had cooked to a golden brown, he removed them from the oil, dipped them in sugar and set them on a plate. Realizing the recipe was making far more than he expected, he decided to take some into the living room where the usual crowd had gathered. "Hey, Seti—have a *malasada*."

He tossed the treat, and his roommate's eyes widened as he caught it. "Whoa—this is still warm."

Jordan smiled. "Made fresh today. I'll have another batch out in a minute."

The kitchen suddenly became very crowded, and Jordan found his *malasadas* disappearing as fast as he could make them. As he got to the end of the dough, he had to insist the others leave some for Kehau.

It wasn't until the last *malasada* was done and the kitchen cleaned up that his phone finally played her ringtone. "Hey, here you are. I've got a surprise for you. Do you want me to bring it up?"

"What? Oh, yeah. Great," she said, sounding out of breath. "And I have a surprise for you. I can't wait to see you, Jordan!"

Jordan smiled at the enthusiasm in her voice. "Yeah, well, I can't wait to see you, either."

"Great. Hurry. Meet me in the lounge."

Jordan quickly wrapped the remaining *malasadas* in some napkins, placed the bundle in a paper bag, and hurried onto campus. He trotted from his car to Hale Five and entered the lounge area. Crossing the threshold into the girls' dorm always made him feel slightly uneasy, as if he were going somewhere forbidden—a sensation likely caused by the large signs placed prominently on most doors that read, "Men are not allowed beyond this point."

But the lounge was the one exception to this rule, and Jordan walked quickly toward Kehau, who embraced him in a flying hug.

"Oh, Jordan! I'm going. I'm going!" Kehau stepped back and wiped a tear from her eye, laughing nervously.

Jordan's eyebrows lowered, his mind fighting off uneasy confusion. "Wait—going where?"

"On a mission. Jordan, my dad called me today after church. They found someone who's willing to pay for the rest of my mission. I'm really going!"

Her renewed embrace seemed to suffocate him, squeezing out

the happiness he'd felt just moments before. He wrapped his arm around her and buried his fingers in the hair that now reached the middle of her back, as though he could keep her from leaving by holding her tightly enough. But he knew this would not happen, and suddenly her closeness was agony to him.

Releasing his grip and taking a step back, he forced a smile and tried desperately to purge the hurt from his eyes. "So, who . . . ?" Jordan started, but couldn't find the words to finish. *Who's stabbing me in the heart?*

Kehau wiped at her eyes and shrugged her shoulders. "I don't know—my dad wouldn't tell me. Probably somebody in their ward." She took a deep breath and her smile broadened. "But who cares? The important thing is, I'm going—right?" Jordan tried to look into her eyes, but the hurt in his chest grew too great, and he had to look down. His shoulders fell, and he fiddled with the parcel in his hand. "Jordan, what's wrong?"

Jordan shrugged, and reached out to set the *malasadas* on a nearby end table. He stared at the greasy bag and sighed. "I'm glad you get to go. I'm happy for you—really I am. It's just . . ." He drew a ragged breath, and forced himself to look at her. "Where does that leave us?"

Kehau's eyebrows bunched together, and her lips curled into a sympathetic smile. "We," she said, taking his hands in hers, "are going to put our trust in God and have faith that He will guide us to the future that's right for us."

Jordan's chest tightened, and he looked down. Kehau moved closer and took his head in her hands, bringing his face directly in front of hers. He saw tears forming in her eyes. "And in the meantime," she said, her voice strained, "we are going to make the most of every minute we have together."

She closed her eyes and pulled him close, guiding his lips onto to hers. Jordan hesitated before returning her kiss, the ecstasy of her sudden affection overshadowed by the pain of her imminent loss. The urge to push her away welled inside him, but before he could act, the impulse was washed away by his overwhelming longing.

Their kiss was cut short by whoops from a group of girls on the far side of the lounge. Kehau's face flushed, and she looked down at the floor. Jordan stared at her, wrestling with the conflicting emotions that tore at him inside.

When Kehau raised her head again, Jordan saw hope in her eyes and fought hard to share that hope. After all, Robert and Malia had survived a mission. Perhaps he and Kehau could too. And she was right—they still had all the time before she left, and it could possibly be months before she got her call.

And in those months, it just might be possible to get her to change her mind.

forty-one

Sandwiched in the back seat of Robert and Malia's silver Altima, Jordan held Kehau's hand and stared blankly out the window, barely noticing the lush green vegetation as it slipped past in the fading light of evening. The other three burst into laughter, but Jordan hadn't been following their conversation.

"Hey." He felt Kehau squeeze his hand and turned to look at her. "Are you okay?"

Jordan forced a smile. "Yeah, just tired."

Kehau placed her other hand on top of his and furrowed her brow. "Are you sure? Is something bothering you?"

Yes—you and your mission, he thought, though he couldn't bring himself to say it. So he brought up the other major stressor in his life. "I'm worried about my video project. The girls in my group pretty much dropped out, and David Cho thinks he's the master of the comedy short and can't be bothered with a 'lame documentary.'" Jordan sighed. "At least I've had some extra time to work on it this week."

Malia turned around in her seat, grabbing the headrest with her hand. "When do you start your new job, Jordan?"

"Monday," he said, trying to keep the disappointment from his voice.

"So, only out of work for a week—that's not too bad."

Jordan rolled his eyes. "No, that's the good part. And it's more hours, though not as much per hour. With any luck I'll get something else in the fall."

Kehau put her arm on his shoulder. "Well, until then you'll be the cutest rubbish picker on campus."

Jordan couldn't help but smile. He put his arm around her and pulled her close, yet feeling her warmth at his side was decidedly bittersweet.

As Malia turned forward in her seat, she suddenly screamed.

"What? What is it?" Robert struggled to pay attention to both his wife and the narrow, winding road.

"My diamond! It's gone!"

"What?" Robert repeated. He swiftly pulled into a tourist gift shop on the side of the highway, and parked squarely in the middle of two spaces.

"It's gone—look!" Malia thrust her hand toward her husband, who grabbed her fingers and stared at the wedding ring. Even from the back seat, Jordan could see that the prongs rising from the gold band were empty.

Robert muttered a curse fitting the situation. "Was it there when you got in the car?"

"I don't know."

"Yes—yes it was," Kehau said. "I remember seeing reflections when we were waiting for Jordan. The sun hit it, and there were little sparkles all over the front of the car."

Robert took a couple of calming breaths. "Okay, then it's still in here. Don't move." He slowly reached in front of Malia and gingerly opened the glove box, as if any sudden movement would scare the diamond away. Robert rummaged around for a few seconds before removing a thick metal flashlight.

The light cast a bright beam that cut through the gathering twilight, and Jordan watched as Robert ran the light up and down Malia, along the seat next to her, and down onto the floor.

"Do you see it?"

"No, not yet."

"Maybe you're sitting on it," Kehau offered.

"Let me move so you can see." Malia popped her door.

"No! Don't get out. If it's on you, it'll fall outside, and we'll never find it."

"Then what do you want me to do?"

"Just stand up so I can see."

Malia raised herself up by arching her back, and quickly lost her balance. She let out a frustrated sound and awkwardly turned around so she practically sat on the dash, her face and hands near the headrest. "Do you see it?"

Robert ran the light over the seat, shaking his head. He cursed again. "I hope it didn't fall down between."

"Robert, do you want me to look under the seat?" Jordan offered.

Robert pursed his lips and hesitated for a moment. "Yeah, here. Try."

Jordan took the flashlight, and Kehau picked up her slippers and placed her bare feet on the seat back in front of her so Jordan could have access to the floor. He crouched down and shined the light under the seat. The complete lack of dirt, crumbs, and debris surprised him, and as he slowly swept the beam across the floor, he saw nothing but the light blue carpet.

"Anything?" Kehau asked.

"No," Jordan said. With an exhale of air, Jordan pulled himself off the floor. As he did so, he caught a bright flash out of the corner of his eye. "Wait—what was that?"

Kehau froze, her feet suspended behind the seat. As Jordan passed the light over them, the bright flash returned. "Hold still." Jordan gingerly reached out and plucked Malia's diamond from the bottom of Kehau's left foot. "I got it."

Malia held out her hand, and Jordan carefully set the stone in her palm. Once she confirmed it really was her diamond, she let out a deep breath. "Oh, my gosh. Oh, my gosh—thank you, Jordan."

"How did it get back here?" Kehau asked.

Jordan shrugged. "Maybe when Malia turned around."

Robert started the car and backed out of his parking space. "Sorry, everyone—movie's cancelled. Goin' to the jewelry store instead."

They filed into one of the many jewelers at Ala Moana, where Robert and Malia explained their situation to a tall, dark, and suitably apologetic salesman. Jordan did his best to exercise patience, staying close to Kehau as she admired the contents of the display cases. "Ooh, I like that one."

Jordan moved in close so he could see what had caught her

attention. She was looking at a three-ring wedding set fashioned in the Hawaiian Heirloom style, with delicate plumeria carved in two-tone white and yellow gold. In addition to the broad his-and-hers wedding bands, the slender engagement ring held a small, channel mount solitaire.

"Yeah, that is nice." Examining the rings, Jordan's heart beat faster. He looked up, caught the eye of the shorter salesman, and motioned him over. "Hi. Can we take a look at this set right there?"

Jordan half expected Kehau to protest, and when she didn't, his optimism grew. The man gently set the box on the glass and removed the engagement ring, handing it to her. Ignoring the sales pitch about karats and craftsmanship, Jordan watched intently as Kehau studied the ring, trying in vain to read her thoughts.

"Why don't you try it on?" Kehau drew in her lower lip, hesitated, and then shook her head, returning the ring to the box.

"It's very beautiful. Thank you."

The salesman nodded politely and returned the ring to its home. Kehau glanced at Jordan and then quickly looked away, her face slightly flushed.

Before Jordan could say anything to Kehau, Robert and Malia joined them. "Okay, guys. I think we're done," Robert said. "Let's go eat, and then maybe we'll catch a late show."

Jordan's eyes lingered on Kehau for a moment before he turned to face the others. "That sounds like a good idea." As the group spilled out into the mall, Jordan took Kehau's hand and felt a smile creep across his face. Maybe his situation wasn't as hopeless as he had feared.

forty-two

"**W**hy are you looking at me like that?" Kehau had just emerged from the back door of Hale Five wearing a simple but flattering blue floral print dress.

A slight smile crept onto Jordan's lips. "I've never seen you in that dress before. I like it." He lifted the tuberose and carnation lei he held in his hand and gently lowered it over her head. He pressed his lips to hers and held them there for several seconds.

Kehau leaned back. "If you like this one, you should see the dress I bought for the Winter Ball a few months ago."

Jordan cocked his head. "I thought you said you didn't go to the Winter Ball?"

"I didn't." She took his hand, and together they began walking. "I was going to go with Scott, but . . ." Kehau trailed off, and Jordan squeezed her hand. "I thought about wearing the dress tonight, but it'd be overkill for a casual dance like this."

As they walked toward the Cannon Center, Jordan heard a car horn honk behind him. He ignored it until a voice called out, "Hey, MacDonald!"

He turned and saw a beat-up old Cavalier convertible, with Brandon behind the wheel. Stacie sat in the passenger seat, grinning. The car, which looked like it had once been black, had a yellow trunk and large primer spots all over it. The seats were torn, and as Jordan approached, he noticed the faint smell of burning transmission fluid.

"Where did you get this thing?" Jordan asked.

"I picked it up from a guy in Hau'ula. I figured me and Stacie will need a car once we're married, and I wasn't going to get anything until we came back in the fall, but then I found this and decided to get it. The guy practically gave her to me."

"Yeah, gee, I wonder why," said Jordan.

Brandon laughed. "She's pretty rough, but I think I can clean her up fairly good. It's your fault, you know. You proved to me the only way to drive in Hawai'i is with the top down."

Kehau pulled on Jordan's arm and said in his ear, "I need to go. That burning smell is starting to make me sick."

"Okay," he told her. Turning back to Brandon, he said, "Hey, we'll catch you inside."

As Brandon drove away, Kehau said, "I'm sorry, it's just that some smells really get to me. Cigarette smoke is the worst, but some car smells bug me too."

They made their way into the Cannon Center, and Jordan was impressed with the building's transformation. The basketball court and bleachers were hardly recognizable behind all the black and silver decorations.

The two of them danced and mingled throughout the night, spending time with both Kehau's and Jordan's friends. Kehau was very interested to learn that Brandon had known Jordan on his mission.

"You were one of Jordan's mission companions?" she asked.

"Yup. I was his trainer."

"Why didn't I know this?" Kehau asked. Brandon and Jordan both shrugged. "So, what kind of missionary was he?"

"Jordan? He was a good greenie. Studied hard. Obeyed the rules. But believe it or not, he was a bit shy."

Kehau smiled. "Oh, no. Not Jordan!" Jordan felt his ears burn.

"Oh, man. Let me tell you. His first day out in the field, I took him out tracting. We were in Corvallis, about two hours south of Portland, and we picked this street with these little old houses. I figured it would be a safe street for him to start out with." Brandon smiled and shook his head. "So I do the first few doors, just to show him how it's done. You know—we introduce ourselves and ask if we can share a message, and the people say 'no' and we're off to the next house. So anyway, after a few times, I tell Elder MacDonald to take the next one . . ."

"You know, Brandon," Jordan interrupted. "I'm not sure Kehau really wants to hear this story."

"Yes, I do. What happened? Tell me."

"Okay, so we get to the next house, right? And I ring the doorbell. Then I look at Jordan, and he's pale as a turnip, and this little old lady comes to the door . . ." Brandon paused for effect. "And Jordan faints."

"What?!"

"Yeah, his eyes roll, his knees buckle, and I have to catch him before he falls into the begonias."

Jordan's entire face flushed as the girls howled with laughter.

"No, wait—but the best part is, here's this old lady, standing at the door with the Mormon boys on her porch, and one of them is passed out cold, and so what else can she do? She has to let us in, right? So I lay Jordan out on the couch, and he starts to get some color back, but this lady says, 'You just lay right there until you get to feeling better,' and so Jordan covers his eyes and nods, and while he's laying there, on the couch, I go ahead and teach this lady the first discussion, and set up an appointment to teach her the second."

Both Kehau and Stacie laughed so hard, Jordan thought they would hurt themselves. And even though he wanted to be upset with Brandon for telling the story, he couldn't help but smile as well.

Later that evening, Kehau said, "That was fun, hearing about your mission. Why didn't you ever tell me any of those stories?"

"Do you really have to ask?"

"Aw, but those were so good," she said, taking his hand. "I can't wait until August when I turn twenty-one so I can send in my papers."

The happiness Jordan had felt just moments before was suddenly replaced by a sense of dread. "Are you still thinking of going?"

"Of course. Why wouldn't I?" she asked.

Jordan shrugged. "I don't know. I guess I just thought maybe you liked me enough to stay here instead."

"Jordan, I do like you," she said, wrapping her arms around his waist and resting her head on his chest. "I like you a lot. But this is important to me. It's something I have to do, now that I actually have the chance."

Biting his lip, Jordan reached up and stroked her hair. The thought of losing Kehau hurt more than anything, and Jordan hoped he could figure out a way to keep her from leaving.

forty-three

On a Saturday in early June, Jordan stood at the end of a wedding line in his own back yard. His mom had surprised him by offering it to Brandon and Stacie for their reception. But even with teachers and friends and both families in attendance, the gathering was still quite small. Standing next to Jordan was the best man, Brandon's brother, Paul, who was even bigger than Brandon and kept his head completely shaved.

"So," asked Paul during a lull in the visitors, "was it just me, or did it seem like there were a lot of weddings today?"

"No, it was busy," Jordan said. "But it's the Saturday between terms, so I guess that's what happens."

Paul nodded. "I've never been to Hawai'i before, so I'm glad they had the wedding here." He turned to Jordan. "My parents were trying to get him to have it at the Mesa temple, and I guess Stacie's parents wanted them to get married in Canada."

Brandon peeked around his brother's shoulder. "So I finally announced that the wedding would be in Hawai'i, that everyone was welcome to come, and if they behaved themselves then we would have receptions in both Arizona and Alberta."

Just then, Kehau arrived with Malia and Robert. Kehau was in the same red mu'u mu'u she had worn the night Jordan first kissed her, and seeing her made him feel slightly dizzy.

"Wow—there's a couple of cuties," Paul said.

Kehau led the group as they made their way through the line. She gave both Stacie and Brandon large hugs, shook Paul's hand, and approached Jordan. She held out her hand and said, "Hello. My name is Kehau."

Jordan looked at her quizzically, but decided to play along. He took her hand and shook it stiffly. "Kehau, it's nice to meet you. I'm Jordan."

"You look very handsome in your tuxedo, Jordan."

"Why, thank you. I have to say, I've never met a more beautiful girl in my life. Is it really possible that you're here alone?" Jordan looked around.

Kehau lowered her head, nodding. "Yes, I'm afraid so. My boyfriend is busy today."

Jordan scowled. "That's terrible. I can't believe it. Tell you what—when I'm done here, why don't I be your boyfriend."

Kehau looked up, her face brightening. "You'd do that for me?"

Jordan cocked his head. "Baby, I'd do anything for you."

Kehau's smile lit up her face. "That's great. Thank you. I'll wait for you right over here." She turned to leave, but Jordan caught her hand.

"Hey, wait. Why don't you give me a little kiss. You know—to hold me over until I'm done."

"Oh, okay," she said. Kehau reached up and pressed her lips to his and held them there just long enough to get a whoop from Brandon. "I'll be waiting," she said as she turned and walked into the crowd.

Malia rolled her eyes and pulled Robert along behind her without even bothering to tell Jordan "Hello." Through the crowd, Jordan thought he saw his mother scowl at him, but she disappeared before he could tell for sure. Jordan watched Kehau as she walked toward the dessert table, greeting a professor and his wife along the way.

"Dude! How did you do that?" Paul asked.

Without taking his eyes off Kehau, Jordan said, "It's a gift."

"Yeah, right," said Brandon, punching Jordan in the shoulder. "Paul, don't pay any attention to this phony." Then Brandon put his arm around Jordan and, nodding toward Kehau, said, "You know, this marriage thing is pretty good. You should try it sometime." He clapped Jordan on the back, and then said, "Oh, hey, before I forget—while we're gone, do you think you could keep an eye on my car? Just change parking spots once in a while so it doesn't look abandoned."

"Brandon, any time that thing's not moving, it looks abandoned."

After a while, the slow trickle of guests finally petered out, and Kehau made her way back to Jordan's side.

Brandon gave Jordan a wink. "Think about what I said."

"Hey, Kehau," Julie called out. She had made it home from college just in time to help out with the wedding. "Get over here. Stacie's throwing the bouquet."

Kehau walked over to stand between Julie and Brandon's sister, Melissa, who giggled as Kehau approached. Rebecca began walking toward them, but Beth said, "Rebecca, no! You're only seventeen—you stay away from that bouquet." Rebecca made a big deal of acting offended but couldn't help laughing as she walked back to her seat.

Julie and Melissa positioned Kehau between them, and when Stacie threw the flowers they ran to either side, leaving Kehau alone in the middle.

"There you go," said Brandon when Kehau held the bouquet over her head in triumph. "What more do you need?"

As Kehau returned to Jordan's side, Brother Boyce approached him. "Jordan, do you have a second? I need to talk to you."

Jordan couldn't think of what Brother Boyce would want to talk to him about, except possibly his group's video assignment. Jordan had done his best, but the video the group handed in turned out to be pretty rough.

"I know this term has been hard on everyone, and nobody's project came together very well. Your group's especially was very uneven, and I really needed you to do much more than what you did, just to get a passing grade." Jordan looked down and fiddled with his hands, a knot forming in the pit of his stomach. Why did Brother Boyce have to do this now, and in front of Kehau?

Brother Boyce took a breath, and Jordan steeled himself, knowing he was about to fail a class for the first time in his life. However, the teacher said, "I've given everyone in the class an incomplete. I'd like to see all of these projects finished."

It took Jordan a few seconds to comprehend what he had just heard. "Thank you, Brother Boyce."

Kehau took Jordan's hand in support.

"I'll be repeating the class during Summer term, and I'm hoping I can get you to redo your project by the end of the month. I'm not sure if anyone else from your group will be taking this next section, but my wife would like to use your finished video as part of her presentation at the Glen Yamada Fund-raiser Gala on the twenty-fifth. That gives you less than three weeks. Can you do it?"

Jordan thought of the work involved in redoing the project. It had been almost more than he could handle getting it to where it was. He'd had a lot of good ideas but simply lacked the time to put it together. But now he was being offered nearly three more weeks, and he thought he just might be able to pull it off. "Yeah, I think so."

Brother Boyce finally smiled. "Good. I'll let Sister Boyce know. Oh, and by the way. She said she could get you a ticket to the gala if you want. It's a big fancy black-tie affair, and you don't have to go, but she thought you might like to see your video's debut presentation."

"Yeah, I'd like that. It sounds like fun."

"Good. I'll let her know." Then, looking at Kehau, he added, "I'll have her get you two tickets."

Kehau grabbed Jordan's arm, clearly thrilled about attending a black-tie gala. "I can wear the dress I bought for Winter Ball. It will be perfect—you'll love it."

Jordan was sure he would.

forty-four

"**H**ello?" A female voice shattered the silence of the TV studio, making Jordan jump. His heart pounded for a moment before he realized it was Kehau.

"I'm up here," he called out. He listened to the sound of her footsteps on the stairs leading to the editing bay, thankful for a break and glad she had thought to come and check on him. He'd been working on the video, trying to clean it up, shorten it, consolidate it, fix it. He'd changed the music, rearranged the video clips and still images, and basically second-guessed everything the class had done on the project, and he still didn't like the results.

"How's it going?"

"Do I have to answer that?" he asked, turning to watch her as she finished climbing the stairs.

"That bad?"

"Mmm. It's getting better," he said.

She bent down to give him a kiss. "How much longer do you think you'll be?"

"I think I'm finished for now," he said, turning to face the computer. "I've done enough damage for one night."

"Oh, I'm sure it's brilliant," said Kehau. She began rubbing his shoulders while he waited for his work to save.

Jordan relished the feeling of Kehau's touch, a feeling made bittersweet at the thought of her leaving soon.

"Mmm, that feels good," he said. "I want you to do that every day for the rest of my life."

"Every day?"

"Yeah, every day."

"That might get hard when I'm gone."

"Then don't go."

Kehau didn't answer. Jordan's computer finished shutting down, and he turned to face her.

"I mean it," said Jordan. "I don't want you to go."

Kehau considered him for a minute. "Why not?"

"Because I don't want to lose you. Because I love you." Jordan had hoped this declaration would be enough to melt her heart and make her give up her ideas of serving a mission. But instead, she looked away and folded her arms.

"I'm sorry," he said. But really he wasn't. "Tell me what it would take to keep you here, and I'll do it."

She turned to face him and drew in a breath as if she were about to speak. But instead of saying anything she chewed her lips, brow furrowed. Exhaling deeply, she crouched down so they were at eye level, and Jordan held his breath.

"Jordan, I really care for you—a lot. You are a wonderful guy, and I consider myself lucky to have spent these last few months with you." She reached up and brushed her fingers through his hair. "I don't know what the future holds for us, but I have to believe that if we're meant to be together, then it will happen. But if not . . ." She took both of his hands in hers. "If not, then we just have to trust that the Lord knows what he's doing."

Jordan looked deeply into her dark brown eyes and could sense the struggle raging in her heart—a struggle that simply had to go his way. His pulse hammered in his ears, and he pulled his lips into a smile. "Of course we're meant to be together. Why else would the Lord have brought us into each other's lives?" Kehau lowered her head, and Jordan reached out, placing his hand under her chin. He gently lifted her face until their eyes met again. "Don't you see? The Lord does know what he's doing—that's why he brought us together."

Leaning forward, Jordan put his hand behind her head and kissed her deeply, possessively. At first she returned his kiss but after a few seconds, she pulled back. "I'm sorry," she said as she stood and turned away from him.

Jordan took a breath, fanning the small ember of hope glowing inside him. Standing, he put a hand on her shoulder. "C'mon," he said. "Let's go find you a snack."

She looked up at him, smiled weakly, and nodded her head. As they walked down the stairs, Jordan took her hand and breathed a sigh of relief. If everything went well, he might not lose Kehau after all.

forty-five

Jordan paced the many crowded walkways of Ala Moana, anxiously checking his watch. When the appointed time arrived, he returned to the jewelry shop where an hour earlier he had applied for store credit to buy an engagement ring for Kehau. Waiting for the saleswoman to finish with another couple, he stood above the case that held the rings Kehau had shown him just weeks before. Looking at them again, he had to admit the set was perfect.

A round of "thank yous" caught Jordan's attention, and he looked up as the other couple exited the store. The woman behind the counter smiled at him and raised a finger.

"Just a moment, Mr. MacDonald," she said before disappearing through a doorway. She was replaced by a balding man wearing a dark blue suit over a bright yellow aloha shirt.

"Mr. MacDonald," he said, giving Jordan a smile that seemed anything but genuine. "My name is Philip King. I'm the assistant manager here." Jordan held his breath, his pulse pounding in his ears.

The man folded his hands in front of him, and his forehead wrinkled. "As you're probably aware, the last few years have seen most lenders severely limiting the credit they make available." Jordan's heart sank as he anticipated the next sentence. "Unfortunately, our underwriter was only able to extend five-hundred dollars to you."

Jordan took in a deep breath, trying not to let his disappointment show. "I see."

"We do have a number of items that fall within that price range, if you'd care to take a look."

"No, thanks." Jordan tried to force a smile before turning to go.

"Sorry we couldn't be of more help. If there's anything we can do for you in the future, feel free to come back and see us."

The sun beat down on Jordan as he trudged through the crowded parking lot. He'd looked to his ability to buy the rings as a sign—evidence that proposing was the right thing to do. But he'd failed.

Stopping in the middle of the lot, he turned and looked back toward the mall. Maybe he should go back and see what they offered in his price range. With a sigh, he abandoned the thought—those were the rings Kehau wanted. He had only one chance to keep her from leaving, so everything needed to be just right.

As he pulled the keys from his pocket and unlocked his door, a sudden flash of inspiration hit him. Surely he could sell his car for enough money to buy the set.

A mix of elation and dread washed over him. Was he really willing to sell his car? He could always drive Brandon's if he needed to—at least for the summer. If selling his car would let him hang on to Kehau, then that was what he needed to do.

Jordan drove to Hale Honu as quickly as he could, stopping at a car wash on the way. Within two hours, he'd taken a dozen pictures of the Mustang and listed it for sale on eBay, with a reserve price equal to the cost of the rings. This would be his sign. If the car sold for enough money to buy the wedding set, he would ask Kehau to marry him.

That night, he paid special attention to Kehau's hands. "What are you doing?" she asked, as he played with her fingers.

"I like your hands," he said. "They're very beautiful."

"Oh, please," she said, pulling them away. "They look like boy hands. I hate them. Look!" she said, holding her hands up, palms toward Jordan. He touched his palms to hers, and aligned their fingers. "See? My hands are almost as big as yours."

Their hands *were* almost the same size. But more important, Jordan noted her left ring finger was nearly the same size as his right pinkie.

He folded his fingers around hers and looked her in the eye. "I don't care what you say—I think they're beautiful."

While waiting the five days for his auction to end, Jordan kept himself busy planning a romantic picnic breakfast. After four days, the bidding had only reached half of the reserve, and Jordan sighed in frustration. But then on the last day, in typical eBay fashion, the bidding picked up, and the car sold for a few bucks more than he needed.

The buyer lived down in Honolulu, and Jordan agreed to meet him near the Shirokiya department store at Ala Moana. With a thick wad of cash in hand, Jordan practically ran to the jewelry store, where he swapped his pile of hundreds for the wedding ring set.

Making his way home on the Circle Island bus, it was all Jordan could do to keep from taking the rings out of his pocket to admire them. But one look at the collection of interesting characters sharing his ride, and he decided that this time patience really would be a virtue.

Waiting outside the back gate at PCC later that evening, Jordan remembered the night so many months ago when Kehau told him she was seeing someone else, and he began to have second thoughts. But this time as she approached, she gave him a smile that wiped all his doubts away. "I'll see you guys tomorrow," she said to her friends as she turned toward Jordan. She took his hand and kissed him, and Jordan was filled with a grand surge of excitement at the thought of asking her to marry him. He was glad he had left the rings at home or he might have forgone his plan and proposed right then and there.

As they walked to the dorms, Jordan asked in a voice thick with scheming, "So what grand plans do you have for tomorrow morning?"

Kehau shrugged her shoulders and returned his mischievous look. "Nothing. Why? What do you have in mind?"

"Oh, just a little surprise."

"A surprise?"

"Mmm-hmm." he said. "I'll be by to pick you up at seven o'clock."

"Seven? That's early."

Jordan smiled and put his arm around her as they walked, pulling her close. "Well, maybe I want to spend as much time as possible with the most beautiful woman on the island before I have to share her with busloads of tourists."

"Okay—now you're just being ridiculous," she said, but her smile grew.

"Maybe." They had reached the dorm, and Jordan steered her to one of the back doors. "But then again, maybe I really believe it." And with that, he gave her a kiss. "Seven o'clock," he said. Then he turned to walk slowly away.

forty-six

As Jordan walked Kehau from her dorm to the parking lot the next morning, she looked around, brow furrowed. "Where's your car?"

"It's, um—I sold it."

Kehau stopped. "You what?"

"I wanted to buy something else. We'll take Brandon's car. And don't worry—the burning smell is gone. He fixed it somehow," Jordan said. *Probably with a big strip of duct tape.*

They drove to the temple, where Jordan took a cooler and blanket from the trunk. Then together they walked the winding pathway to the gazebo. He spread the blanket on a nearby grassy area, and they sat down. She smiled when he brought out the *pani popo*, but Jordan noticed Kehau seemed a bit guarded and suspicious. He had second thoughts about what he was about to do but pushed them aside, intent to follow through with his plan.

After their meal of grapes and cheese and ham, he took Kehau's hand in his. "I just can't believe I ever met someone like you. I never imagined I could have someone as wonderful as you in my life."

Kehau smiled. "That's sweet."

"You've made me happier than I ever thought possible. And now I want to return the favor."

"Really? How?"

"With this," Jordan said, and he reached into the cooler and took out the box with the rings in it.

"Jordan, what is that?" she asked, sounding torn between intrigue and concern.

"It's a proposal," said Jordan. Climbing onto one knee, he opened the box to expose the rings. "Kehau, please stay and marry me."

Kehau frowned, and her lips pursed. She shook her head. "You sold your car to buy these, didn't you? Jordan, why are you doing this?"

"Because I love you, and I want to spend the rest of my life with you. The rest of eternity with you."

"Jordan, I don't know what to say."

"Say yes."

Jordan's heart pounded in his chest as Kehau stared at the rings. At last she drew in a deep breath and shook her head. "I can't."

Jordan's insides clenched. "Why not?"

"You know why not."

"No, I don't." Pain shot through Jordan's chest, and he fought to keep his voice steady. "Kehau, you don't have to go. You haven't even sent in your mission papers yet." He set the rings aside, leaned forward, and took her hand. "Stay here and marry me."

Her eyes were pleading. "Jordan, please. Don't do this."

"Don't do what? Tell you that I love you? Tell you that you are the most wonderful thing to ever happen to me, and I can't bear the thought of letting you go?"

"Jordan . . ." she said, shaking her head.

"Oh, I get it. You didn't really mean it when you said you cared for me."

"Yes, I did. I love you Jordan. I love you so much, and that's what makes this so hard."

"Then stay."

"Jordan, please!" Kehau's brow furrowed, and Jordan saw her eyes were reddening.

"If it's really so hard for you to go, then why do it? You're a girl—it's not like you have to."

"No, I don't. But I want to! Don't you understand?"

"But Kehau, I love you. And if you love me, you'll stay here with me. Let someone else go. Someone who doesn't have a boyfriend who wants to marry her."

Kehau gasped. "This isn't some kind of consolation prize. 'Oh, nobody wants to marry me. I guess I'll go on a mission.' I've always known I wanted to go. I've watched five brothers serve faithfully, and from the moment I found out that girls could serve a mission, I wanted to go too. And now that I can actually afford it, I wouldn't trade this chance for anything in the world."

Jordan stared at her. He had known this was a possible outcome, yet the hurt still threatened to overwhelm him. With tears welling in his eyes, he asked, "So that's it then?"

Kehau's lips quivered as she tried to smile. "That's it."

"Okay, fine," said Jordan. The pain he felt suddenly became too much to bear, and all he could think of was getting away as quickly as he could. He threw open the lid to the cooler and began hastily filling it with food.

"Jordan," Kehau said. "I'm sorry. I do love you. Really I do. But this is so important to me."

"No, I understand," said Jordan, his voice biting. "I'm sorry too." He stood and picked up the cooler. The humiliation suddenly growing unbearable, he couldn't even look at her. "Good-bye, Kehau."

And with that, Jordan turned and stormed down the hill, not waiting for Kehau to stand or bothering to retrieve his blanket. "No, Jordan. Wait!" she called after him, but he ignored her. "Jordan, please!" But Jordan kept walking, not looking back even as he clambered into the car. He tossed the cooler onto the seat, and it landed on its side, the contents spilling onto the floor. Looking at the small box in his hand, the pain in his chest swelled to fill his entire body. What had he been thinking? Jordan righted the cooler, threw the food back inside and pitched the rings in too. Then he slammed the lid and drove off.

The windward coast meandered past, and Jordan let the wind blow his tears along his face. Deep down, he had known this plan wouldn't work—Kehau was determined to serve her mission. Her focus and drive were part of what attracted him to her, but the thought of losing her hurt terribly.

Around the island he went, taking Kalanianaole Highway around Makapu'u and the eastern tip of the island. As he drove, his hurt slowly flaked away, and the gravity of what he had just done started to sink in.

Asking Kehau to marry him was stupid—probably the most stupid thing he had done during this whole stupid year. But leaving her back at the temple was worse. Leaving despite her calling to him. Turning his back on her and simply walking away. How could he have been so cruel?

Because I'm hurt, that's how!

But the pain wasn't her fault—he had brought it onto himself. As he drove through Honolulu, Jordan's frustration ebbed away enough that he finally decided to call her.

With the top down, he knew it would be impossible to call while driving, so he took the next exit off the freeway. Jordan found himself driving back out toward the airport. He stopped in the parking lot by La'aloa and dialed her number, but his call went straight to voice mail. He sent a text message, telling her he was sorry. He hoped she would reply quickly, but as he sat and waited, no return message came.

He thought about hurrying back to find her but couldn't bring himself to do it. What good would it do, anyway? The sting of her rejection still ached in his heart, and he decided to let her make the next move. If he hadn't heard from her by that evening, he'd catch her after work.

Before driving back home, Jordan went to use the restroom in the flight school. Walking toward the hangar, he remembered the rings in the car and ran back to get them. Rather than try to fish them out of the cooler, he simply grabbed the whole thing.

As he came out of the bathroom, Roach called from inside the office. "Hey, MacDonald. What's up with you? You don't look so good."

Jordan walked into the small room and told Roach about his entire misadventure.

"That's the Pulakaumaka girl, isn't it?"

"Yeah," Jordan said, and a wave of curiosity swept over him. "Roach? What's up with you and Joe Pulakaumaka?"

Roach stiffened and looked back at his computer screen. "That's a long story, MacDonald."

"It's okay," said Jordan, setting his cooler on the desk and flopping into a chair. "I've got time."

forty-seven

"**T**he first time I ever laid eyes on Joe Pulakaumaka was in March, 1969. I had just arrived at the Pleiku Air Base in Vietnam. I was very lucky to be there—a lot of my friends ended up being drafted into the infantry. Most came home in boxes.

"But I had experience as a mechanic, so before they could draft me, I signed up with the Air Force. I figured as an aircraft mechanic, I would have a decent shot at coming home in one piece, and for the most part, I was right." As he spoke, Roach leaned across the desk and picked up the model airplane.

"Joe was one of the senior flight line mechanics working on this baby here." Roach held the model out for Jordan to see.

"Rockwell OV-10 Bronco. Designed and built specifically to fly low and slow, picking out targets for the jets." He smiled a far away smile and said, "The first time I saw one of these things, I thought it was the strangest plane I had ever seen." Roach set the model down. "I fell in love with it right then and there. It was this plane that convinced me I wanted to fly.

"Anyway, Joe picked me out and took me under his wing. Probably because I was a—a 'person of color.' There were only four of us in the whole unit, and we were like the four musketeers. We called ourselves the—" Roach stopped himself, then shook his head and smiled sadly. "Well, it probably wasn't the best name. We didn't give much thought to being 'sensitive' and 'politically correct' back then.

"But we stuck together for the most part, me and Joe and Ty and Diego." Roach sat back and thought for a moment. "Except Joe was different. We'd go to the enlisted men's club, and Joe would always get a Sprite. Everyone else would have beer or liquor, but not Joe. Every time—Sprite, Sprite, Sprite. I finally asked him about it, and he explained that he was a Mormon and about that health code thing you have. Every time he ordered a Sprite, Ty made fun of him—well, we all did, really. But he never got upset when we teased him, and I respected him for that as much as I did his sticking to Sprite." Roach was smiling, enjoying his reminiscence, but then he stopped and took a deep breath.

"One night, Ty convinced us other two to play a little joke on Joe. Ty offered to get the drinks that night—his treat. But when he returned there was no Sprite. 'They're out,' he told Joe, 'but don't worry. I got you some root beer instead. It's special stuff they usually reserve for the officers, but I had 'em get some for you—since they ran out of Sprite and all.'"

"Ty had put just a little bit of vodka in the root beer. Joe said something about it tasting funny, and Ty assured him that's how it was supposed to taste. We had four rounds that night, and each time one of us put just a little more vodka in, and by the time we were done, Joe was drunk. And I mean, not a little drunk, either. We really hadn't given him that much, but I guess since it was the only alcohol he'd ever had in his life, it hit him kind of hard.

"Well, we all thought it was pretty funny, watching Joe try to work his way through the bar, stumbling around between the tables. Then he ran into Munchie."

The smile that had been on Roach's face suddenly dropped, and he stared blankly across the room for so long, Jordan wondered if he would ever find out about the Munchie character.

"Munchie was one of those hot-headed little kids who always felt they had something to prove. Joe had just bumped him accidentally, but in a flash, Munchie was on his feet, and before we knew what was going on, he had his fists up and was cursing and swearing at Joe, and Joe was just standing there, staring at him. Then Munchie calls him a name and pushes him. Now Joe, he's one of the most mellow guys I've ever met. I saw pilots and officers wipe their feet all over him, and he didn't even blink. So none of us could believe it when

Joe hauled back and knocked this Munchie clean off his feet. Broke his jaw and everything.

"Well, a couple of MPs were there in the club, and they come over to arrest Joe, and he starts knocking them around, and before we know it the whole place looks like a barroom brawl from some bad spaghetti western. It finally takes a half-dozen MPs to come and get Joe down.

"So Joe ends up in a court-martial, and Ty convinces us not to say anything about adding the alcohol to Joe's drinks. I agreed only because I figured the truth would come out in Joe's testimony, but he never says anything about us putting the booze in his root beer. I couldn't believe it. I mean, he's not stupid—he had to know what really happened. But I still didn't say anything because I figured they'd slap his wrist or maybe give him a few weeks in the brig. That's usually what happened with that kind of thing."

Roach stopped, looking at the model in his hand.

"So what did happen?" Jordan asked.

"The judge threw the book at him. Busted him down to corporal, made him finish his tour in the brig—three months!—and slapped him with a dishonorable discharge. He lost his chance for a military career. We were all stunned. Nobody could believe what had happened. It turns out this judge was like some cousin to Munchie's mom, and he decided to make an example out of Joe."

Roach shook his head at the memory. "Ty figured race played into it too. And he was probably right."

"So that's it?" Jordan asked. "They locked him up, and you just let them? You didn't tell anyone what really happened?"

Roach shook his head. "No, I didn't, though now I wish to God I had." Roach looked at the ceiling. "I was scared, MacDonald. We all were. Obstruction of justice is a big deal, and Ty convinced us that even if we did fess up, the judge wasn't going to let Joe off. He'd just throw the rest of us in with him."

Roach looked down at his hands. "And maybe he was right, I don't know." Roach looked up at Jordan, and a single tear escaped the corner of his eye. "What I do know is I should have said something, even if it did mean getting myself thrown in jail too. I lost my best friends that day, MacDonald. And not a day goes by that I don't regret it."

They sat in silence for a few minutes. Then Jordan's phone rang.

Jordan quickly pulled his phone out and checked the caller. It was Malia.

"Hello?"

"What did you do to her?"

"I, uh . . ." Jordan got up and walked out of the hangar.

"She's been crying for the last hour and a half, and she won't tell me anything."

"Malia, look. I'm sorry. I guess I was kind of a jerk. I've been trying to call and apologize, but she won't take my calls. Is she there now? Can I talk to her?"

"No, you can't talk to her. She's gone."

Jordan paced in front of the hangar. "Well, when she gets back, can you have her call me?"

"She's not coming back. She's gone."

"What? Gone where?"

"Home—back to the Big Island." Jordan's heart began to race. She was really gone. Then Malia continued. "Robert and I just dropped her off at the airport."

Jordan felt a sudden surge of hope. "Wait! When did you drop her off?"

"Just now—like five minutes ago."

Jordan began running toward his car. "What airline?"

"Hawaiian. Why?"

"I'm going to come and see her."

"What? There's no way you can get to the airport that fast."

"Then it's a good thing I'm already here. I'll meet you in five minutes. Wait for me by the curb!" Jordan hung up the phone and drove as quickly as he dared around the south side of the airport toward the interisland terminal. He was relieved to see Malia standing on the sidewalk, looking perplexed. Jordan stopped and got out, leaving the car running.

"Jordan! What—?" Malia began, but Jordan cut her off as he dashed past.

"Watch the car. I'll be back in a minute." He raced through the front doors and stopped, scanning the area. Ahead of him was the Hawaiian Air ticket counter, and Jordan quickly searched the line for Kehau but didn't see her. The security checkpoint to the right was closed, so Jordan jogged left.

She stood second in line for the metal detector when he saw her. "Kehau!" he called, breaking into a sprint. "Kehau!" he yelled again. She turned, and their eyes met. Jordan saw the pain on her face and felt a stabbing guilt. Then Kehau whipped her head forward and gave the agent her ticket.

"Kehau, no! Please," Jordan yelled, as he pushed his way through the line, ignoring the angry calls of the security agents as he did so. But when he saw Kehau walk coolly through the metal detectors and on toward the gate without turning around, he knew she was gone.

The security guard nearest him grabbed his arm. "What do you think you're doing?"

Jordan looked at him. "I guess I'm going home."

The man's grip on Jordan's arm tightened, and he began to object. But at a word from one of the other agents, he released Jordan with a little shove and said, "Go home then."

Jordan walked back out toward the curb, and it wasn't long before he saw Robert in their Altima, followed closely by Malia in Brandon's car. They pulled up to the curb, and Malia got out. "Jordan MacDonald, what the heck is going on?"

Jordan shrugged his shoulders. His insides were numb. "I asked Kehau to marry me. She said no. I got mad and left, and so she got mad and left. I guess that's pretty much it."

"Wait—you what? You asked her to marry you?" Malia and Robert exchanged confused looks.

"Yup," said Jordan. "I've got the rings right here. Do you want to see them?" he asked, leaning over the door. Panic hit as he realized the cooler wasn't in the seat or on the floor. He looked in the back and then felt under the seat, even though he knew it was too big to fit.

Then he remembered, he had taken the cooler in to La'aloa. He quickly walked around to the driver's door. "Um, I, uh—thanks for watching my car. I gotta go." Quickly Jordan pulled away from the curb, eliciting an angry honk from the taxi he cut off, and sped back to La'aloa.

To his relief, the hangar door was still open. Jordan ran in and found the cooler right where he had left it.

"So, did you catch her?" Roach asked.

"Huh? No," said Jordan. He opened the cooler, fished out the ring box, and slipped it into his pocket.

"Why don't you take The Bomb?"

"What?"

"Take The Blue Bomb and go."

Jordan toyed with the idea, but then he remembered the way Kehau had turned and walked through security, leaving him behind. The anger he had felt earlier resurfaced.

"No."

"C'mon—you can't let things end this way."

Roach's words caused a rush of anger to flare inside of Jordan, and he said the first thing that came to his mind. "Tell you what—we'll both go."

"What?" asked Roach.

"Yeah, we'll both go. I'll make up with Kehau, and you can make up with her dad. Joe seems like a pretty good guy—I'm sure he'd love to see you." Jordan hated himself for saying this, but in his frustration it seemed like a good way to lash out.

Roach glared at him and Jordan glared back. Then to Jordan's surprise, Roach looked down.

Jordan gave a bitter smile. "Yeah, that's what I thought." Jordan turned and stormed out of the office, but as he walked, he found himself slowing down, waiting for Roach to call after him, to stop him and fly him over to the Big Island to make his peace with Kehau. Out the door, across the tarmac, through the gate and into the parking lot, Jordan held out hope that Roach would stop him.

But he never did.

forty-eight

Jordan's return to Hale Honu was met by Scott's howls of laughter. Tomasi and Seti sat with him in the living room but didn't seem to share his amusement. Could Scott possibly know what had happened with Kehau? Jordan couldn't think of any other explanation. Robert and Seti were pretty good friends, and news like this didn't take long to spread around La'ie.

As Scott cackled Jordan fought back the urge to lunge at him or to say something vulgar and offensive. Instead he said, "Go ahead and laugh. I suppose to your small mind, this must be hilarious."

Scott jumped to his feet. "What? You think you're funny, *Pono*?" Jordan ignored him and walked back to his room.

Jordan heard Seti say, "Leave him alone. That's gotta be rough, man." He sat on his bed but quickly stood again, unsure what to do next. He began gathering a few things and putting them in a bag, overcome with a desire to leave the house. But where would he go? There really was only one place to go—home. He grabbed his bag, and walked out.

"What? Running home to mommy?" Scott asked as Jordan came back into the living room.

Jordan glanced at Scott but refused to dignify his comment with a response.

"Yeah, you go home and cry to your mommy. You know something, *Pono*? She was too good for you anyway."

Jordan stopped at the door and turned to look Scott straight in the eye. "Maybe she was too good for either one of us," he said.

By the time Jordan got to his mother's house, the last of the color was fading from the clouds and darkness rolled over the island. Jordan sat in the car for a long time, emotionally drained and finding comfort in his solitude. As the sky faded to deep indigo, Jordan hauled himself from the car and made his way to the front door.

His mom sat in her chair reading a book when he came in. "Jordan, this is a surprise. To what do I owe the privilege?"

"Hi, Mom. Hey, um, is it okay if I stay here tonight?"

Beth put her book down. "Of course, Jordan. What's wrong?"

Jordan sat down on the couch and looked at his hands. The thought of telling his mom what had happened mortified him, but he knew it wouldn't take long for the story to get back to her, so he might as well be the one to fill her in. Yet he couldn't find the words to say. Remembering the rings in his pocket, he took the box out and handed it to her.

Beth raised her eyebrows as she took it from him and examined the rings inside. She closed the box and handed it back to Jordan, and he thought he saw a smile briefly tug at the corners of her mouth. "Am I to assume things didn't go the way you had hoped?"

Jordan shook his head.

Beth said, "When I talked to Kehau a couple of months ago, she seemed very excited about going on a mission. Is that still part of her plan?"

"That is her plan." Jordan looked up at his mother. "Mom, I don't understand it. Everything was going so well, and I really felt like we had something special. I fasted and I prayed about this, and I really felt like I needed . . . like I was supposed to ask her to marry me."

"Well, what about her mission?"

"What about it? She doesn't have her call—she doesn't even turn twenty-one for two more months. And I thought . . ." Jordan's voice trailed off and he looked back down at his hands.

"And you thought if she loved you she'd give that up?"

"I guess. I don't know." Jordan opened the ring box and ran his finger over the delicately carved pattern before snapping it shut.

His mother let out a sigh and leaned forward to pat his hand. "Well, I suppose it's all for the best."

Her words grated across his raw emotions, and the anger Jordan felt at Kehau's rejection quickly rose to the surface. "What do you mean, 'for the best'?"

Beth looked at him over her reading glasses and smiled. "Oh, Jordan. Kehau's a nice girl, but you can do so much better."

Jordan's eyes opened wide. "What?"

"Look, I know it hurts now, but you'll be over it in a week or two, and there are plenty of girls who would love to take her place. I mean, just the other day, I was telling Elissa that once Kehau was out of the way . . ."

"Mom!" Jordan said, incredulity creasing his brow. "I just got totally rejected—try to show a little compassion here."

"Oh, Jordan," she said, her lips curling sympathetically. "It's hard, I know. But you will get over it, I promise. And when you do, you'll see that this was all for your good. Believe me, sweetie, you're better off this way. Some day you'll thank those people who paid for her to go."

"No," he said, coming to his feet. "No, I won't." Jordan stormed toward the door, the shock of his mother's words swirling in his head. Opening the screen, he took a step onto the front porch and stopped.

With sudden clarity, he turned around and stepped back into the house, slamming the door behind him. "You," he said, pointing at his mom. "You're the one, aren't you?"

Beth raised her eyebrows, and the corners of her mouth turned in an involuntary grin. "I'm the one what?"

"You're the one paying for the rest of Kehau's mission. You're paying for her mission so you can keep us apart." His mom bit her lips in an attempt to hide a smile, and Jordan's anger swelled to a crescendo. "Well, congratulations—you've succeeded. Thank you very much!"

Jordan burst from the house and drove back to Hale Honu, where the usual evening crowd filled the living room. As he walked through the front door, Scott's voice taunted from across the room, "What, *Pono*? Back already? Even Mommy rejected you?"

Rage welled up inside him. Dropping his bag, Jordan pushed his way through the crowd. Scott sprang to his feet, and Jordan charged toward him. A dark-haired girl screamed, and Jordan felt a pair of strong arms grab him from behind, pulling him back just as Scott's powerful fist passed harmlessly in front of his face.

Jordan struggle to break free, intent in his fury on reaching Scott, not caring what harm might come to him. But a second set of arms encircled his chest, and Tomasi's voice entered his ear. "Jordan—*sole*—chill, man. Chill."

Just a few feet away, Seti stood with his arms wrapped around Scott's chest and biceps. Jordan locked eyes with Scott and channeled every bit of anger he could find into the glare. Scott returned his gaze, and Jordan thought he saw more surprise than anything else. After several tense moments, Scott relaxed, gave Jordan a crooked smile, and said, "Maybe you're not such a wimp after all, eh, *Pono*?" He wiggled loose from Seti's slackened grip, motioned to the dark-haired girl, and laughed as he and the girl walked out the door together.

Jordan felt the grip around his waist loosen, and as he looked around the room, he noticed that everyone was staring at him. Never before had he lost his temper so thoroughly, and the realization of what he had done both embarrassed and scared him.

"I, uh . . ." He forced a smile as he took a step toward his abandoned bag. "I'm just gonna go."

Jordan carelessly discarded his bag at the foot of his bed and then flopped onto the mattress. He lay on his back for a long time, staring at the ceiling and trying to sort through the events of the day.

The door to the room opened, but Jordan kept his gaze on the ceiling. After a few seconds, Seti's voice came from across the room. "*Po'a Palagi*, you're crazy, man." He laughed softly and then said, "I think I'd be crazy too."

Jordan drew in a deep breath, exhaling loudly, but didn't respond.

"She really loves you, you know. Malia told her she should stay home, not go on a mission. But Robert said she really wants to go. So what can you do? If you try to hold her back, you only drive her away."

Jordan closed his eyes, fighting back tears. After a moment passed, he heard Seti leave the room. Once alone, he turned off the light and let the tears flow.

Jordan didn't remember falling asleep, and when he awoke the next morning, he was still unsure of what to do. He showered, dressed, and looked at the tuxedo hanging in the closet. He had been so excited to spend the evening with Kehau at the fund-raiser, and now that she was gone, he didn't even want to go. He was still staring into the closet when the doorbell rang. He listened but didn't hear anyone else in the house. Then the bell rang again, and Jordan quickly walked out to the door.

Standing on the front porch was Lindsay. "This wasn't scheduled for delivery, but Malia said I should probably bring it. Here," she said, handing him a clear plastic bag. Jordan stared at the string of flowers inside. "It's *na pua lei.*"

"Huh?" Jordan looked up at her, confused.

"*Na pua lei*. It's Hawaiian for 'the flower lei.' I learned that in my hula class."

"Uh, yeah, right. Thanks." said Jordan. His eyes returned to the bag, which contained the double tuberose and rosebud lei he'd ordered for Kehau to wear to the gala. Jordan opened the bag, and the sweet smell of flowers took over, filling his mind with images and memories of her: Brandon's wedding, Spring Ball, Malia's wedding, all the way back to the airport and their first movie date, when Jordan held Kehau's hand for the first time.

Maybe Seti was right. Maybe he had to let her go. But maybe Roach was right too. If he couldn't keep her from leaving, he could at least try to patch things up before she went.

forty-nine

Jordan drove warily toward La'aloa. He'd tried to call, but the phone simply rang, and the online reservation system was down. Looking through the fence, he saw that the spaces usually occupied by Roach's planes were empty. His heart sank but quickly lifted again when he saw The Blue Bomb sitting by the fuel station. He parked and hurried to the hangar, letting out a sigh of relief when the door opened for him.

Inside was yet another new face from the temp agency. This one looked sorely out of place, with her trendy pink clothes and her dark brown hair styled into a stiff mane, as if she'd come straight into work after an all-nighter in Waikiki. Jordan thought she would have been rather pretty if not for the sneer clouding her face. Clearly working in an old airplane hangar was not what she had in mind when she left for work that morning.

"Hi," Jordan said. "Do you know if the plane out there is available?"

She gave Jordan a look of bored disdain, smacking her gum a few times before answering. "That plane has been reserved for the whole day, and I've been given strict orders not to let anyone else take it."

Jordan sighed, deflated. But soon a thought came to him. He looked at the rental board, but it was blank. "Can you tell me who the plane's reserved for?" Jordan hoped the other pilot would be someone he knew. Maybe he could work something out with him.

The girl held a folded piece of paper to her chest and said, "Nope. Confidential information."

Jordan's mouth fell open, and he felt his ears grow hot. Renter's names were usually right up on the board—there was nothing confidential about them. This chick was on some kind of sadistic power trip. "Can you at least tell me where they're going?"

"Nope," she said. "I have no idea where they're going, or when they'll be leaving, or when they'll be getting back. I just know the plane is reserved, and you can't have it."

Where on earth is Roach getting these people? Trying to remain calm, he said, "Okay, here's what I would like you to do." He spoke slowly and authoritatively, as if instructing a child. "Please call the people who have the plane scheduled—I'm assuming you have the number. Ask them when they will be leaving, where they are going, and when they will be getting back."

She started to protest, but Jordan cut her off. "Just do it," he ordered, and then added a bit softer, "please."

He stared into her cloudy green eyes, letting her know he would not back down. Finally, with a huff, she turned her back to Jordan, opened the piece of paper, and dialed. Jordan waited for a second, hoping to listen to the conversation, but then his phone began to ring. Thinking it might be Kehau, he stepped away from the desk and quickly pulled it from his pocket. But instead he saw La'aloa Aviation on the caller ID screen.

After a brief moment of confusion, Jordan fully grasped the situation and smiled.

"Hello," he said, answering the call.

"Hello, this is La'aloa Aviation calling for Jordan MacDonald, just to let you know that your plane is still reserved for the entire day, and that it will be here whenever you arrive." She spoke this last part loudly, no doubt for Jordan's benefit.

"Great!" he said. "I'll be there in three seconds."

Jordan counted silently to himself, smiling as he watched Nightclub Girl look at the phone, trying to figure out why she had just heard his voice through both ears. All of a sudden she whipped around, eyes wide.

"Hi," he said, approaching the desk for the second time. "I'm Jordan MacDonald. I'm here for my plane." He couldn't suppress a smile. "In case anyone asks, I'm flying to the Big Island, leaving now, and should be back in time for dinner."

As he walked toward the plane, Jordan noticed the unsightly square bulge on the front of his right leg. He'd put the ring box in his pocket as he left Hale Honu but decided he needed to move it somewhere less conspicuous, afraid if Kehau saw it, the whole trip would be in vain. Pulling the box from his pocket, he unzipped his flight bag and shoved it into the end compartment where he kept some spare change and breath mints.

After forcing himself to slow down enough for a proper preflight, Jordan leapt into the sky and pointed The Bomb at Kamuela. On the seat next to him sat the thick tuberose lei Lindsay had delivered that morning. Over and over in his mind, he repeated the conversation he hoped to have once he got to Kehau. Should he tell her about his mom paying for her mission? Would it make a difference if he did?

The trade winds blew strong and steady at a right angle to Jordan's flight path. They gave him no help and would probably not help on the way back, either. With his nerves growing more jumpy by the second, Jordan made a lousy landing and nearly had to abort and go around again. Finally he got the plane on the ground and taxied back up the runway to the transient tie-downs. He pulled in between a burgundy Piper and an old gold-colored Bonanza and made his way to the airport's FBO, where he attempted to borrow their courtesy car.

"Sorry, the car's out for the morning," said the wiry dark-haired youth behind the counter. "I can have a taxi here in fifteen minutes if you want."

"Yeah, great. Thanks."

While waiting, Jordan tried Kehau again, but his call still went straight to voice mail. He attempted to entertain himself with the worn flying magazines on the lounge table but couldn't stop thinking of Kehau and the things he had said to her the day before.

After what seemed an eternity, a dark blue jeep bumped up to the FBO. A wrinkled old Filipino man got out and poked his head in the door. "Who call a taxi?" he asked.

"Me," said Jordan, collecting his things. The man flashed him a smile with a couple of missing teeth and waved Jordan over.

"Where you like go?" the driver asked as he climbed into the Jeep.

"Kohala," Jordan replied. "Mana'olana Street."

"Oh, yeah. Mana'olana Street. Yeah, yeah, yeah. Okay." Jordan held tight to the lei as the jeep sped off. Looking down at it, he was suddenly filled with a tremendous case of nerves. Would Kehau even talk to him, or would she shut him out like she had at the airport? Could he blame her if she did?

Between the wind rushing in his ears and the man's thick pidgin, Jordan could barely make out any of his steady stream of babble, but he nodded with interest and laughed whenever his driver laughed. As they approached the house, Jordan thought it might be best to have the taxi hang around for a minute or two. If the reception was chilly, he would know soon enough, and he wanted to be able to make a clean, quick getaway.

"Oh, okay. I wait," said the driver, who left the motor running.

Jordan approached the house and heard the sound of men laughing in the back. He knocked on the door and heard someone say, "Hey. Come back here."

As he rounded the house, he caught sight of Kehau's dad sitting on the *lanai*. "Oh, yeah. It's Jordan," he said with a big smile.

"It took you long enough," said Roach, who was sitting just around the corner of the *lanai*. "I tell you, you need to learn to fly the Bonanza. Of course, I had it this morning, so I guess it wouldn't have done you any good."

The men both laughed at this, clearly in a mood to laugh at just about anything.

"Come, Jordan. Have a seat," Joe called out. "I'm just catching up with my good friend, Melvin Roach." Jordan climbed onto the *lanai* and sat down across from the two men. "You know, I met Roach when he was about your age and didn't know nothin' about airplanes. Now look at him—he owns a repair shop and a flight school, and from what I can tell, he turns out some pretty good pilots."

"Oh, yeah? Well look at you," Roach said. "A beautiful wife. Eleven kids. And how many grandkids?"

"Twenty-three."

"That's right—twenty-three grandkids."

"And Malia—my oldest granddaughter—she just got married, so there could be a great-grandbaby any time now."

Jordan sat up quickly. "What?"

Joe leaned forward in his seat. "Oh, no—that's not an announce-ment or anything. Just an old man's wishful thinking." The two friends laughed again. "But look at you, Jordan. You didn't come all this way to listen to us old men talk story. You're here to see Kehau."

"Uh, yes, sir," Jordan said.

"She's not here. Took the car and went somewhere this morning. She didn't say where. But she should be back for dinner. You wanna wait?"

Jordan shook his head and stood. "No, I need to get back. Besides, I have an idea where she might be. Thanks."

"If you find her, tell her to bring home some more dry squid. Roach here ate my whole stash." Jordan shook his head and left the two men laughing on the *lanai*. He waved and walked back to the waiting jeep.

"Pau already?" the driver asked.

"No," said Jordan. "I need to go to Waipio Valley."

They bounced along the highway for nearly twenty minutes before the Waipio overlook park came into view. He tried to find Kehau, but the lookout was crowded with both tourists and locals.

As they pulled into the parking lot, Jordan finally made out a girl sitting on the wall of the overlook. It had to be Kehau.

"You like me wait?" the driver asked.

"Please," said Jordan, climbing out. As he walked across the empty grass leading to the girl, he looked down to check on the lei. The bag had deflated, but the flowers still looked pretty good. He untied the plastic and spun the bag to capture some air. Then he tied it up again.

As he neared the wall, his heart beat faster—there could be no doubt that this was Kehau. She sat cross-legged, looking out over the deep, wide valley and holding something to her chest. As Jordan neared, he noticed it was her scriptures.

"I see what you mean about this place," Jordan said when he reached her. "It's really beautiful."

Kehau didn't respond.

He stood for several moments, feeling the wind on his face, wishing he could somehow unsay the things he had said, take back the way he had walked away from her.

He drew a breath and began his apology the way he had rehearsed.

"I understand Waipio Valley was once *Pu'uhonua O Pakaalana*. A place of refuge." Though she didn't turn to look at him, her rigid stature softened slightly, and Jordan felt encouraged. "If someone had broken a *kapu*, they could come here, make restitution, and ask for forgiveness."

Slowly, she turned her head and looked at him, their eyes meeting for a moment before she blinked and looked away. He could see that she had been crying, and the stabbing guilt returned.

"Kehau, I'm sorry. I thought by asking you to marry me, I was doing what the Lord wanted me to, but I see now that it was just what I wanted. And then afterward, I should never have said what I did. I didn't mean it. I . . ." He tried to think of what he should say and then decided to just say what he felt. "I was scared, Kehau. Scared that I would lose you. Because I love you."

Kehau shook her head. "Jordan, don't—"

"No, I have to say it. Because it's true. I really, truly do love you." She bowed her head and shook it, the tears falling again. "And because I love you, I have to let you go."

Jordan put his hand on Kehau's shoulder, kissed the top of her head, and said, "Good-bye." He set the bag with the lei on the wall next to her, turned and walked away. He could feel the tears welling up in his eyes, but he fought them off by focusing instead on Kehau, imagining her picking up the lei and running after him. He willed her to call out to him, to call him back and forgive him, to let him take her in his arms. But when he reached the Jeep and climbed inside, finally allowing himself to look, Kehau was still sitting on the wall where he had left her.

As the Jeep rumbled back toward the airport, Jordan was grateful for the wind whipping his face and carrying away the tears that he now allowed to flow freely.

On his return flight, Jordan left the autopilot off, preferring instead to focus his attention and energy on maintaining a more precise altitude and heading than was necessary. It was tedious work, but it kept his mind from drifting back to the things he had said to Kehau the day before and his cold reception when he tried to apologize. He flew back slowly, unable to get excited about returning home, and especially not about the gala that night.

As a result of his cold, detached focus, Jordan managed a landing that barely squeaked the tires. *Of course*, he thought to himself. *When no one is around to see it.*

He taxied back to La'aloa aviation and tied down next to the Bonanza. Plodding across the tarmac, he checked his watch. The gala would be starting in little more than an hour—there was no way he could make it home, change, and get back down to Waikiki in time. At the realization, he felt a twinge of guilt and sadness, but mostly he felt relief. He wasn't in the mood to get all dressed up and go out alone.

The large hangar door was still closed, so Jordan walked through the small man-door, and was greeted by Roach's gruff but enthusiastic voice. "'Bout time you got back. How was the flight?"

"Okay, I guess."

"And you found your girlfriend. That's good."

Jordan was puzzled for just a second until he remembered seeing Roach at the Pulakaumaka's. "Yeah, I found her." Had the Bonanza still been in Kamuela when he left? Jordan didn't remember.

"So," Roach continued, "don't you have some big fancy party tonight?"

"Yeah, but I don't think I'm going."

"What?" asked Roach. "Not go? You can't not go!"

"Why not?" Jordan shot back. He didn't feel like going, and he certainly didn't need a lecture from Roach about it.

Roach shrugged. "Well, I guess you don't have to go," he said, his eyes dancing. "But if I had a date with a girl who looked like that, nothing could keep me away."

Confused, Jordan turned to follow Roach's gaze. Behind him, in front of the bathroom door, stood Kehau. Jordan caught his breath. She wore a flattering red silk dress that shimmered even in the cold fluorescent light. Her hair was done simply, with a matching red barrette. She was wearing makeup too—a touch of bronze on her eyelids, and some extremely kissable lipstick.

Jordan stared, mouth open. "But, how . . .?"

"I'm tellin' ya," came Roach's voice from behind. "If you want to get anywhere fast, you need to learn to fly the Bonanza."

Kehau's roommate, Zoe, slipped out of the bathroom carrying an empty hanger and a large duffle bag, solving the other half of the mystery. She gave Kehau a hug, winked at Jordan, and hurried away.

Jordan's happiness and surprise at seeing Kehau faded, replaced by a sinking feeling in his gut. "Oh, no."

"What's wrong?" Kehau asked.

Jordan pointed north. "My tuxedo . . ."

"Is right here." Jordan turned to see Julie and Rebecca walking through the hangar door. Julie thrust the tuxedo bag at him.

Jordan's eyes widened in surprise. "But how did you—?"

"We got a call," Rebecca said, handing him his shoes a bit more carefully.

"You owe me for this one." Julie punched his shoulder and smiled.

"Kehau, you look beautiful!" said Rebecca.

"Thank you."

Jordan shook his head. "Wow—I can't believe this. Thanks."

As he made his way to the bathroom to change, Roach called after him. "Hey, MacDonald. Take advantage of the shower in there—you smell like a Cessna."

Jordan showered and dressed quickly, admiring himself in the tiny mirror as best he could. He stepped out of the bathroom to catcalls from Julie, who urged him to stand by Kehau. "An event like this needs photographic evidence, and then Beks and I are out of here." She scowled as she looked around the cluttered hanger for a suitable backdrop. "Where can we have you stand?"

Kehau's suggestion surprised Jordan, but he had to admit it was perfect. "Let's go out by the planes."

As they walked onto the tarmac, the sun hung low in the western sky, giving the world a rich, golden glow. Arriving at the aircraft, Rebecca pointed to the plastic bag in Kehau's hand and said, "Kehau, your lei—do you want to put it on for the picture?"

"Oh. I almost forgot." Kehau stopped and took out the thick, double tuberose lei and handed it to Jordan. "I thought I'd wait until you could give it to me the right way."

Jordan took the flowers from her, and the look in her eyes made his heart leap. He carefully slipped the fragrant strand over her head and, completely ignoring the presence of his sisters, wrapped his arms around Kehau and kissed her full on the mouth.

There was a soft beep and a bright flash. "Mom's gonna love that one," Julie said. "Okay, let's take some now where we can see your faces."

fifty

After the pictures, Jordan got Kehau situated in the car. The sky faded to black as they drove to the big Glenn Yamada Fund-raiser Gala at the Kahala Resort on the far side of Waikiki. Jordan's ears went pink at the look on the valet's face when he handed over the keys to Brandon's car, but his embarrassment was forgotten as he turned and took Kehau's hand.

They walked into the grand hotel foyer and followed the signs to an elegant ballroom, which was full of important looking people posturing and schmoozing with one another. Jordan felt completely out of place, but when Kehau slipped her arm around his waist, he figured he could put up with anything as long as she was with him. The food on the seven course menu was excellent, and there were some long-winded speeches from the other four beneficiaries. After all of the day's excitement, Jordan fought to stay awake.

When Kahuku Hospital was finally announced as the fifth recipient, Sister Boyce came forward and gave a short thank you. Then she introduced Jordan's video.

The lights dimmed, the wall behind the podium lit up, and Jordan heard his own voice carried over the loudspeaker. Seeing his months of hard work displayed larger than life filled Jordan with a mix of pride and embarrassment. He was acutely aware of every weak spot in the video, but he had to admit it really wasn't too bad—certainly more entertaining than the previous speeches—and pride finally won out.

The presentation was met with polite applause, and the program proceeded quickly to the conclusion.

The rest of the evening was dedicated to dancing, but Jordan was exhausted and ready to call it a night. Kehau, however, had been building up steam ever since she learned the party involved a dance, and Jordan consented to stay. The crowd adjourned to the neighboring ballroom, where a large swing orchestra presided over a long, narrow dance floor. The band was lively, and Jordan did his best while dancing with Kehau, but he could see her looking longingly at the people around them, showing off proper swing steps.

After several energetic numbers, they stopped and took a set of chairs to watch. A dark haired man and his tired looking wife came over from the dance floor and took the chairs next to them. The man turned to Jordan and said, "That was a nice presentation. Thank you." He reached over and shook Jordan's hand. "I'm Glenn Yamada, and this is my wife, Carol." Jordan shook both of their hands, in awe at meeting the Silicon Valley mogul and their host for the evening.

"It's great to meet you," Jordan said. "This is my girlfriend, Kehau."

"Nice to meet you, Kehau." He shook her hand, and then turned back to Jordan. "I met another girl from BYU—Hawaii a couple of months ago. Heather Martin, I think her name was. She and her parents flew with us back to the mainland. Her story was one of the reasons I added the hospital to this year's beneficiaries."

Kehau squeezed Jordan's hand, and a chill ran down his back.

Across the ballroom, the band began playing "In the Mood." Glenn sat up and looked at his wife, who shook her head. "Sorry, dear. I'm not up for any more."

"Oh, c'mon," he said, but her head shaking continued. "Fine," he said in mock contempt. "I'll find somebody else to dance with." Turning to Kehau, he said, "You don't swing dance, do you?"

Kehau looked quickly at Jordan and then back at Glenn. "Yeah, I do."

Glenn's eyes widened, and both he and Kehau looked at Jordan expectantly. Jordan shrugged his shoulders and said, "Happy dancing."

As Jordan sat watching Kehau dance with Glenn, his brain finally began to relax. Soon he was staring glassy-eyed at the dance floor, trying to keep himself awake.

Carol Yamada leaned over and said, "She's a pretty good dancer, isn't she?"

Jordan started from his stupor. "Uh, yeah. She really is."

Carol sighed as she watched her husband. "Glenn has always loved dancing. That's how he first captured my attention—and how he's held it for the last thirty years." She watched them dancing for another minute and then asked, "Do you dance, Mr. MacDonald?"

"Uh, no. Not really," Jordan replied.

"You should learn, then," she said with a smile.

Jordan thought about what she said as he watched Glenn and Kehau dance, but soon his glassy-eyed stupor returned. Carol said, "You know, I think I'd better get you a room for the night."

"Huh?" said Jordan, pulling himself back to reality.

"Glenn always gets a block of rooms for people who need to sleep off the festivities."

"Oh. No, that's okay. I haven't had anything to drink."

"That may be so, but it's clear to me you are in no shape to be driving. Now," she said with a sly smile, "will you be sharing a room? Or should I also get a room for your girlfriend?"

Jordan blushed at the suggestion. "You'd better get a room for her too."

She patted his shoulder. "That's what I thought. Did you bring a change of clothes? I can have the concierge take them up to your room."

"Oh, yeah," said Jordan as he fished out his valet ticket. He described his flight bag and the small bag Kehau had brought with her, which sat in Brandon's trunk.

At the thought of not having to make the hour-long drive home, a wave of relief washed over Jordan. He checked his watch—eleven forty. The party only went until midnight, and he decided not to miss out on the last dance.

Carol came back with two room keys, and handed them to Jordan. "Here you go," she said, adding with a wink, "I got you adjoining rooms, just in case."

Jordan pocketed the keys. "Thank you. Now, what do you say we go and get our dates back?" He offered her his arm and led her out to the floor next to Kehau and Glenn. Rather than cut in right away, though, he began dancing with Mrs. Yamada.

When that song ended, Jordan turned to Mr. Yamada and said, "Let's trade." But the music didn't start up right away. Instead, the MC got on the mike and thanked everyone for coming. Then he announced one more song. Jordan took Kehau by the hand and danced slow and close to "Moonlight Serenade."

He held her next to him, her head resting on his chest, and together they moved to the music. For a fraction of a second, he was tempted to try to only use one room but quickly dismissed the thought with a smile.

Kehau was surprised when Jordan told her about staying the night, but she saw the wisdom of it. When they arrived at their rooms, they found that their bags had already been delivered. Unfortunately, the rooms were in the smoking section.

"Do you want me to see if I can get some other rooms? It's not a problem . . ."

"No," Kehau interrupted. "It doesn't smell too bad. I think I'll be okay." She wrapped her arms around his waist and said, "Thank you for a wonderful evening."

"My pleasure," said Jordan, returning her embrace. "I'm glad you were able to make it."

Standing in the hallway, Jordan kissed her gently and then again more intensely. He barely felt his feet touch the floor as he went to his own room, where he quickly fell asleep.

Soon, however, the sound of his cell phone startled Jordan awake. Instinctively he reached for the source of the noise before even registering where he was. His hand found his phone, which he lifted to his ear. It took a couple of tries before his voice engaged enough to manage a croaked "Hello?"

"Jordan, I need you to take me home." The voice on the other end belonged to Kehau. Jordan's mind raced, the events of the previous day gradually coming back to him. Thinking he had somehow slept late, he looked at the clock. It read four seventeen.

"Are you okay?" Jordan asked as he stumbled out of bed. Kehau's voice sounded more regretful than urgent, but he was concerned nonetheless.

"Yeah, I'm fine," she replied, "but there's a lot of smoke in my room now, and I've got a really bad headache, and I just want to go home."

Without thinking, Jordan took a deep breath and had to agree that the tobacco smell was much stronger than it had been a few hours earlier. "I'll be over in about five minutes."

"Thanks, Jordan," she said, before hanging up.

Jordan got dressed and managed to partially subdue his bed-head hair. He quickly brushed his teeth, collected his flight bag and tuxedo jacket, and knocked quietly on Kehau's door. She answered immediately, her eyes swollen and bloodshot. "I'm sorry," she said.

"Don't worry about it," Jordan said, pulling her close and kissing the top of her head.

As he reached to take her bag, she asked, "Are you going to be okay driving home?"

"Yeah, I'll be fine. It's amazing what a couple hours of sleep can do." Jordan had asked himself this question more than once since her call just a few minutes before, and his answer to Kehau showed more confidence than what he really felt.

A light breeze drifted past them as they stood waiting for the car, and Kehau asked Jordan to put the top down, hoping the mild June air would help clear the smoke out of their clothes. They tried to keep each other awake with conversation, but the roaring wind made talking difficult, and soon Kehau was asleep in her seat, leaving Jordan to stay awake on his own. To this end, he began singing to himself, the sound of his voice swept away by the roaring wind.

As he drove past Hau'ula Beach Park, Jordan noticed the sky beginning to lighten, and the clouds took on a pinkish tint. He looked at Kehau, sleeping peacefully at his side, and suddenly had an idea.

Instead of turning toward the school when they got to La'ie, he continued to the middle of town and turned right.

"Where are we going?" Kehau asked. Her eyes remained closed, but she was apparently awake enough to register the change in destination.

"To my favorite place," Jordan replied. At this, Kehau opened one eye. She sat up and smiled as they drove up the road to La'ie Point.

After climbing the short, winding hill, Jordan turned down Nau-paka Street, between houses crowded along either side, to the wall at the end of the road. He stopped, turned off the car, and looked east across the jagged rocks to the ocean beyond. Kehau undid her seat belt and leaned across the center console. Jordan put his arm around her, and together they watched the sky turn from dark blue to teal, and the clouds from gray to magenta. His mind raced to capture every detail of the moment: her warmth against him in the cool morning breeze, the sound of the gentle ocean waves crashing against the rocks, even the slight smell of tobacco smoke mingled with Kehau's guava shampoo and the tuberose in her lei.

"I had a great time last night," she said, resting her head against his chest.

"Yeah, me too."

"Thanks for coming to get me."

"No problem. I'm sorry I was such a jerk."

Jordan turned his head to kiss her, but at the last second she pulled away.

"Sorry," she said, sitting up, her hand to her mouth. Looking embarrassed, she asked, "Uh, do you have any gum?"

Jordan smiled once he understood her hesitation. "No, but I have some mints in my bag. They're in the end pocket." He reached around and lifted his flight bag off of the back seat and held it out to Kehau. She unzipped the pocket and reached in, but instead of the mints her hand emerged holding a small box. Jordan held his breath, unable to read her expression as she gingerly opened it.

Kehau studied the rings for several seconds, and then snatched the mints from the bag, nimbly climbing over the center console to the back seat.

"What are you doing?" Jordan asked, a curious smile stealing across his lips.

"C'mon back," she said, popping a mint into her mouth. "Those seats are okay for driving, but not so good for parking."

Jordan climbed out of the car, slid the driver's seat forward, and slipped into the back next to Kehau. The mint did the trick, and she kissed him wholeheartedly as soon as he sat down.

Kehau nestled against Jordan, and he sighed, unsure just how to say what he wanted to. After a few quiet minutes passed, he decided there was no point in holding back.

"Kehau," he said.

"Yes?"

"I love you."

Jordan expected Kehau to tense as she had the last time he told her this, but she didn't. For a second he wasn't sure she was going to react at all. But soon she said, "I know. And I love you too, Jordan." She opened the ring box again, and as she took out the engagement band and slipped it on her finger, Jordan felt a surge of hope.

"Look at that—it fits perfectly," Kehau said. "How did you know the right size?"

"I guessed," said Jordan with a smile. "And your ring finger looked like it was about the same size as my pinkie." Jordan took the wedding band from the box and slipped it on the little finger of his right hand. "See?"

Kehau laughed—that clear, beautiful laugh that first caught his attention all those months ago. She took the groom's ring from the box, trying it on until she found that it fit perfectly on her right middle finger. "That is just so funny—our rings fit each other."

She looked at her hands and bit her lip. She gently fingered the stone on the engagement ring for several long seconds. "You remember yesterday, when you said you thought you were doing what the Lord wanted by asking me to marry you, but then you thought maybe it was just what you wanted?" She glanced up at Jordan.

He nodded slightly. "Yeah."

"After you said that, I realized I'd never really prayed about going on a mission. I'd just prayed about where to get the money. When I got that answer, I thought it meant I was supposed to go." She took a deep breath and swallowed hard. "But yesterday, after I saw you, I actually prayed about whether or not I should serve a mission."

Kehau wiped a tear and looked down. Jordan waited for a minute, but she didn't say anything else. "And?" he prompted.

"And, so, I prayed. Right there on the wall at Waipio lookout. I prayed about my mission; I prayed about you; I prayed about me." Her lip quivered, and Jordan could see more tears welling in her eyes. "This mission is important to me, and I want to go so bad."

The hope Jordan felt just moments before began to drain away.

"I learned something yesterday, Jordan." She looked down. "I found out it's your mother paying for me to go."

Jordan stiffened. "Yeah, I know."

Kehau turned to look at him, her eyebrows raised. "You knew?"

He nodded. "I found out a couple of days ago."

"If you knew, why didn't you tell me?"

Jordan breathed in deeply and then exhaled. "I thought about it, but knowing how much your mission means to you, I figured it didn't really matter where the money was coming from. It was wrong for me to try to stop you."

She smiled as tears streamed down her face. "Thank you," she whispered. "Thank you so much." She pressed her face against Jordan's chest, and he felt her tears soak into his shirt. He placed his hand on her head, and gently stroked her hair.

After a moment, Kehau raised her head and shook it gently. "But I can't go. Not now, not knowing what I know."

Jordan swallowed hard. "Sure you can. If she wants to spend her money that way, then—"

"No," Kehau said. "It's not the money. It's . . ." She paused and then looked deep into his eyes. "I prayed about what I should do, and I know we're supposed to be together."

The hope that had abandoned Jordan just moments before came flooding back. "Really?"

Kehau nodded and then wiped away another tear before letting a nervous laugh escape.

Jordan pulled her close, holding her tightly to him. His head felt light, his brain racing to grasp the full meaning of Kehau's decision. He took her left hand in his and tapped the ring. "So, does that mean you're going to stay here and wear this?"

She looked at the ring, not answering right away, and Jordan held his breath. But then Kehau's mouth spread into a smile. "Yeah," she said, "I guess it does."

The kiss she then gave him was, by far, the most satisfying of his entire life.

discussion questions

1. How is the story influenced by the setting? What elements of the story would change if it were told in a different setting? What would remain the same?
2. Why do you think Beth felt it necesary to interfere in Jordan's relationship with Kehau? How might she have better handled her concerns?
3. Despite considering himself an honest person, Jordan puts a lot of energy into lying about his flight lessons. Why do you think he tries to hide his actions? Would he have been better off abandoning his pursuit or openly defying his mother?
4. Why did Jordan allow Heather to dictate so much of his life? Do you know anyone who has acted in a similar way?
5. Why do you think Jordan felt such a strong sense of responsibility to Heather after her accident?
6. Jordan's real growth came when he took himself out of his comfort zone. When have you had to make a similar change? Why is leaving what is comfortable and familiar often so difficult?
7. Waipio Valley was once *Pu'uhonua O Pakaalana*—a place of refuge where someone could go to make restitution and ask for forgiveness. When you feel the need to make restitution or ask forgiveness, where do you go? What do you do?
8. Do you feel Kehau made the right decision regarding her mission? Why or why not?

acknowledgments

I began writing because it was a creative outlet I could pursue alone, and yet the beautiful irony of that decision is how writing has introduced me to so many wonderful new friends. Many of these friends have blessed *Bumpy Landings* throughout its life and helped turn a stream of homesick ramblings into a coherent, publishable book.

I want to thank Tristi for running her quarterly writing challenge, and giving me the spark to take my writing seriously. Thank you to Annette, Josi, and Julie for providing inspiration and encouragement when I was just learning the basics of this writing adventure. And thank you to everyone involved with the LDStorymakers writers conferences.

Thank you to my alpha and beta readers for telling me straight what didn't work and needed to be fixed: Neil and the North Texas Writers Guild, Stephanie, Nicole, Jewel, Andrea, Dan, Shari, and Amy. Thank you to Joe for helping me get the flying bits right, and to Melanie for helping me dry up the tears.

Thank you to Cedar Fort for taking a chance on me and my story: Shersta, Heidi, Emily, Danie, Lyle, and everyone else who has worked to make this book a reality.

And a special thanks to Kara for supporting me and my crazy writing dream—even during the most difficult time of her life. Thank you. I love you.

about the author

When he was eleven years old, Donald Carey moved with his family to the Hawaiian town of La'ie, where his father taught at BYU—Hawaii. Donald is a graduate of Kahuku High School where, when he wasn't in the band room, he could be found in the library with his nose in a book.

Donald was awarded the David O. McKay scholarship to attend BYU—Hawaii, where he met his lovely wife, Kara. During college, he scratched his creative itch by participating in a number of musical organizations, including the Polynesian Cultural Center Brass Band, and added a music minor to his degree in computer science.

Once the responsibilities of work and family took over his life, Donald found the creative itch was better handled through writing fiction and has enjoyed working to develop this talent.

Donald currently lives in a small town outside Ft. Worth, Texas, with his wife and two daughters. His day job involves writing computer programs, which is almost the same as writing fiction but with a lot more semicolons.

0 26575 54136 6